CALL AFTER MIDNIGHT

CALL AFTER MIDNIGHT

Tess Gerritsen

This first world hardcover edition published 2011
in Great Britain and in the USA by
SEVERN HOUSE PUBLISHERS LTD of
9–15 High Street, Sutton, Surrey, England, SM1 1DF,
by arrangement with Harlequin Books.
First published 1987 in the USA in mass market format only.

British Library Cataloguing in Publication Data

Gerritsen, Tess.
  Call after midnight.
  1. Romantic suspense novels.
  I. Title
  813.5'4-dc22

ISBN-13: 978-0-7278-8045-1   (cased)

All Severn House titles are printed on acid-free paper.

Severn House Publishers support The Forest Stewardship Council [FSC],
the leading international forest certification organisation. All our titles that
are printed on Greenpeace-approved FSC-certified paper carry the FSC logo.

MIX
Paper from
responsible sources
FSC
www.fsc.org   FSC® C018575

Printed and bound in Great Britain by
MPG Books Ltd., Bodmin, Cornwall.

To Jacob,
who was always there

Prologue

Berlin

IT TAKES TWENTY SECONDS OF PRESSURE on the carotid arteries to render a man unconscious. Two minutes longer, and death is inevitable. Simon Dance didn't need a medical textbook to tell him these facts—he knew them from experience. He also knew there could be no slack in the garrote. If the cord wasn't taut, if it allowed just a short spurt of precious blood to reach the victim's brain, the struggle would be prolonged. It made the whole process sloppy, even dangerous. There was nothing as savage as a dying man.

As he crouched in the darkness, Dance wound the garrote twice around his hands and glanced at the luminous dial of his watch. Two hours had passed since he'd turned off the lights. His assassin was obviously a cautious man who wanted to be sure Dance was deeply asleep. If the man was a professional, he would know that the first two hours of sleep are the heaviest. Now was the time to strike.

In the hallway outside, a footstep creaked. Dance stiffened, then rose slowly and waited in the darkness beside the door. He ignored the pounding of his own heart. He felt the familiar spurt of adrenaline as it kicked his reflexes into high gear. He stretched the garrote between his hands.

A key was easing into the lock. Dance heard the metallic click of the teeth grating softly across metal. The key turned, and the lock opened with a soft clunk. Slowly the door swung in, and light from the hall spilled into the room. A shadow moved through the doorway and turned toward the bed, where a man appeared to be sleeping. The shadow raised its arm. Three bullets from a silencer thudded into the pillows. As the third bullet struck, so did Dance.

He whipped the garrote around the intruder's neck and snapped the cord up and back. It tightened precisely around the most exposed portion of the carotid artery, by the angle of the jaw. The gun fell to the floor. The man thrashed as if he were a hooked fish and tore frantically at the garrote. He reached back and tried to claw Dance's face. His arms and legs went out of control, wildly jerking and thrusting in all directions. Then gradually the legs crumpled, and the arms reached out one last time before going limp. As Dance counted the minutes, he felt the body's last spasms, the seizures of starved and dying brain cells. He held on.

When three minutes had passed, Dance released the garrote, and the body dropped to the floor. Dance turned on the lights and gazed down at the man he'd just killed.

The mottled face was vaguely familiar. Perhaps he'd seen the man on a street or on a train somewhere, but he didn't know his name. Quickly he went through the man's clothes but found only money, car keys and a few tools of the trade: extra ammunition clips, a switchblade, a lock pick. A nameless professional, thought Dance, wondering offhandedly how much the man had been paid.

He dragged the body onto the bed and tossed aside the three pillows that had been fluffed up beneath the covers. He estimated the body's size to be six feet plus or minus an inch. The same height. Good. Dance exchanged clothes with the corpse; it was probably unnecessary, but he was a thorough man. Then he took off his wedding ring and tried to slip it onto the corpse's finger, but it wouldn't quite fit over the knuckle. He went to the bathroom, soaped the ring and finally managed to jam it on the dead man's finger. Then he sat down and smoked a few cigarettes. He tried to think of any details he might have missed.

The three bullets, of course. Hunting around in the pillows and ticking, Dance managed to retrieve two of the bullets. The third was probably embedded somewhere in the mattress. Before he could probe any deeper, he heard footsteps in the hallway. Did the assassin have an accomplice? Dance swept up the gun, aimed at the door and waited. The footsteps moved on and faded down the corridor. A false alarm. Still, he should leave now; to stay any longer would be foolish.

From the dresser drawer, he pulled out a bottle of methanol. It would burn rapidly and leave no residue. He poured it over the body, the bed and the surrounding rug. The room contained no smoke alarms or automatic sprinklers—Dance had chosen the old hotel for just that reason. He set the ashtray beside the bed and gathered the dead man's belongings, along with the empty methanol bottle, and put them in a trash bag. Then he set the bed on fire.

With a whoosh the flames took off, and in seconds the

body was engulfed. Dance waited just long enough to be certain there'd be nothing recognizable left.

Carrying the trash bag, he left the room, locked the door and walked down the hall to the fire alarm. He didn't see the point of killing innocent people, so he broke the glass and pulled the alarm lever. Then he took the stairs down to the ground floor.

From an alley across the street, he watched the flames shoot from his window. The hotel was evacuated, and the street filled with sleepy-eyed people wrapped in blankets. Three fire trucks responded within ten minutes. By that time his room was a blazing inferno.

It took an hour to extinguish the fire. A crowd of curious onlookers joined the shivering hotel guests, and Dance studied their faces, filing them away in his memory. If he saw any of them again, he would be warned.

Then, through the knot of people, he spotted a black limousine crawling slowly down the street. He recognized the man sitting in the back seat. So the CIA was here. Interesting.

He had seen enough. It was late, and he needed to be on his way, back to Amsterdam.

Three blocks away, he threw the trash bag with the empty methanol bottle into a dumpster. With that the last detail was taken care of. He'd done what he had come to Berlin to do. He'd killed off Geoffrey Fontaine. Now it was time to vanish. He walked off whistling into the darkness.

Amsterdam

THE OLD MAN was awakened at three in the morning with the news. "Geoffrey Fontaine is dead."

"How?" asked the old man.

"A hotel fire. They say he was smoking in bed."

"An accident? Impossible! Where is the body?"

"Berlin morgue. Very badly burned."

Of course, thought the old man. He should have known the body would not be recognizable. Simon Dance, as usual, had done a superb job of covering his tracks. So they had lost him again.

But the old man still had one card to play. "You told me there was an American wife," he said. "Where does she live?"

"Washington."

"I will have her followed."

"But why? I just told you the man's dead."

"He's *not* dead. He's alive. I'm sure of it. And this woman may know where he is. I want her watched."

"I'll have my men—"

"No. I will send my own man. Someone I can count on."

There was a pause. "I will get you her address."

After he'd hung up, the old man could not go back to sleep. For five years he'd waited. For five years he'd been searching. To have come so close, only to fail again! Now everything depended on what this woman in Washington knew.

He had to be patient and wait for her to betray herself. He would send Kronen, a man who'd never failed him. Kronen had his own methods to extract information—methods difficult to resist. But then, that was Kronen's special talent. Persuasion.

Chapter One

Washington

IT WAS AFTER MIDNIGHT WHEN THE telephone rang.

Through a heavy curtain of sleep, Sarah heard it ring. The sound seemed impossibly far away, as if it were a distant alarm going off in a room beyond her reach. She struggled to wake up, but she was trapped somewhere in a world between sleep and wakefulness. She had to answer the phone; she knew her husband, Geoffrey, was calling.

All evening she'd waited to hear Geoffrey's voice. It was Wednesday night, and on his monthly trips to London, Geoffrey always called home on Wednesday. Tonight, however, she'd crawled into bed early, sniffling and coughing, a victim of the latest flu virus to hit Washington. It was influenza A-63 from Hong Kong, a particularly miserable strain that she now shared with half her colleagues in the microbiology lab. For an hour she'd sat up reading in bed, fighting valiantly to stay awake. But the combination of a cold capsule plus the most recent *Journal of Microbiology* had worked faster than any sleeping pill. Within minutes she'd fallen back on the pillows with her glasses still perched on her nose. It would be just a short rest, she had promised herself, just a catnap.... In the end, sleep had crept up and ambushed her.

She woke with a start to find that the bedside lamp was on, *Journal of Microbiology* still draped across her chest. The room was slightly out of focus. Pushing her glasses back in place, Sarah glanced at the clock on the nightstand. Twelve-thirty. The telephone was dead silent. Had she been dreaming?

She jumped as the phone rang again. Eagerly she grabbed the receiver.

"Mrs. Sarah Fontaine?" asked a man's voice.

It wasn't Geoffrey. Sudden alarm shot through her like a jolt of electricity. Something was terribly wrong. She sat up at once, fully awake. "Yes. Speaking," she said.

"Mrs. Fontaine, this is Nicholas O'Hara, U.S. State Department. I'm sorry to call you at this hour, but..." He paused. It was the silence that terrified her most, for it was too deliberate, too practiced, a strategically placed buffer to ready her for a blow. "I'm afraid I have some bad news," he finished.

Her throat tightened. She felt like shouting, *Just tell me! Tell me what's happened!* But all she could manage was a whisper. "Yes. I'm listening."

"It's about your husband, Geoffrey," he said. "There's been an accident."

This isn't real, she thought, closing her eyes. *If Geoffrey were hurt, I would have felt it. Somehow I would have known....*

"It happened about six hours ago," he continued. "There was a fire in your husband's hotel." Another pause. Then, with concern in his voice, he asked, "Mrs. Fontaine? Are you still there?"

"Yes. Please go on."

The man cleared his throat. "I'm sorry to tell you this, Mrs. Fontaine. Your husband...he didn't make it."

He allowed her a moment of silence, a moment in which she struggled to contain her grief. It was a stupid, irrational act of pride that made her press her hand over her mouth to stifle the sob. This pain was too private to share with any stranger.

"Mrs. Fontaine?" he asked gently. "Are you all right?"

At last she managed to take a shaky breath. "Yes," she whispered.

"You don't have to worry about the...arrangements. I'll coordinate all the details with our consulate in Berlin. There'll be a delay, of course, but once the German authorities clear the body's release, there should be no—"

"Berlin?" she broke in.

"It's in their jurisdiction, you see. There'll be a full report as soon as the Berlin police—"

"But this isn't possible!"

Nicholas O'Hara was struggling to be patient. "I'm sorry, Mrs. Fontaine. His identity's been confirmed. Really, there's no question about—"

"Geoffrey was in *London*," she cried.

A long silence followed. "Mrs. Fontaine," he said at last in an irritatingly calm voice, "the accident occurred in Berlin."

"Then they've made a mistake. Geoffrey was in London. He couldn't have been in Germany!"

Again there was a pause, longer this time. Now she could tell he was puzzled. The receiver was pressed so tightly to her ear that all she heard for a few seconds was the pounding of her heart. There had to be a mistake. Some crazy, stupid misunderstanding. Geoffrey had to be alive. She pictured him, laughing at the absurd reports of his own death. Yes, they would laugh about it together when he came home. If he came home.

"Mrs. Fontaine," the man said at last, "which hotel was he staying at in London?"

"The—the Savoy. I have the phone number somewhere here—I have to look it up—"

"That's all right, I'll find it. Let me do some calling around. Perhaps I should see you in the morning." His words were measured and cautious, spoken in the unemotional monotone of a bureaucrat who'd learned how to reveal nothing. "Can you come by my office?"

"How—how do I find it?"

"You'll be driving?"

"No. I don't have a car."

"I'll have one sent by."

"It's a mistake, isn't it? I mean…you do make mistakes, don't you?" A bit of hope, that was all she was asking him for. Some small thread to cling to. At least he could have given her that much. He could have shown her a little kindness.

But all he said was "I'll see you in the morning, Mrs. Fontaine. Around eleven."

"Wait, please! I'm sorry, I can't even think. Your name—what was it again?"

"Nicholas O'Hara."

"Where was your office?"

"Don't worry about it," he said. "The driver will see you get here. Good night."

"Mr. O'Hara?"

Sarah heard the dial tone and knew that he had already hung up. She immediately dialed the number of the Savoy Hotel in London. One phone call, and the matter would be settled. *Please*, she prayed as the phone connection went through, *let me hear your voice*....

"Savoy Hotel," answered a woman from halfway around the world.

Sarah's hand was shaking so hard she could barely hold the receiver. "Hello. Mr. Geoffrey Fontaine's room, please," she blurted out.

"I'm sorry, ma'am," the voice said. "Mr. Fontaine checked out two days ago."

"Checked *out*?" she cried. "But where did he go?"

"He gave us no destination. However, if you wish to send a message, we'd be happy to forward it to his permanent address...."

She never remembered saying goodbye. She found herself staring down at the telephone as if it were something alien, something she'd never seen before. Slowly her gaze wandered to Geoffrey's pillow. The king-sized bed seemed to stretch forever. Sarah had always curled herself into one small part of it. Even when Geoffrey was away from home and she had the bed to herself, she still never moved from her spot.

Now Geoffrey might never come home.

Sarah was left alone in a bed that was too large, in an apartment that was too quiet. She shuddered as a silent wave of pain rose and caught in her throat. She wanted desperately to cry, but the tears refused to fall.

She collapsed onto the bed with her face against the pillows. They smelled of Geoffrey. They smelled of his skin and his hair and his laughter. She clutched one of the pillows in her arms and curled up in the very center of the bed, in the spot where Geoffrey always lay. The sheets were ice-cold.

Geoffrey might never come home. They had been married only two months.

NICK O'HARA DRAINED his third cup of coffee and jerked his tie loose. After a two-week vacation wearing nothing but bathing trunks, his tie felt like a hangman's noose. He'd been back in Washington only three days, and already he was edgy. Vacations were supposed to recharge the old batteries. That's why he'd gone to the Bahamas. He'd spent two glorious weeks doing absolutely nothing except lie around half-naked in the sun. He'd needed the time to be alone, to ask himself some hard questions and come to some conclusions.

But the only conclusion he'd reached was that he was unhappy.

After eight years with the State Department, Nick O'Hara was fed up with his job. He was headed in circles, a ship without a rudder. His career was at a standstill, but the fault was not entirely his. Bit by bit he'd lost his patience for political games of state—he wasn't in the mood to play. He'd hung in there, though, because he'd believed in his job, in its intrinsic worth. From peace marches in his youth to peace tables in his prime.

But ideals, he had discovered, got people nowhere. Hell, diplomacy didn't run on ideals. It ran, like everything else, on protocol and party-line politics. While he'd perfected his protocol, he hadn't gotten the politics quite right. It wasn't that he couldn't. He wouldn't.

In that regard Nick knew he was a lousy diplomat. Unfortunately those in authority apparently agreed with him. So he had been banished to this bottom-of-the-barrel consular post in D.C., calling bad news to new widows. It was a not-so-subtle slap in the face. Sure, he could have refused the assignment. He could've gone back to teaching, to his comfortable old niche at American University. He had needed to think about it. Yes, he'd needed those two weeks alone in the Bahamas.

What he didn't need was to come home to this.

With a sigh, he flipped open the file labeled Fontaine, Geoffrey H. One small item had bothered him all morning. Since 1:00 a.m. he'd been staring at a computer terminal, digging out everything he could get from the vast government files. He'd also spent half an hour on the phone with his buddy Wes Corrigan in the Berlin consulate. In frustration he'd finally turned to a few unusual sources. What had started off as a routine call to the widow to give her his regrets was turning into something a bit more complicated, a puzzle for which Nick didn't have all the pieces.

In fact, except for the well-established details of Geoffrey Fontaine's death, there were hardly any pieces at all to play with. Nick didn't like incomplete puzzles. They drove him crazy. When it came to poking around for more information, more facts, he could be insatiable. But now, as he lifted the thin Fontaine file, he felt as if he were holding a bagful of air: nothing of substance but a name.

And a death.

Nick's eyes were burning; he leaned back in his chair and yawned. When he was twenty and in college, staying up half the night used to give him a high. Now that he was thirty-eight, it only made him crotchety. And hungry. At 6:00 a.m. he'd wolfed down three doughnuts. The surge of sugar into his system, plus the coffee, had been enough to keep him going. And now he was too curious to stop. Puzzles always did that to him. He wasn't sure he liked it.

He looked up as the door opened. His pal Tim Greenstein strode in.

"Bingo! I found it!" said Tim. He dropped a file on the desk and gave Nick one of those big, dumb grins he was so famous for. Most of the time, that grin was directed at a computer screen. Tim was a troubleshooter, the man everyone called when the data weren't where they should be. Heavy glasses distorted his eyes, the consequence of infantile cataracts. A bushy black beard obscured much of the rest of his face, except for a pale forehead and nose.

"Told you I'd get it," said Tim, plopping into the leather chair across from Nick. "I had my buddy at the FBI do a little fishing. He came up with zilch, so I did a little poking around on my own. Not easy, I'll tell ya, getting this out of classified. They've got some new idiot up there who insists on doing his job."

Nick frowned. "You had to get this through security?"

"Yep. There's more, but I couldn't access it. Found out central intelligence has a file on your man."

Nick flipped the folder open and stared in amazement. What he saw raised more questions than ever, questions for which there seemed to be no answers. "What the hell does this mean?" he muttered.

"That's why you couldn't find anything about Geoffrey H. Fontaine," said Tim. "Until a year ago, the guy didn't exist."

Nick's jaw snapped up. "Can you get me more?"

"Hey, Nick, I think we're trespassing on someone else's turf. Those Company boys might get hot under the collar."

"So let 'em sue me." Nick wasn't in the least intimidated by the CIA. Not after all the incompetent Company men he'd met. "Anyway," he said with a shrug, "I'm just doing my job. I've got a grieving widow, remember?"

"But this Fontaine stuff goes pretty deep."

"So do you, Tim."

Tim grinned. "What is it, Nick? Turning detective?"

"No. Just curious." He scowled at the day's pile of work on his desk. It was all bureaucratic crap—the bane of his existence—but it had to be done. This Fontaine case was distracting him. He should just give the grieving widow a pat on the shoulder, murmur a kind word and send her out the door. Then he should forget the whole thing. Geoffrey Fontaine, whatever his real name, was dead.

But Tim had set Nick's curiosity on fire. He glanced at his friend. "Say, how about hunting up a few things about the guy's wife? Sarah Fontaine. That might get us somewhere."

"Why don't you get it yourself?"

"You're the one with all that hot computer access."

"Yeah, but you've got the woman herself." Tim nodded toward the door. "I heard the secretary take down her name. Sarah Fontaine's sitting in your waiting room right now."

THE SECRETARY WAS a graying, middle-aged woman with china-blue eyes and a mouth that seemed permanently etched in two straight lines. She glanced up from her type-writer just long enough to take Sarah's name and direct her toward a nearby couch.

Stacked neatly on a coffee table by the couch were the usual waiting room magazines, as well as a few issues of *Foreign Affairs* and *World Press Review*, to which the address labels were still attached: Dr. Nicholas O'Hara.

As the secretary turned back to her typewriter, Sarah sank into the cushions of the couch and stared dully at her hands, which were now folded in her lap. She hadn't yet shaken the flu, and she was still cold and miserable. But in the past ten hours, a layer of numbness had built up around her, a protective shell that made sights and sounds seem distant. Even physical pain bore a strange dullness. When she'd stubbed her toe in the shower this morning, she'd felt the throb, but somehow she hadn't cared.

Last night, after the phone call, the pain had overwhelmed her. Now she was only numb. Gazing down, she saw for the first time what a mess she'd made of getting dressed. None of her clothes quite matched. Yet on a subconscious level, she'd chosen to wear things that gave her solace: a favorite gray wool skirt, an old pullover, brown walking shoes. Life had suddenly turned frightening for Sarah; she needed to be comforted by the familiar.

The secretary's intercom buzzed, and a voice said, "Angie? Can you send Mrs. Fontaine in?"

"Yes, Mr. O'Hara." Angie nodded at Sarah. "You can go in now," she said.

Sarah slipped on her glasses, rose to her feet and entered the office marked N. O'Hara. Just inside the door, she paused on the thick carpet and looked calmly at the man on the other side of the desk.

He stood before the window. The sun shone in through pencil-sketch trees, blinding her. At first she saw only the man's silhouette. He was tall and slender, and his shoulders slouched a little—he looked tired. Moving from the window, he came around the desk to meet her. His blue shirt was wrinkled; a nondescript tie hung loosely around his neck, as if he'd been tugging at it.

"Mrs. Fontaine," he said, "I'm Nick O'Hara." Instantly she recognized the voice from the telephone, the same voice that had shattered her world just ten hours earlier.

He held his hand out to her, a gesture that struck Sarah as too automatic, a mere formality that he no doubt extended to all widows. But his grip was firm. As he shifted toward the window, the light fell fully on his face. She saw long, thin features, an angular jaw, a sober mouth. She judged him to be in his late thirties, perhaps older. His dark brown hair was woven with gray at the temples. Beneath the slate-colored eyes were dark circles.

He motioned her to a chair. As she sat down, she noticed for the first time that a third person was in the room, a man with glasses and a bushy black beard who was sitting quietly in a corner chair. She'd seen him when he'd passed through the reception room earlier.

Nick settled on the edge of the desk and looked at her. "I'm very sorry about your husband, Mrs. Fontaine," he said gently. "It's a terrible shock, I know. Most people don't want to believe us when they get that phone call. I felt I had to meet you face-to-face. I have questions. I'm sure you have, too." He nodded at the man with the beard. "You don't mind Mr. Greenstein listening in, do you?"

She shrugged, wondering vaguely why Mr. Greenstein was there.

"We're both with state," Nick continued. "I'm with consular affairs in the foreign service. Mr. Greenstein's with our technical support division."

"I see." Shivering, she pulled her sweater tighter. The chills were starting again, and her throat was sore. Why were government offices always so cold? she wondered.

"Are you all right, Mrs. Fontaine?" Nick asked.

She looked up miserably at him. "Your office is chilly."

"Can I get you a cup of coffee?"

"No, thank you. Please, I just want to know about my husband. I still can't believe it, Mr. O'Hara. I keep thinking something's wrong. That there's been a mistake."

He nodded sympathetically. "That's a common reaction, to think it's all a mistake."

"Is it?"

"Denial. Everyone goes through it. That's what you're feeling now."

"But you don't ask every widow to your office, do you? There must be something different about Geoffrey."

"Yes," he admitted. "There is."

He turned and swept up a file folder from his desk. After flipping through it, he pulled out a page covered with notes. The handwriting was an illegible scrawl; it had to be his writing, she thought. No one but the writer himself would ever be able to decipher it.

"After I called you, Mrs. Fontaine, I got in touch with our consulate in Berlin. What you said last night bothered me. Enough to make me recheck the facts." His pause made her gaze up at him expectantly. She found two steady eyes, tired and troubled, watching her. "I talked to Wes Corrigan, our consul in Berlin. Here's what he told me." He glanced down at his notes. "Yesterday, about 8:00 p.m. Berlin time, a man named Geoffrey Fontaine checked into Hotel Regina. He paid with a traveler's check. The signature matched. For identification he used his passport. About four hours later, at midnight, the fire department answered a call at the hotel. Your husband's room was in flames. By the time they got it under control, the room was totally destroyed. The official explanation was that he'd fallen asleep while smoking in bed. Your husband, I'm afraid, was burned beyond recognition."

"Then how can they be sure it was him?" Sarah blurted. Until that instant she'd been listening with growing despair. But Nick O'Hara had just introduced too many other possibilities. "Someone could have stolen his passport," she pointed out.

"Mrs. Fontaine, let me finish."

"But you just said they couldn't even identify the body."

"Let's try and be logical, here."

"I *am* being logical!"

"You're being emotional. Look, it's normal for widows to clutch at straws like this, but—"

"I'm not yet convinced I *am* a widow."

He held up his hands in frustration. "Okay, okay, look at the evidence, then. The hard evidence. First, they found his briefcase in the room. It was aluminum, fire resistant."

"Geoffrey never owned anything like that."

"The contents survived the fire. Your husband's passport was inside."

"But—"

"Then there's the coroner's report. A Berlin pathologist briefly examined the body—what was left of it. While there weren't any dental records for comparison, the body's height was the same as your husband's."

"That doesn't mean a thing."

"Finally—"

"Mr. O'Hara—"

"Finally," he said with sudden force, "we have one last bit of evidence, something found on the body itself. I'm sorry, Mrs. Fontaine, but I think it'll convince you."

All at once she wanted to clap her hands over her ears, to shout at him to stop. Until now she'd withstood the evidence. But she couldn't listen any longer. She couldn't stand having all her hopes collapse.

"It was a wedding ring. The inscription was still readable. Sarah. 2-14." He looked up from his notes. "That *is* your wedding date, isn't it?"

Everything blurred as her eyes filled with tears. In silence she bowed her head. The glasses slipped off her nose and fell to her lap. Blindly she hunted in her purse for a tissue, only to find that Nick O'Hara had somehow produced a whole box of Kleenex out of thin air.

"Take what you need," he said softly.

He watched as she wiped away her tears and tried, somehow, to blow her nose gracefully. Under his scrutiny she felt so clumsy and stupid. Even her fingers refused to work properly. Her glasses slid from her lap to the floor. Her purse wouldn't snap shut. Desperate to leave, she fumbled for her things and rose from the chair.

"Please, Mrs. Fontaine, sit down. I'm not quite finished," he said.

As if she were an obedient child, Sarah returned to her seat and stared at the floor. "If it's about the burial arrangements…"

"No, you can take care of that later, after we fly the body back. There's something else I need to ask you. It's about your husband's trip. Why was he in Europe?"

"Business."

"What kind of business?"

"He was a—a representative for the Bank of London."

"So he traveled a lot?"

"Yes. Every month or so he was in London."

"Only London?"

"Yes."

"Tell me why he was in Germany, Mrs. Fontaine."

"I don't know."

"You must have an idea."

"I don't know."

"Was it his habit not to tell you where he was going?"

"No."

"Then why was he in Germany? There must have been a reason. Other business, perhaps? Other…"

She looked up sharply. "Other women? That's what you want to ask, isn't it?"

He didn't answer.

"*Isn't it?*"

"It's a reasonable suspicion."

"Not about Geoffrey!"

"About anyone." His eyes met hers head-on. She refused to turn away. "You were married a total of two months," he said. "How well did you know your husband?"

"Know him? I loved him, Mr. O'Hara."

"I'm not talking about love, whatever that means. I'm asking how well you *knew* the man. Who he was, what he did. How long ago did you meet?"

"It was…I guess six months ago. I met him at a coffee shop, near where I work."

"Where do you work?"

"NIH. I'm a research microbiologist."

His eyes narrowed. "What kind of research?"

"Bacterial genomes.... We splice DNA.... Why are you asking these questions?"

"Is it classified research?"

"I still don't understand why—"

"Is it *classified*, Mrs. Fontaine?"

She stared at him, shocked into silence by the sharp tone of his voice. Softly she said, "Yes. Some of it."

He nodded and pulled another sheet from the folder. Calmly he continued. "I had Mr. Corrigan in Berlin check your husband's passport. Whenever you fly into a new country, a page is stamped with an entry date. Your husband's passport had several stamps. London. Schiphol, near Amsterdam. And last, Berlin. All were dated within the last week. Any explanation why he'd visit those particular cities?"

She shook her head, bewildered.

"When did he call you last?"

"A week ago. From London."

"Can you be sure he was in London?"

"No. It was direct dial. There was no operator involved."

"Did your husband have a life-insurance policy?"

"No. I mean, I don't know. He never mentioned it."

"Did anyone stand to benefit from his death? Financially, I mean."

"I don't think so."

He took this in with a frown. Settling back onto the desk, he crossed his arms and looked away for a moment. She could almost see his mind churning over the facts, juggling the puzzle pieces. She was just as confused as he was. None of this made sense; none of it seemed possible. Geoffrey had been her husband, and now she was beginning to wonder if Nick O'Hara was right. That she'd never really known him. That all she and Geoffrey had shared was a bed and a home, but never their hearts.

No, this was all wrong; it was a betrayal of his memory. She believed in Geoffrey. Why should she believe this stranger? Why was this man telling her these things? Was there another purpose to all this? Suddenly she disliked Nick O'Hara. Intensely. He was flinging these questions at her for some unspoken reason.

"If you're finished…" she said, starting to rise again.

He glanced at her with a start, as if he'd forgotten she was still there. "No. I'm not."

"I'm not feeling well. I'd like to go home."

"Do you have a picture of your husband?" he asked abruptly.

Taken aback by his sudden request, Sarah opened her purse and pulled a photograph from her wallet. It was a good likeness of Geoffrey, taken on a Florida beach during their three-day honeymoon. His brilliant blue eyes stared directly at the camera. His hair was bright gold, and the sunlight fell at an angle across his face, throwing shadows on his uncommonly handsome features. He was smiling. From the start she'd been drawn to that face—not by just the good looks, but by the strength and intelligence she'd seen in the eyes.

Nick O'Hara took the picture and studied it without comment. Watching him, she thought, *He's so unlike Geoffrey. Not golden haired but dark, not smiling but very, very sober.* A troubled cloud seemed to hang over Nick O'Hara, a cloud of unhappiness. She wondered what he was thinking as he gazed at the picture. He showed little emotion, and except for the lines of fatigue, Sarah could read very little in his face. His eyes were a flat, impenetrable gray. He passed the photo briefly to Mr. Greenstein, then silently handed Geoffrey's picture back to her.

She closed her purse and looked at him. "Why are you asking all these questions?"

"I have to. I'm sorry, but it really is necessary."

"For whom?" she asked tightly. "For you?"

"For you, too. And maybe even for Geoffrey."

"That doesn't make sense."

"It will when you've heard the Berlin police report."

"Is there something else?"

"Yes. It's about the circumstances of your husband's death."

"But you said it was an accident."

"I said it *looked* like an accident." He watched her carefully while he spoke, as if afraid to miss any change in her face, any flicker of her eye. "When I spoke to Mr. Corrigan a few hours ago, there had been a new development. During a routine investigation of the fire, the debris from the room was examined. When they sifted through the mattress remains, they found a bullet."

She stared at him in disbelief. "A bullet?" she said. "You mean…"

He nodded. "They think it was murder."

Chapter Two

SARAH STARTED TO SPEAK, BUT HER voice refused to work. Like a statue, she sat frozen in her chair, unable to move, unable to do anything but stare at him.

"I thought you should know," said Nick. "I had to tell you in any event, because now we'll need your help. The Berlin police want information about your husband's activities, his enemies…why he might have been killed."

She shook her head numbly. "I can't think of… I mean I just don't know…. My God!" she whispered.

The gentle touch of his hand on her shoulder made Sarah flinch. She looked up and saw the concern in his eyes. *He's worried I'll faint*, she thought. *He's worried I'll get sick all over his nice thick carpet and embarrass us both*. With sudden irritation she shook off his hand. She didn't need anyone's rehearsed sympathy. She needed to be alone—away from bureaucrats and their impersonal file folders. She rose unin his pockets and hunched over a little as the wind bit through his wool jacket.

Vaguely he wondered whether Sarah Fontaine had reached her apartment yet, whether she was lying across her bed now, sobbing her eyes out. He knew he'd been rough on her. It had bothered him, hounding her like that, but someone had to break through all of her denial. She had to understand the facts. It was the only way she'd ever really recover from her grief.

"Where we going, Nick?" asked Tim.

"How about Mary Jo's?"

"That salad place? What, are you on a diet or something?"

"No, but it's quiet there. I'm not into loud conversation right now."

After two more blocks, they turned into the restaurant and sat down at a table. Fifteen minutes later the waitress brought their salads, which were cloaked in homemade mayonnaise and tarragon. Tim looked at the lettuce and arugula on his fork and sighed.

"This is rabbit food. Give me a greasy burger any day." He stuffed a forkful of the salad into his mouth and looked across the table at Nick. "So what's bugging you? The new post got you down already?"

"It's a damned slap in the face, that's what it is," said Nick. He drained his cup of coffee and motioned to the waitress for another. "To go straight from being number two man in London to shuffling papers in D.C."

"So why didn't you resign?"

"I just might. Since that fiasco in London, my career's been shot. And now I've got to put up with this bastard, Ambrose."

"Is he still out of town?"

steadily to her feet. No, she was not going to faint, not in front of this man.

Nick reached for her arm and nudged her gently back into the chair. "Please, Mrs. Fontaine. Another minute, that's all I need."

"Let me go."

"Mrs. Fontaine—"

"*Let me go.*"

The sharpness of her voice seemed to shock him. He released her but did not back away. As she sat there, she was acutely aware of various aspects of his presence—the faint smell of after-shave and fatigue, the dull gleam of his belt buckle, the wrinkled shirt sleeves.

"I'm sorry," he said. "I didn't mean to crowd you. I was just worried that…well…"

"Yes?" She looked up into those slate eyes. Something she saw there—a steadiness, a strength—made her suddenly, and against all instinct, want to trust him. "I'm not going to faint, if that's what you mean," she said. "Please, I'd like to go home now."

"Yes, of course. But I have just a few more questions."

"I don't have any answers. Don't you understand?"

He was silent for a moment. "Then I'll contact you later," he said at last. "We have to talk about the arrangements for the body."

"Oh. Yes, the body." She stood up, blinking back a new wave of tears.

"I'll have the car take you home now, Mrs. Fontaine." He moved toward her slowly, as if afraid of scaring her. "I'm sorry about your husband. Truly sorry. Feel free to call me if you have any questions."

She knew none of those words came from the heart, that

none of them held any genuine sympathy. Nicholas O'Hara was a diplomat, saying what he'd been taught to say. Whatever the catastrophe, the U.S. State Department always had the right words ready. He'd probably said the same thing to a hundred other widows.

Now he was waiting for her response, so she did what was expected of any widow. She pulled herself together. Reaching out, she shook his hand and thanked him. Then she turned and walked out the door.

"Do you think she knows?"

Nick stared at the door that had just closed behind Sarah Fontaine's retreating figure. He turned and glanced at Tim Greenstein. "Knows what?"

"That her husband was a spook?"

"Hell, *we* don't even know that."

"Nick my man, this whole thing reeks of espionage. Geoffrey Fontaine was a total nonentity till a year ago. Then his name shows up on a wedding license, he has a brand new Social Security number, a passport and what have you. The FBI doesn't seem to know a damn thing. But intelligence—they've got the guy's file under classified! Am I dumb or what?"

"Maybe I'm the dumb one," grunted Nick. He walked to his desk and dropped into the chair. Then he scowled at the Fontaine file. Tim was right, of course. The case stank to high heaven of funny business. Espionage? International crime? An ex-federal witness, hiding from the mob?

Who the hell *was* Geoffrey Fontaine?

Nick slouched down and threw his head back against the chair. Damn, he was tired. But he couldn't get Geof-

frey Fontaine out of his head. Or Sarah Fontaine, fo[r] matter.

He'd been surprised when she walked into the office; been expecting someone with a little more sophistica[tion]. Her husband had been a world-class traveler, a guy wh[o] whisked through London and Berlin and Amsterdam[. A] man like that should have a wife who was sleek and elega[nt.] Instead, in had walked this skinny, awkward creature w[ho] was almost, but not quite, pretty. Her face had been too fu[ll] of angles: high, sharp cheeks, a narrow nose, a square for[e]head softened only by a gentle widow's peak. Her long hai[r] had been a rich, coppery color; even tied back in a ponytail, it had been beautiful. Her horn-rimmed glasses had somehow amused him. They had framed two wide, amber-colored eyes—her best feature. With no makeup and with that pale, delicate complexion, she'd seemed much younger than the thirty or so years she must be.

No, she was not quite pretty. But throughout the interview Nick had found himself staring at her face and wondering about her marriage. And about her.

Tim rose. "Hey, all this grief is making me hungry. Let's hit the cafeteria."

"Not the cafeteria. Let's go out. I've been sitting in this building all morning, and I'm going stir-crazy." Nick pulled on his jacket, and together they walked out past Angie's desk and headed for the stairs.

Outside a brisk spring wind blew in their faces as they strode down the sidewalk. The buds were just starting to swell on the cherry trees. In another week the whole city would be awash in pink and white flowers. It was Nick's first D.C. springtime in eight years—he'd forgotten how pretty it could be, walking through the trees. He thrust his hands

"One more week. Till then I can do the job my way. Without all that bureaucratic nonsense. Hell, if he rewrites any more of my reports to make 'em 'conform to administration policy,' I'm going to puke." Nick put his fork down and scowled at the salad. The mention of his boss had just ruined his appetite. From the very first day, Nick and Ambrose had rubbed each other the wrong way. Charles Ambrose reveled in the bureaucratic merry-go-round, whereas Nick always insisted on getting straight to the point, however unpleasant. The clash had been inevitable.

"Your trouble, Nick, is that even though you're an egghead, you don't talk gobbledegook like all the others. You've got 'em all confused. They don't like guys they can understand. Plus you're a bleeding-heart liberal."

"So? You are, too."

"But I'm also a certified nerd. They make allowances for nerds. If they don't, I shut down their computers."

Nick laughed, suddenly glad for the company of his old buddy, Tim. Four years of being college roommates had left strong bonds. Even after eight years abroad, Nick had come home to find Tim Greenstein just as bushy and likable as ever.

He picked up his fork and finished off the salad.

"So what're you going to do with this Fontaine case?" Tim asked over dessert.

"I'm going to do my job and look into it."

"You gonna tell Ambrose? He'll want to hear about it. So will the guys at the Company, if they don't already know."

"Let 'em find out on their own. It's my case."

"It sounds like espionage to me, Nick. That's not exactly a consular affair."

But Nick didn't like the idea of turning Sarah Fontaine over to some CIA case officer. She seemed too fragile, too vulnerable. "It's my case," he repeated.

Tim grinned. "Ah, the widow Fontaine. Could it be she's your type? Though I can't quite see the attraction. What I really can't see is how she hooked that husband. Blond Adonis, wasn't he? Not the kind of guy to go for a woman in horn-rimmed glasses. My deduction is that he married her for reasons other than the usual."

"The usual? You mean love?"

"Naw. Sex."

"Just what the hell are you getting at?"

"Hmm. Touchy. You liked her, didn't you?"

"No comment."

"Seems to me the old love life's been pretty barren since your divorce."

Nick set his coffee cup down with a clatter. "What's with all these questions?"

"Just trying to see where your head's at, Nick. Haven't you heard? It's the latest thing. Men opening up to each other."

Nick sighed. "Don't tell me. You've been to another one of those sensitivity training sessions."

"Yeah. Great place to meet women. You should try it."

"No, thanks. The last thing I need is to join some big cry-in with a bunch of neurotic females."

Tim gave his friend a sympathetic look. "Let me tell you, Nick. You need to do something. You can't just sit around and be celibate the rest of your life."

"Why not?"

Tim laughed. "Because, dammit, we both know you're not the priestly type!"

Tim was right. In the four years since his split-up with Lauren, Nick had avoided any close relationships with women, sexual or otherwise, and it was starting to show. He was irritable. He'd thrown himself into salvaging what was left of his career, but work, he'd discovered, was a poor substitute for what he really wanted—a warm, soft body to hold; laughter in the night; thoughts shared in bed. To avoid being hurt again, he'd learned to live without these things. It was the only way to stay sane. But those old male instincts didn't die easily. No, Nick was not the priestly type.

"Heard from Lauren lately?" asked Tim.

Nick looked up with a scowl. "Yeah. Last month. Told me she misses me. What she really misses, I think, is the embassy life."

"So she called you. Sounds promising. Sounds like a reconciliation in the works."

"Yeah? It sounded more to me like her latest romance wasn't going so well."

"Either way, it's obvious she regrets the divorce. Did you follow up on it?"

Nick pushed away what remained of his chocolate mousse cake. "No."

"Why not?"

"Didn't feel like it."

Tim leaned back and laughed. "He didn't feel like it." He sighed to no one in particular. "Four years of moaning and groaning about being divorced, and now he tells me this."

"Look, every time things go bad for her, she decides to call good old Nick, her ever-loyal chump. I can't handle that anymore. I told her I was no longer available. For her or anyone else."

Tim shook his head. "You've sworn off women. That's a very bad sign."

"Nobody's ever died of it." Nick grunted as he threw a few bills on the table and rose. He wasn't going to think about women right now. He had too many other things on his mind, and he sure as hell didn't need another bad love affair.

But outside, as they walked back through the cherry trees, he found himself thinking about Sarah Fontaine. Not about Sarah, the grieving widow, but about Sarah, the woman. The name fit her. Sarah with the amber eyes.

Nick quickly shook off the thoughts. Of all the women in Washington, she was the last one he should be thinking about. In his line of work, objectivity was the key to doing the job right. Whether it was issuing visas or arguing a jailed American's case before a magistrate, getting personally involved was almost always a mistake. No, Sarah Fontaine was nothing more to him than a name in a file.

She would have to remain that way.

Amsterdam

THE OLD MAN loved roses. He loved the dusky smell of the petals, which he often plucked and rubbed between his fingers. So cool, so fragrant, not like those insipid tulips that his gardener had planted on the banks of the duck pond. Tulips were all color, no character. They threw up stalks, bloomed and vanished. But roses! Even through winter they persisted, bare and thorny, like angry old women crouched in the cold.

He paused among the rosebushes and breathed in deeply, enjoying the smell of damp earth. In a few weeks, there'd be flowers. How his wife would have loved this garden! He could picture her standing on this very spot, smiling at the roses. She would have worn her old straw hat and a house-dress with four pockets, and she would have carried her plastic bucket. *My uniform*, she'd have said. *I'm just an old soldier, going out to fight the snails and beetles.* He remembered how the rose clippers used to clunk against the bucket when she walked down the steps of their old house—the house he'd left behind. *Nienke, my sweet Nienke*, he thought. *How I miss you.*

"It is a cold day," said a voice in Dutch.

The old man turned and looked at the pale-haired young man walking toward him through the bushes. "Kronen," he said. "At last you've come."

"I am sorry, *meneer*. A day late, but it couldn't be helped." Kronen took off his sunglasses and peered up at the sky. As usual, he avoided looking directly at the old man's face. Since the accident, everyone avoided looking at his face, and it never failed to annoy him. It had been five years since anyone had stared him boldly in the eye, five years since he'd been able to meet another person's gaze without detecting the invariable flinching. Even Kronen, whom he'd come to regard almost as a son, made it a point to look anywhere else. But then, young men of Kronen's generation always fussed too much about appearances.

"I take it things went well in Basra," said the old man.

"Yes. Minor delays, that's all. And there were problems with the last shipment . . . the computer chips in the aiming mechanism.... One of the missiles failed to lock in."

"Embarrassing."

"Yes. I have already spoken to the manufacturer."

They followed a path from the rosebushes toward the duck pond. The cold air made the old man's throat sore. He wrapped his scarf a little tighter around his neck and forced out a thin, dry cough. "I have a new assignment for you," he said. "A woman."

Kronen paused, sudden interest in his eyes. His hair looked almost white in the sunshine. "Who is she?"

"The name is Sarah Fontaine. Geoffrey Fontaine's wife. I want you to see where she leads you."

Kronen frowned. "I don't understand, sir. I was told Fontaine was dead."

"Follow her anyway. My American source tells me she has a modest apartment in Georgetown. She is a microbiologist, thirty-two years old. Except for her marriage, she has no apparent intelligence connections. But one can never be certain."

"May I contact this source?"

"No. His position is too...delicate."

Kronen nodded, at once dropping the subject. He'd worked for the old man long enough to know the way things were done. Each man had his own territory, his own small box in which to operate. Never must one try to break out. Even Kronen, trusted as he was, saw only a part of the picture. Only the old man saw it all.

They walked together along the banks of the pond. The old man reached into his coat pocket and pulled out the bag of bread he'd brought from the house. Silently he flung a handful into the water and watched the crumbs swell. The ducks splashed among the reeds. When Nienke was alive, she had walked to the park every morning, just to feed the ducks her breakfast toast. She had worried that the weak ones would not get enough to eat. Look there, Frans, she would say. The little ones grow so fat! All on our breakfast crumbs!

steadily to her feet. No, she was not going to faint, not in front of this man.

Nick reached for her arm and nudged her gently back into the chair. "Please, Mrs. Fontaine. Another minute, that's all I need."

"Let me go."

"Mrs. Fontaine—"

"*Let me go.*"

The sharpness of her voice seemed to shock him. He released her but did not back away. As she sat there, she was acutely aware of various aspects of his presence—the faint smell of after-shave and fatigue, the dull gleam of his belt buckle, the wrinkled shirt sleeves.

"I'm sorry," he said. "I didn't mean to crowd you. I was just worried that…well…"

"Yes?" She looked up into those slate eyes. Something she saw there—a steadiness, a strength—made her suddenly, and against all instinct, want to trust him. "I'm not going to faint, if that's what you mean," she said. "Please, I'd like to go home now."

"Yes, of course. But I have just a few more questions."

"I don't have any answers. Don't you understand?"

He was silent for a moment. "Then I'll contact you later," he said at last. "We have to talk about the arrangements for the body."

"Oh. Yes, the body." She stood up, blinking back a new wave of tears.

"I'll have the car take you home now, Mrs. Fontaine." He moved toward her slowly, as if afraid of scaring her. "I'm sorry about your husband. Truly sorry. Feel free to call me if you have any questions."

She knew none of those words came from the heart, that

none of them held any genuine sympathy. Nicholas O'Hara was a diplomat, saying what he'd been taught to say. Whatever the catastrophe, the U.S. State Department always had the right words ready. He'd probably said the same thing to a hundred other widows.

Now he was waiting for her response, so she did what was expected of any widow. She pulled herself together. Reaching out, she shook his hand and thanked him. Then she turned and walked out the door.

"Do you think she knows?"

Nick stared at the door that had just closed behind Sarah Fontaine's retreating figure. He turned and glanced at Tim Greenstein. "Knows what?"

"That her husband was a spook?"

"Hell, we don't even know that."

"Nick my man, this whole thing reeks of espionage. Geoffrey Fontaine was a total nonentity till a year ago. Then his name shows up on a wedding license, he has a brand new Social Security number, a passport and what have you. The FBI doesn't seem to know a damn thing. But intelligence—they've got the guy's file under classified! Am I dumb or what?"

"Maybe I'm the dumb one," grunted Nick. He walked to his desk and dropped into the chair. Then he scowled at the Fontaine file. Tim was right, of course. The case stank to high heaven of funny business. Espionage? International crime? An ex-federal witness, hiding from the mob?

Who the hell was Geoffrey Fontaine?

Nick slouched down and threw his head back against the chair. Damn, he was tired. But he couldn't get Geoffrey Fontaine out of his head. Or Sarah Fontaine, for that matter.

He'd been surprised when she walked into the office; he'd been expecting someone with a little more sophistication. Her husband had been a world-class traveler, a guy who'd whisked through London and Berlin and Amsterdam. A man like that should have a wife who was sleek and elegant. Instead, in had walked this skinny, awkward creature who was almost, but not quite, pretty. Her face had been too full of angles: high, sharp cheeks, a narrow nose, a square forehead softened only by a gentle widow's peak. Her long hair had been a rich, coppery color; even tied back in a ponytail, it had been beautiful. Her horn-rimmed glasses had somehow amused him. They had framed two wide, amber-colored eyes—her best feature. With no makeup and with that pale, delicate complexion, she'd seemed much younger than the thirty or so years she must be.

No, she was not quite pretty. But throughout the interview Nick had found himself staring at her face and wondering about her marriage. And about her.

Tim rose. "Hey, all this grief is making me hungry. Let's hit the cafeteria."

"Not the cafeteria. Let's go out. I've been sitting in this building all morning, and I'm going stir-crazy." Nick pulled on his jacket, and together they walked out past Angie's desk and headed for the stairs.

Outside a brisk spring wind blew in their faces as they strode down the sidewalk. The buds were just starting to swell on the cherry trees. In another week the whole city would be awash in pink and white flowers. It was Nick's first D.C. springtime in eight years—he'd forgotten how pretty it could be, walking through the trees. He thrust his hands in his pockets and hunched over a little as the wind bit through his wool jacket.

Vaguely he wondered whether Sarah Fontaine had reached her apartment yet, whether she was lying across her bed now, sobbing her eyes out. He knew he'd been rough on her. It had bothered him, hounding her like that, but someone had to break through all of her denial. She had to understand the facts. It was the only way she'd ever really recover from her grief.

"Where we going, Nick?" asked Tim.

"How about Mary Jo's?"

"That salad place? What, are you on a diet or something?"

"No, but it's quiet there. I'm not into loud conversation right now."

After two more blocks, they turned into the restaurant and sat down at a table. Fifteen minutes later the waitress brought their salads, which were cloaked in homemade mayonnaise and tarragon. Tim looked at the lettuce and arugula on his fork and sighed.

"This is rabbit food. Give me a greasy burger any day." He stuffed a forkful of the salad into his mouth and looked across the table at Nick. "So what's bugging you? The new post got you down already?"

"It's a damned slap in the face, that's what it is," said Nick. He drained his cup of coffee and motioned to the waitress for another. "To go straight from being number two man in London to shuffling papers in D.C."

"So why didn't you resign?"

"I just might. Since that fiasco in London, my career's been shot. And now I've got to put up with this bastard, Ambrose."

"Is he still out of town?"

"One more week. Till then I can do the job my way. Without all that bureaucratic nonsense. Hell, if he rewrites any more of my reports to make 'em 'conform to administration policy,' I'm going to puke." Nick put his fork down and scowled at the salad. The mention of his boss had just ruined his appetite. From the very first day, Nick and Ambrose had rubbed each other the wrong way. Charles Ambrose reveled in the bureaucratic merry-go-round, whereas Nick always insisted on getting straight to the point, however unpleasant. The clash had been inevitable.

"Your trouble, Nick, is that even though you're an egghead, you don't talk gobbledegook like all the others. You've got 'em all confused. They don't like guys they can understand. Plus you're a bleeding-heart liberal."

"So? You are, too."

"But I'm also a certified nerd. They make allowances for nerds. If they don't, I shut down their computers."

Nick laughed, suddenly glad for the company of his old buddy, Tim. Four years of being college roommates had left strong bonds. Even after eight years abroad, Nick had come home to find Tim Greenstein just as bushy and likable as ever.

He picked up his fork and finished off the salad.

"So what're you going to do with this Fontaine case?" Tim asked over dessert.

"I'm going to do my job and look into it."

"You gonna tell Ambrose? He'll want to hear about it. So will the guys at the Company, if they don't already know."

"Let 'em find out on their own. It's my case."

"It sounds like espionage to me, Nick. That's not exactly a consular affair."

But Nick didn't like the idea of turning Sarah Fontaine over to some CIA case officer. She seemed too fragile, too vulnerable. "It's my case," he repeated.

Tim grinned. "Ah, the widow Fontaine. Could it be she's your type? Though I can't quite see the attraction. What I really can't see is how she hooked that husband. Blond Adonis, wasn't he? Not the kind of guy to go for a woman in horn-rimmed glasses. My deduction is that he married her for reasons other than the usual."

"The usual? You mean love?"

"Naw. Sex."

"Just what the hell are you getting at?"

"Hmm. Touchy. You liked her, didn't you?"

"No comment."

"Seems to me the old love life's been pretty barren since your divorce."

Nick set his coffee cup down with a clatter. "What's with all these questions?"

"Just trying to see where your head's at, Nick. Haven't you heard? It's the latest thing. Men opening up to each other."

Nick sighed. "Don't tell me. You've been to another one of those sensitivity training sessions."

"Yeah. Great place to meet women. You should try it."

"No, thanks. The last thing I need is to join some big cry-in with a bunch of neurotic females."

Tim gave his friend a sympathetic look. "Let me tell you, Nick. You need to do something. You can't just sit around and be celibate the rest of your life."

"Why not?"

Tim laughed. "Because, dammit, we both know you're not the priestly type!"

Tim was right. In the four years since his split-up with Lauren, Nick had avoided any close relationships with women, sexual or otherwise, and it was starting to show. He was irritable. He'd thrown himself into salvaging what was left of his career, but work, he'd discovered, was a poor substitute for what he really wanted—a warm, soft body to hold; laughter in the night; thoughts shared in bed. To avoid being hurt again, he'd learned to live without these things. It was the only way to stay sane. But those old male instincts didn't die easily. No, Nick was not the priestly type.

"Heard from Lauren lately?" asked Tim.

Nick looked up with a scowl. "Yeah. Last month. Told me she misses me. What she really misses, I think, is the embassy life."

"So she called you. Sounds promising. Sounds like a reconciliation in the works."

"Yeah? It sounded more to me like her latest romance wasn't going so well."

"Either way, it's obvious she regrets the divorce. Did you follow up on it?"

Nick pushed away what remained of his chocolate mousse cake. "No."

"Why not?"

"Didn't feel like it."

Tim leaned back and laughed. "He didn't feel like it." He sighed to no one in particular. "Four years of moaning and groaning about being divorced, and now he tells me this."

"Look, every time things go bad for her, she decides to call good old Nick, her ever-loyal chump. I can't handle that anymore. I told her I was no longer available. For her or anyone else."

Tim shook his head. "You've sworn off women. That's a very bad sign."

"Nobody's ever died of it." Nick grunted as he threw a few bills on the table and rose. He wasn't going to think about women right now. He had too many other things on his mind, and he sure as hell didn't need another bad love affair.

But outside, as they walked back through the cherry trees, he found himself thinking about Sarah Fontaine. Not about Sarah, the grieving widow, but about Sarah, the woman. The name fit her. Sarah with the amber eyes.

Nick quickly shook off the thoughts. Of all the women in Washington, she was the last one he should be thinking about. In his line of work, objectivity was the key to doing the job right. Whether it was issuing visas or arguing a jailed American's case before a magistrate, getting personally involved was almost always a mistake. No, Sarah Fontaine was nothing more to him than a name in a file.

She would have to remain that way.

Amsterdam

THE OLD MAN loved roses. He loved the dusky smell of the petals, which he often plucked and rubbed between his fingers. So cool, so fragrant, not like those insipid tulips that his gardener had planted on the banks of the duck pond. Tulips were all color, no character. They threw up stalks, bloomed and vanished. But roses! Even through winter they persisted, bare and thorny, like angry old women crouched in the cold.

He paused among the rosebushes and breathed in deeply, enjoying the smell of damp earth. In a few weeks, there'd be flowers. How his wife would have loved this garden! He could picture her standing on this very spot, smiling at the roses. She would have worn her old straw hat and a housedress with four pockets, and she would have carried her plastic bucket. *My uniform*, she'd have said. *I'm just an old soldier, going out to fight the snails and beetles.* He remembered how the rose clippers used to clunk against the bucket when she walked down the steps of their old house—the house he'd left behind. *Nienke, my sweet Nienke*, he thought. *How I miss you.*

"It is a cold day," said a voice in Dutch.

The old man turned and looked at the pale-haired young man walking toward him through the bushes. "Kronen," he said. "At last you've come."

"I am sorry, *meneer*. A day late, but it couldn't be helped." Kronen took off his sunglasses and peered up at the sky. As usual, he avoided looking directly at the old man's face. Since the accident, everyone avoided looking at his face, and it never failed to annoy him. It had been five years since anyone had stared him boldly in the eye, five years since he'd been able to meet another person's gaze without detecting the invariable flinching. Even Kronen, whom he'd come to regard almost as a son, made it a point to look anywhere else. But then, young men of Kronen's generation always fussed too much about appearances.

"I take it things went well in Basra," said the old man.

"Yes. Minor delays, that's all. And there were problems with the last shipment...the computer chips in the aiming mechanism.... One of the missiles failed to lock in."

"Embarrassing."

"Yes. I have already spoken to the manufacturer."

They followed a path from the rosebushes toward the duck pond. The cold air made the old man's throat sore. He wrapped his scarf a little tighter around his neck and forced out a thin, dry cough. "I have a new assignment for you," he said. "A woman."

Kronen paused, sudden interest in his eyes. His hair looked almost white in the sunshine. "Who is she?"

"The name is Sarah Fontaine. Geoffrey Fontaine's wife. I want you to see where she leads you."

Kronen frowned. "I don't understand, sir. I was told Fontaine was dead."

"Follow her anyway. My American source tells me she has a modest apartment in Georgetown. She is a microbiologist, thirty-two years old. Except for her marriage, she has no apparent intelligence connections. But one can never be certain."

"May I contact this source?"

"No. His position is too…delicate."

Kronen nodded, at once dropping the subject. He'd worked for the old man long enough to know the way things were done. Each man had his own territory, his own small box in which to operate. Never must one try to break out. Even Kronen, trusted as he was, saw only a part of the picture. Only the old man saw it all.

They walked together along the banks of the pond. The old man reached into his coat pocket and pulled out the bag of bread he'd brought from the house. Silently he flung a handful into the water and watched the crumbs swell. The ducks splashed among the reeds. When Nienke was alive, she had walked to the park every morning, just to feed the ducks her breakfast toast. She had worried that the weak ones would not get enough to eat. Look there, Frans, she would say. The little ones grow so fat! All on our breakfast crumbs!

Now, here he was, throwing bread on the water to the ducks he cared nothing about, except that Nienke would have loved them. He carefully folded the wrapper and stuffed it back into his pocket. As he did this, it struck him what a very sad and very feeble gesture it was, trying to preserve an old bread wrapper, and for what?

The pond had turned a sullen gray. Where had the sun gone? he wondered. Without looking at Kronen, he said, "I want to know about this woman. Leave soon."

"Of course."

"Be careful in Washington. I understand the crime there has become abominable."

Kronen laughed as he turned to leave. *"Tot ziens, meneer."*

The old man nodded. "Till then."

THE LAB WHERE Sarah worked was spotless. The microscopes were polished, the counters and sinks were repeatedly disinfected, the incubation chambers were wiped clean twice daily. Sarah's job required strict attention to asepsis; by habit she insisted on cleanliness. But as she sat at her lab bench, flipping through the last box of microscope slides, it seemed to Sarah that the sterility of the room had somehow extended to the rest of her life.

She took off her glasses and blinked tiredly. Everywhere she looked, stainless steel seemed to gleam back at her. The lights were harsh and fluorescent. There were no windows, and therefore, no sunshine. It could be noon or midnight outside; in here she'd never know the difference. Except for the hum of the refrigerator, the lab was silent.

She put her glasses on again and began to stack the slides back into the box. From the hallway came the clip of a woman's heels on the floor. The door swung open.

"Sarah? What're you doing here?"

Sarah glanced around at her good friend, Abby Hicks. In her size forty lab coat, Abby filled most of the doorway.

"I'm just catching up on a few things," said Sarah. "So much work's piled up since I've been gone...."

"Oh, for heaven's sake, Sarah! The lab can manage without you for a few weeks. It's already eight o'clock. I'll check the cultures. Go on home."

Sarah closed the box of slides. "I'm not sure I want to go home," she murmured. "It's too quiet there. I'd almost rather be here."

"Well, this place isn't exactly jumping. It's about as lively as a tomb—" At once Abby bit her lip and reddened. Even at age fifty-five, Abby could blush as deeply as a schoolgirl. "Bad choice of words," she mumbled.

Sarah smiled. "It's all right, Abby."

For a moment the two women said nothing. Sarah rose and opened the incubator to deposit the specimen plate she'd been working on. The foul smell of agar drifted out from the warm petri dishes and permeated the room.

"How are you doing, Sarah?" Abby asked gently.

Sarah shut the incubator after setting the plate inside. With a sigh she turned and looked at her friend. "I'm managing, I guess."

"We've all missed you. Even old Grubb says it's not the same without you and your silly bottle of disinfectant. I think everyone's just a little afraid to call you. None of them really knows what to do with grief, I suppose. But we do care, Sarah."

Sarah nodded gratefully. "Oh, Abby, I know you care. And I appreciate everything you've done for me. All the casseroles and cards and flowers. Now I just have to get back on my feet." She gazed sadly around the room. "I thought that coming back to work was what I needed."

"Some people need the old routine. Others need to get away for a while."

"Maybe that's what I should do. Get away from Washington for a while. Away from all the places that remind me of him…." She swallowed back the familiar ache in her throat and tried to smile. "My sister has asked me to visit her in Oregon. You know, I haven't seen my nephew and nieces in years. They must be getting huge."

"Then go. Sarah, it hasn't even been two weeks! You need to give it some time. Go see your sister. Have yourself a few more cries."

"I've spent too many days crying. I've been sitting at home, wondering how to get through this. I still can't bear to see his clothes hanging in the closet." Sarah shook her head. "It's not just losing him that hurts so much. It's the rest…."

"You mean the part about Berlin."

Sarah nodded. "I'll go crazy if I think about it much longer. That's why I came in tonight—to get my mind off the whole thing. I thought it was time to get back to work." She stared at the stack of lab books by her microscope. "But it's strange, Abby. I used to love this place. Now I wonder how I've stood it these past six years. All these cold cabinets and steel sinks. Everything so closed in. I feel as if I can't breathe."

"It's got to be more than the lab. You've always liked this job, Sarah. You're the one who stands humming by the centrifuge."

"I can't picture myself working here the rest of my life. Geoffrey and I had so little time together! Three days for a honeymoon. That's all. Then I had to rush back to finish that damned grant proposal. We were always so busy, no time for vacations. Now we'll never have another chance." Sighing, she went back to her bench and flicked off the microscope lamp. Softly she added, "And I'll never really know why he…" She sat down without finishing the sentence.

"Have you heard anything else from the State Department?"

"That man called again yesterday. The police in Berlin have finally released the—the body. It's coming home tomorrow." Her eyes suddenly filmed with tears. She gazed down, struggling not to cry. "The service will be Friday. You'll be there?"

"Of course I'll be there. We'll all be there. I'll drive you, okay?" Abby came over and laid a hand on her friend's shoulder. "It's still so recent, Sarah. You've got every right to cry."

"There's so much I'll never understand about his death, Abby. That man in the State Department—he kept hounding me for answers, and I couldn't give him a single one! Oh, I know it was just his job, but he brought up these…possibilities that have bothered me ever since. I've started wondering about Geoffrey. More and more."

"You weren't married that long, Sarah. Heck, my husband and I were married thirty years before we split up, and I never did figure out the jerk. It's not surprising you didn't know everything there was to know about Geoffrey."

"But he was my husband!"

Abby fell silent for a moment. Then, with some hesitation, she said, "You know, Sarah, there was always something about him…. I mean, I never felt I could get to *know* him very well."

"He was shy, Abby."

"No, it wasn't just shyness. It was as if—as if he didn't want to give anything away. As if—" She looked at Sarah. "Oh, it's not important."

But Sarah was already thinking about what Abby had said. There was some truth to her observation. Geoffrey had been an aloof man, not given to lengthy or revealing conversations. He'd never talked much about himself. He had always seemed more interested in her—her work, her friends. When they first met, that interest had been flattering; of all the men she'd known, he was the only one who'd ever really *listened*.

Then for some reason, another face sprang to mind. Nick O'Hara. Yes, that was his name. She had a sudden, vivid memory of the way Nick O'Hara had studied her, the way his gray eyes had focused on her every expression. Yes, he'd listened, too; but then, it had been his job. Had it also been his job to torment new widows? She didn't want to think about him. She never wanted to speak to the man again.

Sarah put the plastic cover over the microscope. She thought about taking her data book home. But as she scanned the open page, it occurred to her that the column of entries symbolized the way she was living her life. Neatly, carefully and precisely within the printed boundaries.

She closed the book and put it back on the shelf.

"I think I'm going home," she said.

Abby nodded her approval. "Good. No sense burying yourself in here. Forget about work for a while."

"Are you sure you can handle the extra load?"

"Of course."

Sarah took off her lab coat and hung it by the door. Like everything else in the room, her coat looked too neat, too clean. "Maybe I will take some time off, after the funeral. Another week. Maybe a month."

"Don't stay away too long," said Abby. "We do want you back."

Sarah glanced around one last time to make sure things were tidy. They were. "I'll be back," she said. "I just don't know when."

THE COFFIN SLID down the ramp and landed with a soft thud on the platform. The sound made Nick shudder. Years of packing off dead Americans hadn't dulled his sense of horror. But like everyone else in the consular corps, he'd found his own way to handle the pain. Later today he'd take a long walk, go home and pour himself a drink. Then he'd sit in his old leather chair, turn on the radio and read the newspaper; find out how many earthquakes there'd been, how many plane and train and bus crashes, how many bombs had been dropped. The big picture. It would make this one death seem insignificant. Almost.

"Mr. O'Hara? Sign here, please."

A man in an airline uniform held out a clipboard with the shipment papers. Nick glanced over the documents, quickly noting the deceased's name: Geoffrey Fontaine. He scrawled his signature and handed back the clipboard. Then he turned and watched as the coffin was loaded into a waiting hearse. He didn't want to think about its contents, but all at once an image rose up in his mind, something he'd seen in a magazine, a picture of dead Vietnamese villagers after a bombing. They had all burned to death. Is that what lay inside Geoffrey Fontaine's coffin? A man charred beyond recognition?

He shook off the image. Damn, he needed a drink. It was time to go home. The hearse was headed off safely to a designated mortuary; as previously arranged, Sarah Fontaine would take charge from there. He wondered if he should call her just one more time. But for what? More condolences, more regrets? He'd done his part. She'd already paid the bill. There was nothing else to say.

By the time he got to his apartment, Nick had shoved the whole grisly affair out of his mind. He threw his brief-case onto the couch and went straight to the kitchen, where he poured out a generous glass of whiskey and slid a TV dinner into the oven. Good old Swanson, the bach-elor's friend. He leaned back against the counter and sipped his drink. The refrigerator began to growl, and the oven light clicked off. He thought of turning on the radio, but he couldn't quite force himself to move. So ended an-other day as a public servant. And to think it was only Tuesday.

He wondered how long it had been since he'd been happy. Months? Years? Trying to recall a different state of mind was futile. Sights and sounds were what he remem-bered—the blue of a sky, the smile on a face. His last dis-tinct image of happiness was of riding a bus in London, a bus with torn seats and dirty windows. He'd just left the em-bassy for the day and was on his way home to Lauren....

The apartment buzzer made him jump. Suddenly he felt starved for company, any company, even the paperboy's. He went to the intercom. "Hello?"

"Hey, Nick? It's Tim. Let me in."

"Okay. Come on up."

Nick released the front lock. Would Tim want supper? Dumb question. He always wanted supper. Nick poked in the freezer and was relieved to find two more TV dinners. He put one in the oven.

He went to the front doorway and waited for the elevator to open.

Tim bounded out. "Okay, are you ready for this? Guess what my FBI friend found out?"

Nick sighed. "I'm afraid to ask."

"You know that guy, Geoffrey Fontaine? Well, he's dead all right."

"So what's new?"

"No, I'm talking about the *real* Geoffrey Fontaine."

"Look," said Nick. "I've pretty much closed my file on this case. But if you want to stay for dinner…"

Tim followed him into the apartment. "See, the real Geoffrey Fontaine died—"

"Right," said Nick.

"Forty-two years ago."

The door slammed shut. Nick turned and stared at him. "Ha!" said Tim. "I thought that'd get your attention."

Chapter Three

THE DAY SMELLED OF FLOWERS. On the grass at Sarah's feet lay a mound of carnations and gladioli and lilies. For the rest of her life, the smell would sicken her. It would bring back this hilltop and the marble plaques dotting the shorn grass and the mist hanging in the valley below. Most of all, it would bring back the pain. Everything else—the minister's words, the squeeze of her good friend Abby's hand around her arm, even the first cold drops of rain against her face—she scarcely felt, for it was peripheral to the pain.

She forced herself not to concentrate on the gash of earth at her feet. Instead she stared at the hill across the valley. Through the mist she could see a faint dappling of pink. The cherry trees were blooming. But the view only saddened her; it was a springtime Geoffrey would not see.

The minister's voice receded to a faintly irritating drone. A cold drizzle stung Sarah's cheeks and clouded her glasses; fog moved in, closing off the world. Abby's sudden nudge brought her back to reality. The casket had been lowered. She saw faces, all watching her, all waiting. These were her friends, but in her pain she scarcely recognized them. Even Abby, dear Abby, was a stranger to her now.

Automatically Sarah bent down and took a handful of earth. It was damp and rich and it smelled of rain. She tossed it into the grave. The thud of the casket made her wince.

Faces passed by as if they were ghosts in the mist. Her friends were gentle. They spoke softly. Through it all she stood dry-eyed and numb. The smell of flowers and the mist against her face overpowered her senses, and she was aware of nothing else until she looked around and saw that the others had gone. Only she and Abby were standing beside the grave.

"It's starting to rain," said Abby.

Sarah looked up and saw the clouds descending on them like a cold, silvery blanket. Abby draped her stout arm around Sarah's shoulders and nudged her toward the parking lot.

"A cup of tea, that's what we both need," said Abby. It was her remedy for everything. She had survived a nasty divorce and the departure of her college-bound sons on nothing more potent than Earl Grey. "A cup of tea, and then let's talk."

"A cup of tea does sound nice," admitted Sarah.

Arm in arm, they slowly walked across the lawn. "I know it means nothing to you now," said Abby, "but the pain will pass, Sarah. It really will. We women are strong that way. We have to be."

"What if I'm not?"

"You are. Don't you doubt it."

Sarah shook her head. "I question everything now. And everyone."

"You don't doubt me, do you?"

Sarah looked at Abby's broad, damp face and smiled. "No. Not you."

"Good. When you get to be my age, you'll see that it's all—" Suddenly Abby stopped in her tracks. Her breathing was loud and husky. Sarah followed the direction of her gaze.

A man was walking toward them through the mist.

Sarah took in the windblown dark hair and the gray overcoat, now sparkling with water droplets. She could tell he had been standing outside a long time, probably through the whole funeral. The cold had turned his face ruddy.

"Mrs. Fontaine?" he asked.

"Hello, Mr. O'Hara."

"Look, I realize this is a bad moment, but I've been trying to get hold of you for two days. You haven't returned my calls."

"No," she admitted, "I haven't."

"I need to talk to you. There've been some new developments. I think you should hear about them."

"Sarah, who is this man?" broke in Abby.

Nick turned to the older woman. "Nick O'Hara. I'm with the State Department. If it would be all right, ma'am, I'd like a moment alone with Mrs. Fontaine."

"Maybe she doesn't want to talk to you."

He looked back at Sarah. "It's important."

Something about the way he looked at her, the stubborn angle of his jaw, made Sarah consider his request. She hadn't planned to speak to him again. For the past two days, her answering machine had recorded his half dozen calls, all of which she'd ignored. Geoffrey was dead and buried; that was pain enough. Nick O'Hara would only make things worse by asking his unanswerable questions.

"Please, Mrs. Fontaine."

At last she nodded. With a glance at Abby, she said, "I'll be all right."

"Well, you can't stand around chatting out here. It'll be pouring in a minute!"

"I can drive her home," said Nick. At Abby's dubious look, he smiled. "Really, I'm okay. I'll take care of her."

Abby gave Sarah one last hug and kiss. "I'll call you tonight, sweetheart. Let's have breakfast in the morning." Then, with obvious reluctance, she turned and headed toward her car.

"A good friend, I take it," he said, watching Abby's retreat.

"We've worked together for years."

"At NIH?"

"Yes. The same lab."

He glanced up at the sky, which was now dark with storm clouds. A chill had fallen over them. "Your friend's right. It'll be pouring in a minute. Come on. My car's this way."

Gently he touched her sleeve. She moved ahead mechanically, allowing him to guide her into the front seat of his car. He slid in beside her and pulled his door shut. For a moment they sat in silence. The car was an old Volvo, practical, without frills, a model one chose purely for transportation. It fit him, somehow. A trace of warmth still clung to the interior, and Sarah's glasses clouded over. Pulling them off, she turned and looked at him and saw that his hair was wet.

"You must be cold," he said. "Let's get you home."

The engine roared to life. A blast of air erupted from the heater, gradually warming them as they drove along the winding road from the cemetery. The windshield wiper squeaked back and forth.

"It started out so beautiful this morning," she said, watching the rain fall.

"Unpredictable. Just like everything else."

He smoothly turned the car onto the highway bound for D.C. He was a calm driver, with steady hands. The kind who probably never took risks. Savoring the heater's warmth, Sarah settled back in her seat.

"Why didn't you return my calls?" he asked.

"It was rude of me. I'm sorry."

"You didn't answer my question. Why didn't you call me back?"

"I guess I didn't want to hear any more speculation about Geoffrey. Or about his death."

"Even if they're facts?"

"You weren't giving me facts, Mr. O'Hara. You were guessing."

He stared ahead grimly at the road. "I'm not guessing anymore, Mrs. Fontaine. I've got the facts. All I need is a name."

"What are you talking about?"

"Your husband. You said that six months ago you met Geoffrey Fontaine at a coffee shop. He must have swept you clean off your feet. Four months later you were married. Correct?"

"Yes."

"I don't know how to say this, but Geoffrey Fontaine—the real Geoffrey Fontaine—died forty-two years ago. As an infant."

She couldn't believe what she was hearing. "I don't understand..."

He didn't look at her; he kept his eyes on the road as he talked. "The man you married took the name of a dead infant. It's easy enough to do. You hunt around for the name of a baby who died around the year you were born. Then you get a copy of the birth certificate. With that you apply for a Social Security number, a driver's license, a marriage license. You *become* that infant, grown up. A new identity. A new life. With all the records to prove it."

"But—but how do you know all this?"

"Everything's on computer these days. From a few cross-checks, I found out that Geoffrey Fontaine never registered for the draft. He never attended school. He never held a bank account—until a year ago, when his name suddenly appeared in a dozen different places."

The breath went out of her. "Then who was he?" she whispered at last. "Who did I marry?"

"I don't know," Nick answered.

"Why? Why would he do it? Why would he start a new life?"

"I can think of lots of reasons. My first thought was that he was wanted for some crime. His thumbprints were on record with the driver's license bureau, so I had them run through the FBI computer. He's not on any of their lists."

"Then he wasn't a criminal."

"There's no proof that he was. Another possibility is that he was in some kind of federal witness program, that he was given a new name for protection. It's hard for me to check on that. The data are locked up tight. It would, however, give us a motive for his murder."

"You mean—the people he testified against—they found him."

"That's right."

"But he would have told me about something like that, he would have shared it with me...."

"That's what makes me think of one more possibility. Maybe you can confirm it."

"Go on."

"What if your husband's new name and new life were just part of his job? He might not have been running from anything. He might have been sent here."

"You mean he was a spy," she said softly.

He looked at her and nodded. His eyes were as gray as the storm clouds outside.

"I don't believe this," she said. "None of it!"

"It's real. I assure you."

"Then why are you telling *me*? How do you know I'm not an accomplice or something?"

"I think you're clean, Mrs. Fontaine. I've seen your file—"

"Oh. I have a file, too?" she shot back.

"You got security clearance some years ago, remember? For the research you were working on. Naturally a file was generated."

"Naturally."

"But it's not just your file that makes me think you're clean. It's my own gut feeling. Now convince me I'm right."

"How? Should I hook myself up to a polygraph?"

"Start off by telling me about you and Geoffrey. Were you in love?"

"Of course we were!"

"So it was a real marriage? You had…relations?"

She flushed. "Yes. Like any normal couple. Do you want to know how often? When?"

"I'm not playing games. I'm sticking my neck out for you. If you don't like my approach, perhaps you'd prefer the way the Company handles it."

"Then you haven't told the CIA?"

"No." His chin came up in an unintended gesture of stubbornness. "I don't care much for the way they do things. I may get slapped down for this, but then again, I may not."

"So why are you putting yourself on the line?"

He shrugged. "Curiosity. Maybe a chance to see what I can do on my own."

"Ambition?"

"That's part of it, I guess. Plus..." He glanced at her, and their eyes met. Suddenly he fell silent.

"Plus what?" she asked.

"Nothing."

The rain was coming down in sheets and streamed across the windshield. Nick left the freeway and edged into city-bound traffic. Driving through D.C. rush hour usually made Sarah nervous; today, though, she took it calmly. Something about the way Nick O'Hara drove made her feel safe. In fact, everything about him spoke of safety—the steadiness of his hands on the wheel, the warmth of his car, the low timbre of his voice. Just sitting beside him, she felt secure. She could imagine how safe a woman might feel in his arms.

"Anyway," he continued, "you can see we've got a lot of unanswered questions. You might have some of the answers, whether you know it or not."

"I don't have any answers."

"Let's start off with what you do know."

She shook her head, bewildered. "I was married to him and I can't even tell you his real name!"

"Everyone, Sarah, even the best spy, slips up. He must've let his guard down for a moment. Maybe he talked in his sleep. Maybe he said things you can't explain. *Think*."

She bit her lip, suddenly thinking not about Geoffrey, but about Nick. He'd called her by her first name. Sarah. "Even if there were things," she said, "little things—I might not have considered them significant."

"Such as?"

"Oh, he might have—he might have called me Evie once or twice. But he always apologized right away. He said she was an old girlfriend."

"What about family? Friends? Didn't he talk about them?"

"He said he was born in Vermont, then raised in London. His parents were theater people. They're dead. He never talked about any other relatives. He always seemed so...self-sufficient. He didn't have any close friends, not even from work. At least, none he introduced me to."

"Oh, yes. His work. I've been checking on that. It seems he *was* listed on the Bank of London payroll. He had a desk in some back office. But no one remembers quite what he did."

"Then even that part wasn't real."

"So it seems."

Sarah sank deeper into the seat. Each thing this man told her left another slash in the fabric of her life. Her marriage was dissolving away to nothing. It had been all shadow and no substance. Reality was here and now, the rain hitting the car, the windshield wipers beating back and forth. Most of all, reality was the man sitting silently beside her. He was not an illusion. She scarcely knew him, and yet he'd become the only reality she could cling to.

She wondered about Nick O'Hara. She didn't think he was married. Despite his aloofness she found him attractive enough; any woman would have. But there was more than just the physical attraction. She sensed his need. Something told her he was lonely, troubled. Vague shadows of unhappiness surrounded his eyes, creating a feeling of restlessness; it was the look of a man without a home. He probably had none. The foreign service was a career for nomads, not for people who craved a house in the suburbs. Nick O'Hara was definitely not the suburban type.

Shivering, she longed desperately to be back in her apartment, drinking that cup of tea with Abby. *It won't be long,* she thought as the streets became more and more familiar. Connecticut Avenue glistened in the rain. The downpour had already stripped the cherry trees of half their blossoms; the first rush of spring had been short-lived.

They pulled up in front of her apartment, and Nick dashed around the car to open her door. It was a funny little gesture, the sort of thing Geoffrey used to do, gallant and sweetly impractical. By the time they stamped into the lobby they were both soaked. The rain had plastered his hair in dark curls against his forehead.

"I suppose you have more questions." She sighed as they headed toward the stairs leading to the second floor.

"If you mean do I want to come up, the answer is yes."

"For tea or interrogation?"

He smiled and brushed away the water dripping down his cheek. "A little of both. I've had so much trouble getting hold of you, I'd better ask all my questions now."

They reached the top of the stairs. She was just about to say something when the hallway came into view. What she saw made her freeze.

The door to her apartment was hanging open. Someone had broken in.

Instinctively Sarah retreated, terrified of whatever lay beyond the door. She fell back against Nick and found herself wordlessly clutching his arm. He stared at the open door, his face suddenly tense. Except for the pounding of her own heart, she heard nothing. The apartment was absolutely silent.

Light spilled into the hall through the open doorway. Nick motioned her to stay where she was, then cautiously approached the door. Sarah started to follow him, but he gave her such a dark look of warning that she shrank back at once.

He nudged the door open, and the arc of light widened and spilled across his face. For a few seconds, he stood in the doorway, staring at the room beyond. Then he entered the apartment.

In the hall Sarah waited, frightened by the absolute silence. What was happening inside? A shadow flickered in the doorway, and panic began to overtake her as she watched the outline grow larger. Then, to her relief, Nick poked his head out.

"It's all right, Sarah," he said. "There's no one here."

She ran past him into the apartment. In the living room, she paused, surprised by what she saw. She had expected to find her possessions gone, to find only empty shelves where her TV and stereo had always sat. But nothing had been touched. Even the antique clock was in its place, ticking softly on the bookshelf.

She turned and ran into the bedroom with Nick close behind. He watched from the doorway as she went directly to the jewelry box on her dresser. There, on red velvet, was her string of pearls, right where it should be. Slamming the box shut, she turned and quickly surveyed the room, taking in the king-size bed, the nightstand with its china lamp, the closet. In confusion she looked back at Nick.

"What's missing?" he asked.

She shook her head. "Nothing. Could I have just left the door unlocked?"

He stalked out of her bedroom, back to the hall. She found him crouched in the doorway. "Look," he said, pointing down at the wood splinters and fragments of antique-white paint littering the gray carpet. "It's definitely been forced open."

"But it doesn't make sense! Why break into an apartment and then not take anything?"

"Maybe he didn't have time. Maybe he was interrupted...." Rising, he turned and looked at her. "You look shook up. Are you all right?"

"I'm just—just bewildered."

He touched her hand; his fingers felt hot against hers. "You're also freezing. You'd better get out of those wet clothes."

"I'm fine, Mr. O'Hara. Really."

"Come on. Off with the coat." He insisted. "And sit down while I make a few calls."

Something about his tone seemed to leave Sarah no choice but to obey. She let him tug off her coat, then sat on the couch and watched numbly as he reached for the telephone. Suddenly she felt as though she'd lost control of her actions. As though, just by walking into her apartment, Nick O'Hara had taken over her life. Almost as an act of protest, she rose and headed for the kitchen.

"Sarah?"

"I'm going to make a pot of tea."

"Look, don't go to any trouble—"

"It's no trouble. We could both use a cup, I think."

From the kitchen doorway, she saw him dial his call. As she put the kettle on, she heard him say, "Hello? Tim Greenstein, please. This is Nick O'Hara calling.... Yes, I'll hold."

The next pause seemed to last forever. Nick began to pace back and forth, like an animal in a cage, first pulling off his overcoat, then loosening his tie. His agitation made him entirely out of place in her small, tidy living room.

"Shouldn't you call the police?" she asked.

"That's next on the list. First I'd like an informal chat with the bureau. If I can just get through the damned lines."

"The bureau? You mean the FBI? But why?"

"There's something about all this that bugs me...."

His words were lost when the kettle abruptly whistled. Sarah filled the teapot and carried the tray out to the living room, where Nick was still waiting on the phone.

"Dammit," he muttered to himself. "Where the hell are you, Greenstein?"

"Tea, Mr. O'Hara?"

"Hmm?" He turned and saw the cup she held out to him. "Yeah. Thanks."

She sat down, holding a cup and saucer on her lap. "Does Mr. Greenstein work for the FBI?"

"No. But he has a friend who—hello? Tim? It's about time! Don't you answer your calls anymore?"

In the silence that followed, Nick's face and the way he stood, with his shoulders squared and his back rigid, told Sarah that something was wrong. He was livid. The loud clatter of his teacup on the saucer made her jump.

"How the hell did Ambrose get wind of it?" he snapped into the receiver, turning away from Sarah.

Another silence. She stared at his back, wondering what kind of catastrophe had made Nick O'Hara so angry. Up until now she'd thought of him as a man completely in control of his emotions. No longer. His anger surprised her, yet somehow it also reassured her that he was human.

"Okay," he said into the phone. "I'll be there in half an hour. Look, Tim, something else has come up. Someone's broken into Sarah's apartment. No, nothing's been touched. Can you get me the number of this FBI friend? I want to— Yeah, I'm sorry I got you into this, but…" He turned and gave Sarah a harassed look. "Okay! Half an hour. My trip to the woodshed. Meet you in Ambrose's office." He hung up with a scowl.

"What's wrong?" she asked.

"So end eight glorious years with the State Department," he muttered, furiously snatching up his overcoat and walking toward the door. "I've gotta go. Look, you've still got the chain. Use it. Better yet, stay with your friend tonight. And call the police. I'll get back to you as soon as I can."

She followed him into the hallway. "But Mr. O'Hara—"

"Later!" he called over his shoulder as he stalked away. She heard his footsteps echo in the stairwell, and moments later the lobby door slammed shut.

She closed the door and slid the chain in place, then slowly gazed around the room. Her stack of *Advances in Microbiology* lay on the coffee table. A vase of peonies dropped petals onto the bookshelf. Everything was as it should be.

No, not quite. Something was different. If she could just put her finger on it…

She was halfway across the room when it suddenly struck her—there was an empty space on the bookshelf. Her wedding picture was gone.

A cry of anger welled up in her throat. For the first time since she'd returned to the apartment, she felt a sense of violation, of fury that someone had invaded her house. It had only been a photograph, a pair of happy faces beaming at a camera, yet it meant more to her than anything else she owned. The picture had been all she had left of Geoffrey. Even if her marriage had been mere illusion, she never wanted to forget how she had loved him. Of all the things in her apartment, why would anyone steal a photograph?

Her heart skipped a beat as the phone rang. It was probably Abby, calling as promised. She picked up the receiver.

The first sound she heard was the hiss of a long-distance connection. Sarah froze. For some reason she found herself staring at the empty shelf, at the spot where the photograph should have been.

"Hello?" she said.

"Come to me, Sarah. I love you."

A scream caught in her throat. The room was spinning wildly, and she reached out for support. The receiver slipped from her fingers and thudded on the carpet. *This is impossible!* she thought. *Geoffrey is dead....*

She scrambled on the floor for the receiver, scrambled to hear the voice of what could only be a ghost.

"Hello? *Hello? Geoffrey!*" she screamed.

The long-distance hiss was gone. There was only silence and then, a few seconds later, the hum of the dial tone.

But she had heard enough. Everything that had happened in the past two weeks faded away as if it were a nightmare remembered in the light of day. None of it had been real. The voice she'd just heard, the voice she knew so well—*that* was real.

Geoffrey was alive.

Chapter Four

"YOU'VE HAD IT, O'HARA!" Charles Ambrose stood outside the closed door of his office and looked pointedly at his watch. "And you're twenty minutes late!"

Unperturbed, Nick hung up his coat and said, "Sorry. I couldn't help it. The rain had us backed up for—"

"Do you know who just happens to be waiting in my office right now? I mean, do you have any idea?"

"No. Who?"

"Some son of a—" Ambrose abruptly lowered his voice. "The CIA, that's who! A guy named Van Dam. This morning he calls me up wanting to know about the Fontaine case. What's the Fontaine case, I ask. He had to tell me what's going on in my own department! For God's sake, O'Hara! What the hell do you think you're doing?"

Nick gazed back calmly. "My job, as a matter of fact."

"Your job was to tell the widow you were sorry and to fly the damned body back. That was it, period. Instead, Van

Dam tells me you've been out playing James Bond with Sarah Fontaine."

"I'll admit that I went to the funeral. And I did drive Mrs. Fontaine home. I wouldn't call that playing James Bond."

In reply, Ambrose turned and flung the office door open. "Get in there, O'Hara!"

Without blinking, Nick walked into the office. The blinds were open and the last drab light of day fell on the shoulders of a man sitting at Ambrose's desk. He was in his midforties, tall, silent, and like the day outside, totally without color. His hands were folded in a gesture of prayer. There was no sign of Tim Greenstein. Ambrose closed the door, stalked past Nick and seated himself off to the side. The fact that Ambrose had been evicted from his own desk spoke volumes about his usurper's prestige. *This guy,* thought Nick, *must be hot stuff in the CIA.*

"Please sit down, Mr. O'Hara," said the man. "I'm Jonathan Van Dam." That was the only label he gave himself: a name.

Nick took a chair, but obedience had nothing to do with it. He was simply not going to stand at attention while he was put through the wringer.

For a moment Van Dam silently regarded him with those colorless eyes. Then he picked up a manila folder. It was Nick's employment record. "I hope you're not nervous. It's just a minor thing, really." Van Dam glanced through the folder. "Let's see. You've been with state for eight years."

"Eight years, two months."

"Two years in Honduras, two in Cairo and four years in London. All in the consular service. A good record, with the exception of two adverse personnel memos. It says here that in Honduras you were too—er, sympathetic to native concerns."

"That's because our policy there stinks."

Van Dam smiled. "Believe me, you're not the first person to say that."

The smile threw Nick off guard. He glanced suspiciously at Ambrose, who'd obviously been hoping for an execution and now looked sorely disappointed.

Van Dam sat back. "Mr. O'Hara, this is a country of diverse opinions. I respect men who think for themselves, men like you. Unfortunately, independent thinking is often discouraged in government service. Is that what led to this second memo?"

"I assume it's about that incident in London."

"Yes. Could you elaborate?"

"I'm sure Roy Potter filed a report with your office. His version of the story, anyway."

"Tell me yours."

Nick sat back, the memory of the incident at once reawakening his anger. "It happened the week our consular chief, Dan Lieberman, was out of town. I was filling in for him. A man named Vladimir Sokolov approached me one night, in confidence. He was an attaché with the Russian embassy in London. Oh, I'd met him before, you know, at the usual round of receptions. He'd always struck me as a little nervous. Worried. Well, he took me aside at one of their—I don't know, I guess it was a reception for the ambassador. He wanted to talk asylum. He had information to trade—good information, to my mind. I immediately brought the matter to Roy Potter." Nick glanced at Ambrose. "Potter was chief of intelligence in our London mission." He looked back at Van Dam. "Anyway, Potter was skeptical. He wanted to try using Sokolov as a double agent first. Maybe get some hard intelligence from the Soviets. I tried to convince him the man was in real danger. And he had a family in London, a wife and two kids. But Potter decided to wait before taking him in."

"I can see his point. Sokolov had strong links to the KGB. I would've questioned his motives, too."

"Yeah? If he was a KGB plant, why did his kids find him dead a few days later? Even the Soviets don't dispose of their own operatives without good reason. Your people left him to the wolves."

"It's a dangerous business, Mr. O'Hara. These things do happen."

"I'm sure they do. But I felt personally responsible in this case. And I wasn't going to let Roy Potter off the hook."

"It says here you two had a shouting match in the embassy stairwell." Van Dam shook his head and laughed as he scanned the report. "You called Mr. Potter a large variety of—er, colorful names. My goodness, here's one I've never heard before. And all within public hearing."

"To that I plead guilty."

"Mr. Potter also claims you were…let me quote: 'incensed, out of control and close to violence,' unquote."

"I was not close to violence."

Van Dam closed the file and smiled sympathetically. "I know how it feels, Mr. O'Hara, to be surrounded by incompetents. God knows, not a day goes by that I don't wonder how this country stays afloat. I'm not talking about just the intelligence business. Everything. I'm a widower, you see, and my wife left me with a rather large house to keep up. I can't even find a decent housekeeper, or a gardener who can keep my azaleas alive. Sometimes, at work, I want to throw my hands up and just say, 'Forget it! I'm doing things my own way and the rules be damned!'

Haven't you felt that way, too? Of course you have. I can see you're a nonconformist, like me."

Nick began to feel he'd been trapped in the wrong conversation. Housekeepers? Azaleas? What was the guy leading up to?

"I see you were with American University before you joined the State Department," said Van Dam.

"I was an associate professor. Linguistics."

"Oh, I'm sorry. It's really *Dr.* O'Hara, isn't it?"

"A minor point."

"Even at the university, you were the independent sort. Traits like that don't change. Mr. Ambrose says you don't quite fit into this department. You're an outsider. I imagine that gets a bit lonely."

"Just what are you trying to say, Mr. Van Dam?"

"That a lonely man might find it…tempting, shall we say, to associate with other nonconformists. That, in anger, you might be persuaded to cooperate with outside interests."

Nick stiffened. "I'm not a traitor, if that's what you're implying."

"No, no. I'm not saying that at all! I dislike that word, traitor. It's so imprecise. After all, the definition of traitor varies with one's political orientation."

"I know what a traitor is, Mr. Van Dam! It so happens I don't agree with a lot of our policies, but that doesn't make me disloyal!"

"Well, then. Perhaps you can explain your involvement in the Fontaine case."

Nick forced himself to take a deep breath. They'd finally gotten to the real issue. "I was just doing my job. Two weeks ago Geoffrey Fontaine died in Germany. I got the routine task of calling the widow. Certain things she said bothered me. I ran Fontaine's name through the computer—just checking, you understand. I came up with a lot of blanks. So I called a friend…"

"Mr. Greenstein," offered Van Dam.

"Look, leave him out of this. He was just doing me a favor. He has a buddy in the FBI who looked up Fontaine's name. Not much turned up. I had more questions than answers. So I went straight to the widow."

"Why didn't you come to us?"

"I wasn't aware your authority extended to American soil. Legally speaking, that is."

For the first time, a faint look of irritation flashed in Van Dam's eyes. "You realize, don't you, that you may have done irreparable damage?"

"I don't understand."

"We had things under tight control. Now I'm afraid you've warned her."

"Warned her? But Sarah's as much in the dark as I am."

"Is that an amateur spy's conclusion?"

"It's my gut feeling."

"You don't know all the implications—"

"What *are* the implications?"

"That Geoffrey Fontaine's death is still in question. That his wife may know more about it than you think. And that a lot rides on this case—more than you'll ever know."

Nick stared at him, stunned. What was the man talking about? Was Geoffrey Fontaine dead or alive? Could Sarah possibly be such a good actress that she'd totally fooled Nick?

"Just what does ride on this case?" Nick asked.

"Let's just say the repercussions will be international."

"Was Geoffrey Fontaine a spy?"

Van Dam's mouth tightened. He said nothing.

"Look," said Nick. "I've had enough of this. Why am I being grilled on a routine consular matter?"

"Mr. O'Hara, I'm here to ask the questions, not answer them."

"Pardon me for interfering with your standard operating procedures."

"For a diplomat, you're damned undiplomatic." Van Dam turned to Ambrose. "I can't tell if he's clean. But I agree with your plan of action."

Nick frowned. "What plan of action?"

Ambrose cleared his throat. Nick knew exactly what that meant. It was a sure sign of impending unpleasantness. "Upon review of your personnel record," said Ambrose, "and based on this latest act of—uh, indiscretion, we feel it best you take an extended leave of absence from the department. Your security clearance will need reevaluation. Until we confirm your noninvolvement in anything subversive, you will be on leave. If we find evidence of something more serious than indiscretion, you will be hearing from Mr. Van Dam again. Not to mention the Justice Department."

Nick didn't need a translation—he'd just been labeled a traitor. The logical response would be to protest his innocence and resign, here and now. But damned if he would do it in front of Jonathan Van Dam.

Instead he rose stiffly and said, "I understand. Is that all, *sir?*"

"That's all, O'Hara."

With that brusque dismissal, Nick turned and strode out of the office. *So that's it,* he thought as he walked down the hall to what had been, up to a moment ago, his own office. After eight years with the State Department, a little curiosity had gotten him canned.

The funny part was that except for being called a traitor, he wasn't at all bothered about losing the job. In fact, as he turned the key to unlock his door, he felt strangely buoyant, as though a terrible weight had just been lifted from his shoulders. He was free. The decision he'd struggled so hard to make had just been made for him. In a way it had been inevitable.

Now he could start a new life. He had saved enough money to keep him going another six months or so. Perhaps he'd consider returning to the university. The last eight years had given him a big dose of reality; it would make him a better teacher than he ever could have been.

As he turned to the task of cleaning out his desk, he was actually grinning. One by one he emptied out his drawers, throwing the year's accumulated junk into a cardboard box. Next he threw in his dozens of journals, just part of the huge library of a man addicted to facts. To his surprise he found himself whistling. It would be a great night to go out and get roaring drunk. On second thought, he'd rather skip the hangover. He had too many things to do, too many answers to find. Losing his job he could handle, but he wasn't going to exit with his loyalty in question. He had to set the record straight, to get to the truth. And for that he had to see Sarah Fontaine again.

The prospect was not at all unpleasant. In fact, he looked forward to sharing a little civilized conversation, maybe over dinner.

The urge to see her became instantly compelling. Nick dropped the box on his desk and dialed her number. As usual, he was greeted by her answering machine. With an oath he hung up, suddenly remembering his suggestion that she stay with her friend. If only he knew the friend's number...

Leaning back in his chair, he found himself engaging in a rare moment of fantasy. Sarah. Of all the women in the world, to be thinking of her! This afternoon, at the cemetery, she'd looked so helpless, so thin, walking toward him through the mist. Not beautiful, but very, very vulnerable. In the car she'd huddled beside him like a cold, wet sparrow. Then she'd taken off her glasses and looked at him. And at that moment, as he'd looked into those huge amber eyes, he'd been awestruck. *I'm wrong*, he'd thought. *Dead wrong. In her own quiet way, Sarah Fontaine is the most beautiful woman I have ever seen.*

He was attracted to her, which wasn't very smart. With all of these unanswered questions about her husband—and about Sarah herself—Nick had plenty of reasons to keep his emotional distance. But now, as he leaned back in his chair and propped his feet up on the desk, he couldn't help painting all those mental pictures lonely men like to paint. He saw her standing in his apartment—in his bedroom—with her copper-colored hair loose about her shoulders. He saw the look in her eyes—shy and awkward, yet at the same time somehow eager. Her hands would be cold. He'd warm them against his skin. Then she—

"Nick!"

The fantasy shattered as Tim Greenstein walked into the room. "What're you still doing here?"

Nick looked up, startled. "What does it look like I'm doing? I'm cleaning out my desk."

"Cleaning out your—you mean you got sacked?"

"The moral equivalent. I've been asked to take an 'extended leave of absence,' as Ambrose so politely put it."

"Geez, that's tough!" Tim dropped into a chair. He was looking unusually pale, as if he'd just been shaken up badly.

"Where were you?" asked Nick. "I thought you were meeting me in Ambrose's office."

"I got sidetracked by my supervisor. And the FBI. *And* the CIA. Not pleasant. They even threatened to take away my computer pass card. I mean—that's cruel!"

Nick shook his head and sighed. "It's my fault, isn't it? Sorry, Tim. Looks like we were on forbidden turf. Did your FBI friend get slapped down, too?"

"No. Funny thing is, he may come out of this smelling like a rose. See, all his digging around just happened to embarrass the CIA. Over at the bureau, you get bonus points for making the Company look bad." Tim laughed, but something about the sound made Nick uneasy. His friend's laughter faded.

"What's going on, Tim?"

"It's a bad scene, Nick. We've been poking around in a hornet's nest."

"So it involves a little espionage. We've dealt with spooks before. What's so special about Geoffrey Fontaine?"

"I don't know. And I don't want to know any more than I already do."

"Lost your curiosity?"

"Damn right. So should you."

"I've got a personal interest in this case."

"Back off, Nick. For your own good. It'll blow your career apart."

"My career's already blown. I'm a private citizen now, remember? And I just might spend a little more time with Sarah Fontaine."

"Nick, as a friend I'm telling you to forget her. You're wrong about her. She's no Little Miss Innocent."

"That's what everyone keeps telling me. But I'm the only one who's spent any time with her."

"Look, you're *wrong*, okay?"

Tim's sharp tone puzzled Nick. *What's going on?* he thought. *What's happened?* Leaning forward, he looked his friend straight in the eye. "What are you trying to tell me, Tim?" he asked evenly.

Tim looked miserable. "She pulled one over on you, Nick. My FBI buddy's been keeping tabs on her. Her movements. Her contacts. And he just called and told me..."

"Told you what?"

"She knows something. It's the only explanation for what she did—"

"Dammit, Tim! What happened?"

"Soon after you left her apartment, she took a taxi to the airport. She boarded a plane."

Nick froze in disbelief. Sarah had left town? Why?

"Where did she go?" he snapped.

Tim gave him a sympathetic look. "London."

LONDON. It was the logical place to start. Or so it seemed to Sarah. London had been Geoffrey's favorite city, a town of green parks and cobblestoned alleys, of streets where men in stiff black suits and bowler hats rubbed elbows with turbaned Sikhs. He'd told her of St. Paul's Cathedral, soaring high above the rooftops; of red and yellow tulips blanketing Regent's Park; of Soho, where both the laughter and music were always loud. She'd heard all of these things and now, as she stared out the taxi window, she felt the same stirring that Geoffrey must have felt whenever he came to

London. She saw broad, clean streets, and black umbrellas bobbing along the sidewalks. Over the skyline hung a gentle mist, and in the parks the first spring flowers were bursting open. This was Geoffrey's city. He knew it and loved it. If he were in trouble, this is where he would hide.

The cab dropped her off on the Strand, in front of the Savoy Hotel. At the front desk the clerk, a sweet-faced young woman neatly dressed in a blazer, looked up and smiled at her. Yes, she told Sarah, a room was available. The tourist rush hadn't started yet.

Sarah was filling out the registration form when she said casually, "By the way, my husband was here about two weeks ago."

"Was he, now?" The clerk glanced across the ledger at her name. "Oh! You're Mrs. Fontaine? Is your husband Geoffrey Fontaine?"

"Yes. Do you remember him?"

"Of course we do, ma'am! Your husband's been a regular here. Such a nice man. Queer, though, I never imagined you were American. I always thought…" Her voice trailed off as she turned her attention to Sarah's registration card. "Will your husband be joining you in London?"

"No, not—not yet." Sarah paused. "Actually I was expecting a message of some sort. Could you check for me?"

The clerk glanced over at the mail slots. "I don't see anything."

"Then there haven't been any calls? For either of us?"

"They'd be here in the slot. Sorry." The clerk turned back to her paperwork.

Sarah fell silent for a moment. What next? Search his hotel room? But of course it would have been cleaned weeks ago.

"Anyway," said the clerk, "if there had been a message, we would have forwarded it to your house in Margate. That's what he always had us do."

Sarah blinked in bewilderment. "Margate?"

The clerk was too busy writing to look up. "Yes."

What house in Margate? Sarah wondered. Did Geoffrey own a residence here in England that he'd never told her about?

The clerk was still writing. Sarah steadied her hands on the counter and prayed she could lie convincingly. "I hope—I hope you don't have the wrong address," she said. "We're still in Margate, but we—we moved last month."

"Oh, dear," sighed the clerk, heading toward the back office. "Let me see if the address has been updated...." A moment later, she emerged with a registration card. "Twenty-five Whitstable Lane. Is that the old address or the new?"

Sarah didn't answer. She was too busy committing the address to memory.

"Mrs. Fontaine?" asked the clerk.

"I'm sure it's all right," said Sarah, quickly sweeping up her suitcase and turning for the elevator.

"Mrs. Fontaine, you needn't carry that up! I'll call the boy...."

But Sarah was already stepping into the elevator. "Twenty-five Whitstable Lane," she murmured as the door closed. "Twenty-five Whitstable Lane..."

Was that where she'd find Geoffrey?

THE SEA POUNDED against the white chalk cliffs. From the dirt path where Sarah walked, she could see the waves crashing on the rocks below. Their violence frightened her.

The sun had already burned through the morning fog, and in a dozen cottage gardens, flowers bloomed and thrived despite the salt air and chalk soil.

At the end of Whitstable Lane, Sarah found the house she'd been seeking. It was only a cottage, tucked behind a white picket fence. In the tiny front garden, stately rosebushes mingled with riotous marigolds and cornflowers. The soft clip of garden shears drew her attention to the side of the cottage, where an elderly man was trimming a hedge.

"Hello?" she called across the fence.

The old man stood up and looked at her.

"I'm looking for Geoffrey Fontaine," she said.

"Isn't 't 'ome, miss."

Sarah's hands started to shake. Then Geoffrey *had* been here. But why? she wondered. Why keep a cottage so far from his work in London?

"Where can I find him?" she asked.

"Don't rightly know."

"Do you know when he'll be coming home?"

The old man shrugged. "Neither he nor the missus tells me 'bout their comin's 'n goin's."

"*Missus?*" she repeated stupidly.

"Aye. Mrs. Fontaine."

"You don't mean—his wife?"

The old man looked at her as if she were an idiot. "Aye," he said slowly. "It would seem that way. 'Course, with a little imagination, one could always figure on 'er bein' 'is mother, but I'd say she's a bit young for that." He suddenly burst out laughing, as if the whole thing was quite absurd.

Sarah was clutching the picket fence so hard that the wooden points were biting into her palms. A strange roar rose in her ears, as if a wave had swept over her and was dragging her to the ground. With fumbling hands she dug in her purse and pulled out Geoffrey's photograph. "Is this Mr. Fontaine?" she asked hoarsely.

"That's 'im, all right. I've got a good eye for faces, you know."

She was trembling so hard she could barely stuff the picture back into her purse. She held on to the fence, trying to absorb what the man had said. The knowledge came as a shock, and the pain was more than she could bear.

Another woman. Hadn't someone asked her about that? She couldn't remember. Oh yes, it had been Nick O'Hara. He'd wondered about another woman. He'd called it a logical assumption, and she'd been angry with him.

Nick O'Hara had been right. She was the blind one, the stupid one.

She didn't know how long she had been standing there among the marigolds; she had lost track of time and place. Everything—her hands, her feet, even her face—had gone mercifully numb. Her mind refused to take in any more pain. If it did, she thought she'd go crazy.

Only when the old man called to her a third time did she hear him.

"Miss? Miss? Do you need some 'elp?"

Still in a daze, Sarah looked at him. "No. No, I'll be all right."

"You're sure, now?"

"Yes, I…please, I need to find the Fontaines."

"I don't rightly know 'ow, miss. The lady packed 'er bags and took off 'bout two weeks ago."

"Where did she go?"

"She weren't in the 'abit of leavin' a forwardin' address."

Sarah hunted in her purse for a piece of paper, then scribbled down her name and hotel. "If she—if either of them—shows up, please tell them to call me immediately. Please."

"Aye, miss." The old man folded up the paper without looking at it and slipped it into his pocket.

Like a drunken woman, she stumbled toward the road. At the beginning of Whitstable Lane, she saw a row of mailboxes. Glancing back, she saw that the old man was once more at work, clipping his hedge. She looked inside the box labeled 25 and found only a mail-order catalog from a London department store. It was addressed to Mrs. Eve Fontaine.

Evie.

More than once, Geoffrey had called Sarah by that name.

She shoved the catalog back into the mailbox. As she walked down the cliff road to the Margate train station, she was crying.

SIX HOURS LATER, tired, empty and hungry, Sarah walked into her room at the Savoy. The phone was ringing.

"Hello?" she said.

"Sarah Fontaine?" It was a woman. Her voice was low and husky.

"Yes."

"Geoffrey had a birthmark, left shoulder. What shape?"

"But—"

"What shape?"

"It was—it was a half-moon. Is this Eve?"

"The Lamb and Rose. Dorset Street. Nine o'clock."

"Wait—Eve?"

Click.

Sarah looked at her watch. She had half an hour to get to Dorset Street.

Chapter Five

Fog swirled around the door of the Lamb and Rose. The cabdriver took Sarah's bills, grunted something unintelligible and sped off. Sarah was left standing alone in the dark street.

From the pub came the muffled sounds of laughter and the clink of glassware. Through the haze the window glowed a soft, welcoming yellow. She crossed the cobblestoned street and pushed open the door.

Inside, a fire crackled in the hearth. At the gleaming mahogany bar, two men hunched over glasses of ale. They looked up as she walked in, then just as quickly stared down at their glasses. Sarah paused to warm herself by the fire, all the time searching the room with her eyes. Only a serving girl, standing by the tap, met her gaze. Without a word the girl nodded toward the back of the room.

Sarah returned the nod and walked in the direction the girl had indicated. Several wooden booths lined the wall.

In the first booth sat a couple, staring intently into each other's eyes. In the second an old man in tweeds quietly nursed a whiskey. There was only one booth left. Even before she reached it, she knew Eve would be sitting there. A wisp of cigarette smoke drifted from the shadows. The woman looked up as Sarah approached. Their eyes met, and in that one glance, they both understood. Even in the pub's dimly lighted interior, each could see the other's pain.

Sarah slid onto the bench across from the other woman. Eve nervously took a puff from her cigarette and flicked off the ashes, all the while studying Sarah. She was slender— almost too slender—and fair haired, with greenish eyes that looked tired and pinched. Her hands moved constantly. Every few seconds she glanced toward the pub door, as if expecting someone else to walk inside. The cigarette smoke curled like a serpent between them.

"You're not what I expected," said Eve. Sarah recognized the husky voice from the telephone. The accent was faintly Continental, not English. "You're not as plain as I expected. And you're younger than he said. How old are you? Twenty-seven? Twenty-eight?"

"I'm thirty-two," said Sarah.

"Ah. So he wasn't lying."

"Geoffrey told you about me?"

Eve took another puff and nodded. "Of course. He had to. It was my idea."

Sarah's eyes widened in astonishment. "*Your* idea? You mean—but *why?*"

"You don't know anything at all about Geoffrey, do you?" The green eyes stabbed cruelly into Sarah's. "No," said Eve with a trace of satisfaction. "Obviously you don't. And I suppose I'm scotching it all up now, telling you this. But you seem to have found out about me on your own. And I wanted to see you for myself."

"Why?"

"Call it morbid curiosity. Masochism. I hated to think of you two together. I loved him too much." Her chin came up, a poor attempt at nonchalance. "Tell me. Were you happy with him?"

Sarah nodded, her eyes suddenly stinging. "Yes," she whispered. "We—at least *I* was happy. As for Geoffrey…I don't know anymore. I don't know anything anymore."

"How often did you make love? Every night? Once a week?"

Sarah's mouth tightened. "Why should it matter to you? It was all part of your plan, wasn't it?"

The eyes softened, but only for an instant. "You loved him, too, didn't you?" asked Eve. She glanced down as she flicked off another ash. When she looked up, her eyes were once more as hard as emeralds. "So we both lost out, didn't we? It had to happen some day. It's the nature of the business."

"*What* business?"

Eve leaned back. "You're better off not knowing. But you want to hear it, don't you? If I were you, I'd forget all this. I'd forget it and go home. While you still can."

"Who *is* Geoffrey?"

Eve inhaled the smoke deeply and gazed into the distance, conjuring up the memories. "I met him ten years ago, in Amsterdam. He was a different man then." She smiled wanly, as if amused by some private joke. "By different, I mean both literally and figuratively. His name was Simon Dance. At the time, we were both working for Mossad— the Israeli Secret Service. We were quite a team then, the three of us. Simon and I and another woman, our chief. Mossad's best. And then Simon and I fell in love."

"You were spies?"

"I suppose you could call us that. Yes, let's leave it at that." She stared thoughtfully at the patterns her cigarette smoke was weaving in the air. "We'd been together only a year when one of our assignments went badly. We worried too much about each other, you see. That can't happen, not in our business. The work must be everything. Otherwise, things go wrong. And they did. The old man escaped."

"Escaped? Was that your assignment, to arrest someone?"

Eve laughed. "Arrest? In our business, we do not bother to arrest. We terminate."

Sarah's hands went ice-cold. Surely this wasn't the same Geoffrey they were talking about? No, she reminded herself. He wasn't Geoffrey then. He was *Simon*.

"So the old man lived. Magus, we called him. A holy name for an unholy man. Magus, the magician. To us it was more than just a code name. In a way he was a magician. That case finished us." She stubbed out her cigarette and lighted another, ruining three matches in the process. Her hands were shaking too much. She sighed, gratefully inhaling the smoke. "After that, we all dropped out of the business. Simon and I were married, and for a while we lived in Germany, then France. We changed our names twice. But we kept feeling as though things were closing in. We knew there was a contract out on all of us. Ordered by Magus, of course. We decided to leave Europe."

"So you chose America."

Eve nodded. "Yes. It's all so simple, really. He found a new name. And a plastic surgeon. His cheeks were brought in, the nose narrowed. The difference was dramatic—no one could've recognized him. My face was changed, too. He went first, to America. It takes time to establish a new base, a new identity. I was to going to follow."

"Why did he marry me?"

"He needed an American wife. He needed your home, your bank account, the cover you could provide. I could not pass as an American. My accent, my voice—I could not change them. But Simon—ah, he could sound like a dozen different people!"

"Why did he choose me?"

Eve shrugged. "Convenience. You were lonely, not so pretty. You had no boyfriends. Yes, you were very vulnerable. You fell in love quickly, didn't you?"

Choking back a sob, Sarah nodded. Yes, she had been vulnerable. Before Geoffrey, her days had been spent at work, her nights mostly at home alone. She'd longed for a relationship with a man, for the closeness and caring her parents had had. But her career had been demanding and she'd been single too long; with each year that passed, marriage had seemed less and less likely.

Then Geoffrey had appeared. Geoffrey, who had filled the void. She'd fallen in love at once. Yet all this time, he had thought of her as nothing more than a convenience. She looked up in anger. "You didn't care, did you?" she asked. "Either of you. You didn't care who got hurt."

"We had no choice. We had our own lives—"

"*Your* lives? What about *my* life?"

"Lower your voice."

"My life, Eve. I loved him. And you can sit there, so smug, and justify what you both did!"

"Please lower your voice. They can hear you."

"I don't care."

Eve started to rise. "I think I've said all I care to."

"No, wait!" Sarah grabbed her hand. "Please," she said softly. "Sit down. I have to hear the rest. I have to know."

Slowly Eve sank into the booth. She was silent for a moment, then said, "The truth is, he didn't love you. I was the one he loved. His trips here to London—they were only to see me. He'd check into the Savoy before taking the train to Margate. Every few days he'd return to London to call you or post you a letter. I hated it, these last two months, sharing him with you. But it was necessary and only temporary. We were both surviving. Until..." She looked away. Her eyes suddenly glistened with tears.

"What happened, Eve?"

Eve cleared her throat and lifted her head bravely. "I don't know. All I know is, he left London two weeks ago. He had joined an operation against Magus. Then things went wrong. He was being followed. Someone left explosives, set to go off in his hotel room. He called from Berlin and told me he'd decided to vanish. I was to go into hiding. When the time was right, he'd come for me. But the night before I left Margate, I had a—a premonition. I tried to call him in Berlin. That's when I learned he was dead."

"But he's not dead!" Sarah blurted. "He's alive!"

Eve's hands jerked, almost causing her to drop the cigarette. "What?"

"He called me two days ago. That's why I'm here. He told me to come to him—that he loved me—"

"You're lying."

"It's true!" cried Sarah. "I know his voice."

"A recording, perhaps—some kind of trick. It's easy to imitate a voice. No, it couldn't have been him. He wouldn't call *you*," Eve said coldly.

Sarah fell silent. Why would someone use Geoffrey's voice to draw her to Europe? Then she remembered something else, another piece of the puzzle that made no sense. She looked across the table at Eve. "The day I left Washington, someone broke into my apartment. All they took was a photograph—that's all, just a photograph—and I still don't underst—"

"A photograph?" Eve asked sharply. "Of Geoffrey?"

"Yes. It was our wedding picture."

The woman's face went chalk white. She stubbed out her cigarette and snapped up her purse and sweater.

"Where are you going?" asked Sarah.

"I have to get back—he'll be searching for me."

"Who?"

"Geoffrey."

"But you said he was dead!"

Eve's eyes were suddenly as bright and sparkling as jewels. "No. No, he's alive. He must be! Don't you see? They don't know his face so they've stolen his photograph. It means they're looking for him, too." She threw on her sweater and ran for the door.

"Eve!" Sarah scrambled from the booth and chased after her. But when she stepped outside, the street was empty. She saw only fog, great thick clouds of it, creeping at her feet. "Eve?" she called. There was no answer.

Eve had disappeared.

EVE DIDN'T GET far. Wild and reckless with hope, she ran through the fog of Dorset Street toward the underground station. She didn't stop to listen for footsteps; she didn't take all the usual precautions she'd learned to take during her years as a Mossad operative. Simon was alive—that was all that mattered. He was alive, and he'd be waiting for her. She didn't have the patience to zigzag through the neighborhood, to pause in doorways and see if she was alone. Instead, her path took her in a straight line for the subway station.

After only two blocks of running, her breathing became hard and heavy. It was the cigarettes, she thought. Too many years of smoking had left her easy to tire and short of breath. But she forced herself to keep moving, until the ache started in her chest and she knew she'd have to rest, just for a moment. The pain was an old problem, one she'd lived with since she was a child. It meant nothing. It would ease up a bit and she could keep going.

She paused to lean against a lamppost. Little by little the ache subsided. Her breathing came easier. The roaring in her ears faded. She closed her eyes and took a deep breath.

Then another sound penetrated her awareness, a sound so soft she almost missed it. She stiffened, and her eyes shot open. There it was again, a few yards away. A footstep. But in which direction?

Staring desperately through the mist she tried to make out a face, a figure, but she saw nothing. Reaching into her purse, she withdrew the pistol she always carried. The cold steel felt instantly reassuring in her palm. She realized that the lamplight was a beacon, and she was standing right beneath it. She fled into the shadows. Darkness had always been her ally.

Another sound made her swing the pistol around. *Where is he?* she thought. *Why can't I see him?*

She realized too late that the last sound had been nothing more than a decoy, a trick meant to draw her aim. From behind, something rushed at her. Before she could twist around and fire, she was flung to the ground. The pistol flew from her hand, and then, in the next instant, she felt a blade press firmly against her throat.

A face was smiling down at her, a face she recognized. Even in the darkness, his pale hair gleamed like silver.

"Kronen," she whispered.

She felt the blade slide across her skin, as gentle as a caress. She wanted to scream, but terror had clamped off her throat.

"Little Eva," Kronen murmured. Then he laughed softly, and that was when Eve knew she would not live through the night.

THE WORLD LOOKED different from thirty-five thousand feet. No neon lights, no traffic, no concrete, just an endless black sky glittering with stars.

Nick leaned his head back tiredly and wished he could sleep. Almost everyone else on Flight 201 to London seemed to be snoring blissfully across the Atlantic. On the other side of the dim cabin, he saw a stewardess gently tuck in a child and tiptoe away down the aisle. It was 1:00 a.m., D.C. time, yet Nick was wide awake, with an airline blanket still folded neatly on his lap.

He was too disgusted to sleep. He kept remembering Sarah and how innocent she'd looked, how grief stricken and vulnerable. What a great actress. She'd given an Oscar-winning performance. She'd also stirred up a whole host of male instincts he'd forgotten he had. He'd wanted to protect her, to hold her.

Now he wasn't sure *what* he wanted to do to her. Whatever it was, protection had nothing to do with it.

Because of Sarah Fontaine he was out of a job, his patriotism was in question and worst of all, he felt like a damned fool. Van Dam had been right. As a spy Nick was nothing but a rank amateur.

The more he thought about how she'd fooled him, the angrier he got. He slapped the armrest and stared out the window at the stars.

By God, when he got to London, he'd get the truth out of her. He owed it to himself; he couldn't leave the foreign service without clearing his record.

She wouldn't be expecting him in London. He already knew where to find her; a phone call confirmed that she'd checked into the Savoy, her husband's usual hotel. He looked forward to seeing the look on her face when she opened her door to find him standing there. Surprise, surprise! Nick O'Hara was in town to set the record straight. And this time he wouldn't settle for lies.

But mingled with his anger was another emotion, much deeper and infinitely more disturbing. He kept coming back to that old fantasy, the vision of her standing in his bedroom, gazing at him with those soft amber eyes. The confusion of what he really felt was driving him nuts. He didn't know if he wanted to kiss her or strangle her. Maybe both.

He did know one thing. Boarding this flight to London had surely been the craziest stunt he'd ever pulled. All his life he'd made decisions thoughtfully. He was not, by nature, a careless man. But tonight he'd thrown his clothes into a suitcase, caught a taxi to Dulles and slapped a credit card down on the British Airways ticket counter. It was totally unlike him to do something so impulsive, so emotional. So stupid. He hoped it wasn't the start of a new trend.

THE OLD MAN would not be happy.

As Kronen wiped the woman's blood from his knife, he considered putting off the inevitable phone call for another hour, another day. At least until he'd eaten a stout breakfast or perhaps put away a few pints. But the old man would be hungry for news, and Kronen didn't want to keep him waiting too long. The old man didn't tolerate frustrations very well these days. Ever since the tragedy, he had been impatient and easily irritated. One did not irritate him if one wanted to remain in good health.

Not that Kronen was afraid. He knew the old man needed him too much.

At the age of eight, Kronen had been plucked from the trash heaps of Dublin and adopted by the old man. Perhaps it was the boy's fair, almost white hair that caught his attention; perhaps it was the utter emptiness in the boy's eyes, the sign of a soulless vacuum within a shell of human flesh and bone. The old man recognized, even then, that the boy could someday be dangerous. A boy without a soul had no use for love, and as a man he might someday turn on his guardian.

But a boy without a soul could also be very useful. So the old man took the boy in, fed him, taught him, maybe even loved him a little, but he never quite trusted him.

Kronen, even at a young age, had sensed the old man's distrust. Instead of resenting it, he had worked hard to overcome it. Anything the old man wanted done, Kronen would do. After thirty years of doing his bidding, it had become automatic. Kronen was well compensated. More important, he enjoyed his work. It gave him a sense of pleasure and satisfaction. Especially when it involved women.

Like tonight.

Unfortunately the woman had not talked. She'd been stronger that way than any man he'd ever met. Even an hour of his most persuasive techniques had been to no avail. She'd done a lot of screaming, which had both annoyed and excited him, but she'd given him absolutely no information. And then, when he'd least expected it, she'd died.

That had bothered him most of all. He hadn't meant to kill her. At least not yet. What bad luck to discover too late that his victim had a weak heart. She'd looked healthy enough.

He finished wiping his blade. He believed in cleanliness, especially when it came to his favorite knife. A sharp edge required care. He put the knife in its sheath and stared at the telephone. There was no point in delaying the matter any longer. He decided to call Amsterdam.

The old man answered.

"Eva did not talk," said Kronen.

The silence was enough. He could sense the disappointment through the receiver. "Then she is dead?"

"Yes," said Kronen.

"What about the other?"

"I am still watching her. Dance has not come near."

The old man made a sound of impatience. "I cannot wait forever. We have to force his hand."

"How?"

"Abduct her."

"But she has the CIA following her."

"I'll see they're taken care of. By tomorrow. Then you take the woman."

"And then?"

"See if she knows anything. If she does not, we can still

use her. We will broadcast an ultimatum. If Dance is alive, he'll respond."

Kronen was not so sure. Unlike the old man, he held no faith in something as ridiculous as love. Besides, he'd seen Sarah Fontaine, and he didn't think any man—certainly not Simon Dance—would come to her rescue. No, to risk one's life for a woman was absurd. He didn't think Dance would be so stupid.

Nevertheless, it would be an interesting experiment. And when it was over the old man would let Kronen take care of the woman. Her heart would certainly be stronger than Eva Fontaine's. She would last much longer. Yes, it would be an interesting experiment. It gave him something to look forward to.

IN A DREAM it came back to Sarah. But everything was distorted and strange and swirling with mist. She was running through the streets, running after Geoffrey, crying out his name. She heard his footsteps ahead of her, but he was always out of sight, always beyond her reach. Then the footsteps changed. They were behind her. She was no longer the pursuer, but the pursued. She was running through the fog, and the footsteps were growing closer. Her heart was pounding. Her legs refused to work. She struggled to move forward.

Her path was blocked by a woman with green eyes, a woman who was standing in the middle of the street, laughing at her. The footsteps closed in. Sarah whirled around.

The man who came toward her was someone she knew, someone with tired gray eyes. Slowly he emerged from the mist. And as he did, her fears dissolved. Here was safety, here was warmth. His footsteps echoed on the cobblestoned streets....

Sarah woke up, drenched in sweat. Someone was knocking at her door. She turned on the light. It was 4:00 a.m.

The knock came again, louder. "Mrs. Fontaine?" said a man's voice. "Please open up, ma'am."

"Who is it?" she called.

"The police."

She stumbled out of bed, struggled into a robe and opened the door. Two uniformed policemen stood outside, accompanied by a sleepy-eyed hotel clerk.

"Mrs. Sarah Fontaine?"

"Yes. What is it?"

"Sorry for the intrusion, ma'am, but it will be necessary for you to accompany us to the station headquarters."

"I don't understand. Why?"

"We're obliged to place you under detention."

She clutched the door with both hands and stared at them in amazement. "Do you mean I'm under *arrest*? But for what?"

"For murder. The murder of Mrs. Eve Fontaine."

Chapter Six

THIS CANNOT BE HAPPENING, THOUGHT SARAH.

Surely it was a nightmare, a scenario pulled from the darkest reaches of her subconscious. She was sitting in a hard chair, staring at a bare wooden table. Glaring fluorescent lights shone down on her from the ceiling and illuminated her every movement, like a spotlight waiting for guilt to appear. The room was cold and she felt half-naked, dressed only in her nightgown and robe. A detective with ice-blue eyes brusquely fired question after question, without letting her finish a single sentence. Only after she'd asked him half a dozen times did he let her use the bathroom, and then only with a matron standing outside the stall.

Once back in the interrogation room, she was left shivering and alone for a moment to ponder her situation. *I am going to jail*, she thought. *I am going to be locked up forever, for murdering a woman I met only last night....*

Dropping her head in her hands, she felt another wave of tears threaten to flood her eyes. She was trying so hard to keep from crying that she scarcely heard the door open and close.

But she did hear the voice calling her name. That one word was like a burst of warm sunshine. She looked up.

Nick O'Hara was standing in front of her. By some miracle he'd been transported across an ocean, and here he was, her only friend in London, looking down at her.

Or was he a friend?

Immediately she saw that something was wrong. His mouth was set in two hard lines. His eyes showed no expression. Desperately she searched for some warmth, some comforting look in his face, but what she saw was rage. Little by little she took in the other details: his wrinkled shirt, the slack tie, the British Airways sticker on his briefcase. He had just come off a plane.

He turned and pushed the door shut. The loud slam made her flinch. Then he practically threw his briefcase on the table and glowered at her.

"Lady, you are in one *helluva* mess!" he grunted.

She sniffed pitifully. "I know."

"Is that all you can say? I *know?*"

"Are you going to get me out of here?" she asked in a small voice.

"It all depends."

"On what?"

"On whether or not you did it."

"Of course I didn't do it!" she cried.

He seemed taken aback by her violent outburst. For a moment he was silent. Then he crossed his arms and settled irritably on the edge of the table.

She was afraid to look at him, afraid to see the accusing look in his eyes. The man she'd thought was her friend had suddenly turned into someone she scarcely knew. So he thought she was guilty, too. What hope did she have of convincing complete strangers of her innocence when even Nick O'Hara didn't believe her? Bitterly she told herself how wrong she'd been about him. As for why he was here, the reason was now obvious. The man was just doing his job.

She clenched her hands in a hard knot on the table. She was furious with him for seeing her in this helpless position, for betraying her trust in him as a friend.

"Why are you in London, anyway?" she muttered.

"I could ask you the same question. This time, though, I expect the truth."

"The truth?" She looked up. "I've never lied to you! You were the one—"

"Oh, come on!" he roared. Agitated, he shot to his feet and began to pace the floor. "Don't give me that innocent look, Mrs. Fontaine. You must think I'm pretty damned stupid. First you insist you don't know a thing, and then you take off for London. I just finished talking to the inspector. Now I want to hear your side. You knew about Eve, didn't you?"

"I didn't know! At least, not until yesterday. And you were the one who lied, Mr. O'Hara."

"About what?"

"About Geoffrey. You told me he was dead. Oh, you gave me all that nice evidence, you laid it out so neatly, so perfectly. And I believed you! All this time you knew, didn't you? You *must* have known."

"What are you talking about?"

"Geoffrey's alive!"

The incredulous look on his face was too real. She stared at him, wondering if it was possible that Nick really didn't know Geoffrey was alive.

"I think you'd better explain," he said. "And I want it all, Sarah. Right down to what you ate for breakfast. Because, as you no doubt know, you're in deep trouble. The evidence—"

"The *evidence* is all circumstantial."

"The evidence is this: Eve Fontaine's body was found about midnight in a deserted alley a few blocks from the Lamb and Rose. I won't go into the body's condition; let's just say someone obviously didn't like her. The barmaid in the Lamb and Rose remembered seeing Eve with a woman—an American. That was you. She also remembered that you two had an argument. Eve ran out, you followed. And that's the last anyone saw of Eve Fontaine."

"I lost her outside the Lamb and Rose!"

"Do you have any witnesses?"

"No."

"Too bad. The police called Eve's house in Margate and spoke with the groundskeeper. The old man remembered you, all right. He said he gave Eve your message over the phone. And he just happened to have that slip of paper with your name and hotel."

"I gave it to him so she could call me."

"Well, to the police you've got an obvious motive. Revenge. You found out Geoffrey Fontaine was a bigamist. You decided to get even. That's the evidence. Good, hard and undeniable."

"It doesn't mean I killed her!"

"No?"

"You have to believe me!"

"Why should I?"

"Because no one else does." Without warning, all the fear
and weariness seemed to sweep through her in one over-
powering wave. Lowering her head, she repeated softly, "No
one else does...."

Nick watched her with a disturbing mix of emotions. She
looked so drained, so terrified, as she huddled against the
table. Her robe sagged open, and he caught a glimpse of her
flimsy blue nightgown. A long strand of reddish-brown hair
fell across her face, across that smooth, pale cheek. It was
the first time he'd seen her hair loose, and it reminded him
once again of that fantasy he'd tried so hard to suppress. But
the image came back to him now, warm and compelling.
He forced it out of his mind, trying instead to concentrate
on why he was here. A woman had been murdered, and
Sarah was in very bad trouble. Yet all he could think about
was how she would feel in his arms.

Suddenly all his anger toward her evaporated. He'd hurt
her, and now he felt like a monster. Gently he touched her
head. "Sarah. Sarah, it'll be all right," he murmured. "You'll
be all right." He crouched down and clumsily laid her face
against his shoulder. Her hair felt so soft, so silky; the warm,
feminine scent of her skin was intoxicating. He knew the
emotions coursing through him now were dangerous, but
he couldn't control them. He wanted to take her from this
room, to keep her safe and warm and protected. He was
most definitely not being objective.

Reluctantly he pulled away. "Sarah, talk to me. Tell me
why you think your husband's alive."

She took a deep breath and looked at him. Her eyes were
like a fawn's, soft and moist. He knew then how much

courage it had taken for her to meet his gaze. To keep the tears at bay. He'd been wrong about Sarah. She wasn't broken at all. She had reserves of strength that he'd never suspected.

"He called me," she said. "Two days ago, in Washington—the afternoon of the funeral—"

"Wait. He *called* you?"

"He told me to come to him. It ended so quickly—he never told me where he was—"

"Was it long-distance?"

"I'm sure of it."

"That's why you jumped on a plane? But why to London?"

"It—it was just a feeling. This was his home. This is where he should have been."

"And when did you find out about Eve?"

"After I got here. The hotel clerk showed me an address on Geoffrey's registration card. It was Eve's cottage in Margate."

He absorbed this torrent of new facts with a feeling of growing confusion. Pulling up a chair, he sat down and focused intently on her face.

"You've just thrown me a wild card," he said. "That call from Geoffrey—it's so crazy, I'm beginning to think you must be telling the truth."

"I *am* telling the truth! When are you going to believe me?"

"All right. I'll give you the benefit of the doubt. For now."

He was beginning to believe her. That was all she needed, that tiny kernel of trust. It meant more to her at this moment than anything else in the world. *This is crazy,* she thought. After all she'd been through this morning, only now were the tears beginning to fall. She shook her head and laughed sheepishly. "What is it about you, Mr.

O'Hara?" she asked. "I always seem to be crying when you're around."

"It's okay," he said. "Crying, I mean. Women are always doing that to me. I guess it comes with the job."

She looked up and found him smiling. What a startling transformation, from stranger to friend. Somehow she'd forgotten how attractive he was. Not just physically. There was a new gentleness, an intimacy in his voice, as though he really cared. Did he? Or was she reading too much into all of this? Certainly she could recognize her own response, could feel the blood rising in her face.

He seemed hesitant, almost clumsy, as he leaned toward her. She shivered. Immediately he pulled off his jacket and draped it around her shoulders. It smelled like him; it felt so warm and safe, like a blanket. She pulled it close and a calmness came over her, a feeling that nothing could harm her while Nick O'Hara's jacket was around her shoulders.

"As soon as our man from the consulate shows up, we'll get you out of here," he said.

"But aren't you handling this?"

"Afraid not. This isn't my territory."

"But then, why are you here?"

Before he could answer, the door flew open.

"*Nick O'Hara,*" said a short fireplug of a man. "What the hell are *you* doing here?"

Nick turned to face the man in the doorway. "Hello, Potter," he said after a distinctly uncomfortable pause. "It's been a long time."

"Not long enough." Potter stalked into the room, his critical gaze examining Sarah from head to toe. He tossed his damp hat deliberately on Nick's briefcase. "So you're Sarah Fontaine."

She shot a puzzled glance at Nick.

"Sarah, this is Mr. Roy Potter," Nick said tightly. "The embassy's—er, what is it they call you these days? Political officer?"

"Third secretary," snapped Potter.

"Charming euphemism. So where's Dan Lieberman? I thought he was coming."

"I'm afraid our consul couldn't make it. I'm here instead." Potter gave Sarah a perfunctory handshake. "I hope you've been treated well, Mrs. Fontaine. Sorry you had to go through all this. But I think we'll have it cleared up in no time."

"Cleared up?" Nick asked suspiciously. "How?"

Potter turned grudgingly back to Nick. "Maybe you should leave, O'Hara. Get on with your—uh, vacation, is it?"

"No. I think I'll stick around."

"This is official business. And if I've heard right, you're no longer with us, are you?"

"I don't understand," said Sarah, frowning. "What do you mean he's no longer with you?"

"What he means," Nick said calmly, "is that I've been placed on indefinite leave of absence. News gets around fast, I see."

"It does when it's a matter of national security."

Nick snorted. "I didn't know I was so dangerous."

"Let's just say your name's on a most unflattering list, O'Hara. If I were you, I'd make sure I kept my nose clean. That is, if you expect to keep your job."

"Look, let's get down to business. Sarah's case, remember?"

Potter looked at Sarah. "I've discussed it with Inspector Appleby. He tells me the evidence against you isn't as solid as he'd like. He's willing to release you—provided I take responsibility for your conduct."

Sarah was astonished. "You mean I'm free?"

"That's right."

"And there's nothing—I'm not—"

"The charges have been dropped." He extended his hand. "Congratulations, Mrs. Fontaine. You're a free woman."

She leaped up and grabbed his pudgy hand. "Mr. Potter, thank you! Thank you so much!"

"No problem. Just stay out of trouble, okay?"

"Oh, I will. I will!" She looked joyously at Nick, expecting to see a smile on his face. But he wasn't smiling. Instead he looked completely baffled. And suspicious. Something was bothering him, and she felt instantly uneasy. She turned to Potter. "Is there anything else? Anything I should know?"

"No, Mrs. Fontaine. You can leave right now. In fact, I'll drive you back to the Savoy myself."

"Don't bother," said Nick. "I'll take her back."

Sarah drew closer to Nick. "Thank you, Mr. Potter," she said, "but I'll go with Mr. O'Hara. We're—we're sort of old friends."

Potter frowned. "Friends?"

"He's been so helpful since Geoffrey died."

Scowling, Potter turned and swept his hat off the table. "Okay. Good luck, Mrs. Fontaine." He glanced at Nick. "Say, O'Hara, I'll be sending a report to Mr. Van Dam in Washington. I'm sure he'll be interested to hear you're in London. Will you be returning Stateside soon?"

"I might," said Nick. "Then again, I might not."

Potter headed for the door, then turned one last time and gave Nick a long, hard look. "You know, you've had a decent career with the foreign service. Don't screw it up now. If I were you, I'd watch my step."

Nick dipped his head. "I always do."

"WHAT DOES THAT mean—indefinite leave of absence?" Sarah asked as Nick drove her back to the hotel.

He smiled humorlessly. "Let's just say it's not a promotion."

"Have you been fired?"

"In a word—yes."

"But why?"

He didn't answer. Pausing at the next stoplight, he leaned back and sighed. It was a sound of utter weariness and defeat.

"Nick?" she asked quietly. "Was it because of me?"

He nodded. "You were part of it. Because of you, it seems my patriotism's been called into question. Eight years of good, solid work don't mean a thing to them. But don't let it bother you. I guess, on a subconscious level, I've been working my way out of the job for some time. You were just the last straw."

"I'm sorry."

"Don't be. Getting canned might be the best thing that ever happened to me."

The light changed, and they merged with the morning traffic. It was ten o'clock and the cars were bumper-to-bumper. An oncoming bus roared by on their right, and Sarah felt a momentary flash of panic. The left-sided driving unsettled her. Even Nick seemed uneasy as he frowned at the rearview mirror.

She forced herself to sit back and ignore the road. "I can't believe everything that's happened," she said. "It's all so crazy. And the more I try to figure it out, the more confused I get...." Glancing sideways at Nick, she saw that his frown was deepening. "Nick?"

"The plot has just thickened," he said softly.

"What are you talking about?"

"Keep your eyes straight ahead. Don't look back. We're being followed."

The urge to turn her head was overwhelming, but Sarah managed to focus her attention on the wet road in front of them. *Why is this happening?* she asked herself, as fear made her heart beat faster. "What are you going to do, Nick?"

"Nothing."

"*Nothing?*"

He ignored the dismay in her voice. "That's right. We're going to act like nothing at all is wrong. We're going to stop at your hotel, where you'll change, pack your bags and check out. Then we're going to have some breakfast. I'm starved."

"Breakfast? But you just said we're being followed!"

"Look, if those guys were out for blood, they could've grabbed you last night."

"Like they grabbed Eve?" she asked in a whisper.

"No. That's not going to happen." He looked in his mirror. "Hang on, Sarah. We're gonna see just how good these guys are...."

He swerved into a narrow street, zipped past a row of small shops and cafés, then hit the brakes. The car behind them skidded to a stop, missing their rear bumper by inches. Unexpectedly Nick laughed. Glancing at Sarah, he saw that she was gripping the dashboard. "You all right?"

She nodded, too frightened to say a word.

"We're okay, Sarah. I think I know these guys. I've seen 'em before." He stuck his hand out and flashed an unmistakably obscene gesture at the car behind them. An instant later he grunted with satisfaction at their response, which was equally obscene. "I was right. Those are Company boys. The driver just flipped me the sign of the eagle."

"You mean they're CIA?" she asked with sudden relief.

"Don't go celebrating yet. I don't trust them. Neither should you."

But her panic was already fading. Why should she be afraid of the CIA? Weren't they on the same side? But then why were they following her? She wondered how long she'd been tailed. If it had been since her arrival in London, they might have seen who killed Eve....

She turned to Nick. "What did happen to Eve?" she asked.

"You mean besides murder?"

"You said something about—the way she died. They did more than just kill her, didn't they?"

The look he gave her made Sarah shudder. "Yes," he said. "They did more than just kill her."

The stoplight was red. Nick pulled up behind a long line of cars and let the engine idle. Rain began to fall, big, fat droplets that slid down the windshield. The ubiquitous black umbrellas filled the intersection. Nick sat motionless as he gazed at the street.

"They found her in an alley," he said at last. "Her hands were tied to an iron fence post. Her mouth was gagged. She must have screamed like hell, but no one heard her. Whoever did the job took his time. An hour, maybe longer. He knew how to use a knife. It was not a...good death."

His flint eyes turned and locked on hers. She was aware of his closeness, of the warmth and the smell of his wool coat around her shoulders. A woman had been tortured to death. A car was following them. And yet, at this moment, with this man sitting beside her, she felt infinitely safe. She knew Nick O'Hara was hardly a savior. He was just an ordinary man, someone who'd probably spent his life behind a desk. She didn't even know why he was here, but he was, and for that she was grateful.

The car behind them honked its horn. The light had changed to green. Nick turned his attention reluctantly to the traffic.

"Why did they kill her that way?" murmured Sarah. "Why—why torture her?"

"The police say it looked like the work of a maniac. Someone who gets his thrills from causing pain."

"Or someone out for vengeance," Sarah added. Eve had been playing a deadly game. Perhaps it had caught up with her. "Magus," she said, suddenly remembering the name. At Nick's quizzical glance, she explained, "It's a code name. For a man they called the Magician. Eve told me about him."

"We'll get to all that," he said, glancing at the mirror again. "The Savoy's right up this block. And we're still being followed."

AN HOUR AND a half later, they sat in a booth at the back of a Strand café and finished off a breakfast of eggs and bacon and grilled tomatoes. At last Sarah was starting to feel human again. Her stomach was full, and a cup of hot tea warmed her hands. Most important, she was dressed in a skirt and a shetland gray sweater. She realized now what good police strategy it had been to keep her in her night-clothes. She'd felt so naked and helpless, the right frame of mind to be forced into a confession.

And the ordeal still wasn't over; her troubles were really just beginning.

Nick had eaten quickly, all the while watching the door as he listened to Sarah's story. By the time she'd finished talking, the dishes were cleared and they were working on their second pot of tea.

"So Eve agreed with you that Geoffrey's alive?" he asked.

"Yes. The stolen photograph convinced her."

"Okay," he said, reviewing what she'd just told him. "So according to Eve, someone's out to kill Geoffrey. Someone who doesn't know his face but does know his new name's Fontaine. Geoffrey discovers he's being followed. He goes to Berlin, calls Eve and tells her to vanish. Then he stages his own death."

"That doesn't explain why she was tortured."

"It doesn't explain a lot of things. There are too many holes. Whose body was buried, for one. But at least we've got an explanation for that stolen photograph. If Simon Dance had plastic surgery to change his appearance, then whoever's after him may not recognize his face."

"And why are we being followed? Do they think I'll lead them to Geoffrey?"

He nodded. "And that brings up the detail that really bothers me: your release. I don't buy that story about the police not having enough evidence against you. When I talked to Inspector Appleby, he seemed ready to shut you away for life. Then Potter showed up and—poof! Everything's hunky-dory. Just like that, you're out. I think someone put a little pressure on the good inspector. The order must have come from above—way above. Someone wants you free to move around, and he's waiting for your next move."

Fatigue had drawn new shadows on Nick's face. She wondered how much sleep he'd had. Probably not much, not on a trans-Atlantic flight. She had an impulse to reach out and tenderly stroke his haggard face, to run her fingers across the harsh stubble on his jaw. Instead, hesitantly she reached out and brushed her fingers across his hand. He seemed startled by her touch, by the mingling of their hands on the table. *I've embarrassed him*, she thought as the blood rose to her cheeks. *I've embarrassed us both*. But as she started to pull away, his fingers closed tightly around hers. The warmth of his skin seemed to creep up her arm and invade every part of her body.

"You believe Geoffrey's alive, don't you?" she murmured.

He nodded. "I think he's alive."

She stared down at their hands woven together on the table. "I never believed he was dead," she whispered.

"Now that you've heard the facts, how do you feel about him?"

"I don't know. I don't know anymore...." With sudden intensity, she looked at Nick. "All this time I trusted him. I *believed* in him. Oh, you probably think I was naive, don't you? Maybe I was. But we all have dreams, Nick. Dreams we want to come true. And when you're like me, thirty-two and lonely and not very pretty, when a man says he loves you, you want so much to believe him."

"You're wrong, Sarah," he said gently. "You're very pretty."

She knew he was only being kind. She looked down at the table and wondered what he really thought of her. That only a plain woman could be so gullible? She pulled her hand away and reached for the teacup. Of course she knew what he was thinking—that Geoffrey had picked his target well; that Sarah, foolish woman, had fallen hard and fast. She saw it just as clearly. As clearly as if she were holding up a mirror and could coldly, critically, see herself as a man might see her: not beautiful, but shy and awkward. Not the kind of woman to attract a man like Geoffrey.

"It was a marriage of lies," she said. "Strange, how I feel as though I dreamed the whole thing. As though I was never married at all…"

He nodded. "I've felt that way myself, sometimes."

"You were married, then?"

"Not long. Three years. I've been divorced for four."

"I'm sorry."

His eyes focused on hers. "You really mean that, don't you?"

She nodded. Up till this moment, she hadn't seen the sadness in his eyes. She recognized it now, the same pain she was feeling. His marriage had failed; Sarah's had never existed. They both had their wounds.

But hers wouldn't heal. Not until her questions were answered. Not until she knew why Geoffrey had called her.

"Whatever your feelings about Geoffrey," said Nick, "you know, don't you, that it's a big risk, staying here in London. If someone's after him, you're the one they'll watch. Obviously you've been followed, at least since yesterday. You've already led them to Eve."

She looked up sharply. "Eve?"

"I'm afraid so. Eve was a professional. An ex-Mossad agent, on the run for years. She knew how to drop out of sight, and she did it well. But curiosity—maybe jealousy—made her careless. Against her better judgment, she agreed to meet you. It's no coincidence that the night you two met was the same night she was killed."

"Then I caused her death?" Sarah asked in what was barely a whisper.

"Yes, in a way. They must have tailed you to the Lamb and Rose. Right to Eve."

"Oh, God!" She shook her head miserably. "I almost hated her, Nick. When I thought about her and Geoffrey, I couldn't help it. But to be responsible for her death… I didn't want that!"

"She was the professional, Sarah, not you. You can't blame yourself."

She began to tremble and pulled her sweater tight. "Vengeance," she said softly, remembering the way Eve had died. "That's why they killed her."

"I'm not so sure."

"What else could it be?"

"Consider all the possible motives for torture. Granted, vengeance is one. People like to get even. But let's suppose there were more practical reasons…."

She suddenly understood his point. "You mean interrogation? They thought Eve knew something?"

"Maybe they saw through Geoffrey's faked death. Maybe they think he's still alive, too. So they put the knife to Eve, hoping for information. The question is, did she give them any?"

Sarah thought of Eve, remembering the green eyes, windows to a tough soul that did what was necessary to survive. Eve would have killed without a second thought. The business she was in required that ruthlessness. Tough as she was, though, Eve had also been in love. Last night in the Lamb and Rose, Sarah had sensed, even through her heartache, that Eve loved Geoffrey just as deeply, perhaps even more deeply, than Sarah ever had. Eve must have known where to find him. But whatever the torture, she would have held fast. She never would have betrayed Geoffrey. She had died with her secret.

Would Sarah have been as brave? She thought of the knife, of the pain that a blade could inflict on naked flesh, and she shuddered. There was no way to judge one's own courage, she thought. Courage surfaced only when it was needed, when one was forced to meet one's darkest terrors.

Sarah hoped hers would never be tested.

Chapter Seven

"I WANT ANSWERS, DAN. Starting with who ordered Sarah Fontaine's release and why."

Dan Lieberman, chief of consular affairs, regarded Nick with the passive face of a career man long attached to the State Department. Years of giving nothing away but a smile had left their mark; since the day they had met four years ago, Nick had not seen a single strong emotion emerge on Lieberman's face. The foreign service had turned the man into one hell of a poker player.

Yet Nick's instincts told him that somewhere beneath that polite facade was a voice of integrity trying to scream through the politics. Unlike Nick, Lieberman had learned to live with his demons. At least he still had a job and an enviable post here in London. He hadn't held on to it by rocking the boat. No, he'd kept his opinions to himself, had stayed out of trouble, and he'd survived.

But a little trouble was just what Nick was bringing him today.

"What's going on with her case?" asked Nick. "It seems to me it's being handled in a damned peculiar way."

"There have been irregularities," admitted Lieberman.

"Yeah. Starting with that son of a bitch Potter showing up at the police station."

At this remark Lieberman did crack a faint grin. "I'd forgotten you and Roy Potter knew each other so well. What was it between you guys again?"

"Sokolov. Don't tell me you've forgotten that, too."

"Oh, yeah. The Sokolov case. I remember now. You and Potter had it out in the stairwell. I hear your vocabulary would've made a sailor blush." He shook his head. "Bad move, Nick. Generated a very nasty personnel memo."

"You never met Sokolov, did you?"

"No."

"They say his kids found him New Year's day. He had two sons, ten years old or so. They went down to the basement looking for Daddy. They found him with a bullet in his head. Nice New Year's surprise, don't you think?"

"These things happen, Nick. You shouldn't ruin a career over it."

"Two kids, for God's sake! If Potter had listened to me, those two little boys would be safe in Montana or somewhere. Now they're probably freezing in Siberia, hauled back by the KGB."

"He was a defector. He took a risk and lost. Hey, this is all history. You didn't really come here to grouse about Potter, did you?"

"No. I'm here about Sarah Fontaine. I want to know why Potter's involved."

Lieberman shook his head. "Nick, I shouldn't even be talking to you. I hear from the grapevine that you're as popular as a dead fish. So before I say a thing, tell me why you're interested in the Fontaine case."

"Let's call it a sense of moral outrage."

"What're you outraged about?"

"Right now, Sarah Fontaine's sitting in my hotel room, wondering whether she's a widow. I happen to think her husband's alive. But all I've been hearing from our people is that he's dead. That I should give the widow my condolences and forget about it."

"So why not take the easy way out and do what you're told?"

"I don't like being lied to. And I really don't like being ordered to pass those same lies along. If there's a reason for keeping her in the dark, then I want to hear it. If it's valid, okay, I'll back off. But she's going through hell, and I think she has a right to know the truth."

Lieberman sighed. "Back tilting at windmills, aren't you? Know what we used to call you around here? Don Quixote. Nick, why don't you save yourself an ulcer and just go home?"

"Then you won't help me."

"No, it's not that I don't want to. I just don't have any answers."

"Can you tell me why Potter showed up at the station in your place?"

"Okay, I can tell you that much. I got a call this morning from above that Potter would be handling the case, that I wasn't to get involved."

"A call from above? How far above?"

"Let's just say very far above."

"How was her release arranged?"

"Through the British chain of command, I assume. Someone must've whispered in their ear."

"The Brits?" Nick frowned. "Then it's a cooperative effort?"

"Draw your own conclusions." Lieberman's smile revealed he did not disagree.

"What's Roy Potter's involvement?"

"Who knows? Obviously the Company's very interested in your widow. Enough to spring her from jail. Since Potter himself is doing the footwork, I imagine there must be high stakes involved."

"Have you looked over the Fontaine case?" asked Nick.

"Briefly. Before they called me off of it."

"What did you think?"

"I thought the murder charge had a few major holes. A good barrister could've knocked it to pieces."

"And what did you think about Geoffrey Fontaine's death?"

"Irregular."

"An understatement if ever I've heard one. Did you know anything about Eve Fontaine?"

"Not really. I was told she bought the cottage a year ago. They say she was a recluse. Spent all her time out at Margate. But I'm sure you know a lot more about that than I do. Did you say the widow's staying in your room?"

"That's right. At my old bed and breakfast on Baker Street."

"Oh, the Kenmore." Lieberman filed away this information without a change in expression. "What sort of woman is she?"

Nick thought a moment. "Quiet," he said at last. "Intelligent. At the moment, very bewildered."

"I saw her passport photo. She struck me as rather, well…unremarkable."

"She strikes a lot of people that way."

"May I ask what your involvement is?"

"No."

Lieberman smiled. "Blunt as ever! Look, Nick, that really is all I know." He made a gesture that implied he had more pressing business. "If I have more information, I'll give you a call. How long will you be at the Kenmore?"

Nick rose. "For a few days, probably. After that, I'm not sure."

"And Sarah Fontaine? Will she be staying with you?"

Nick didn't have an answer. If it were up to him, Sarah would be on a plane back to Washington. Just the fact she was sitting alone in his room right now made him nervous. The Kenmore's proprietress, an old acquaintance of Nick's, had assured him that her two beefy sons would handle any trouble. Still, Nick was anxious to get back. Eve Fontaine's gruesome death still weighed on his mind.

"If Sarah decides to stay in London," Nick said, "then I'll be around."

They shook hands. Lieberman's grip was the same as always, firm and connected. It made Nick want to trust him. "By the way," Nick said as they walked to the door, "have you ever heard of someone called Magus?"

Lieberman's brow remained absolutely smooth. Not a ripple passed through his blue eyes. "Magus?" he repeated. "In biblical terms, it refers to a wise man. Or a magician."

"No. I'm referring to a code name."

"Doesn't ring a bell."

Nick paused in the doorway. "One last thing. Could you relay a message to Roy Potter for me?"

"Sure. Just keep the language decent."

"Tell him to call off his bloodhounds. Or at least have them follow us at a more discreet distance."

For the first time, a frown appeared on Lieberman's face. "I'll tell him," he said. "But if I were you, I'd make damn sure it really is the Company on your tail. Because if it isn't, let's just say the alternative might be a lot less pleasant."

"Less pleasant than the Company?" asked Nick. "I doubt it."

WHEN NICK RETURNED to his room at the Kenmore Bed and Breakfast, Sarah was fast asleep. She was sprawled, fully dressed, on the bed by the window, her face nestled against the pillow, her arm trailing over the side. Her glasses had fallen to the floor, as if she'd drifted to sleep still clutching them. The sun shone in brightly and illuminated her coppery hair.

For a moment he stood over the bed and gazed down at her, taking in the baggy sweater and the plain gray skirt. Lieberman had called her unremarkable. *Maybe to everyone else she is,* thought Nick. *Maybe I'm not seeing straight. Maybe I'm too lonely to care about looks anymore.* Whatever the reason, as he watched her now, he was starting to think she was really quite beautiful.

Not in the classical sense. Not like Lauren, the woman he'd once been married to. Black-haired, green-eyed Lauren could walk into a room and make a dozen heads turn. Nick had gotten a kick out of that—for a while. When Lauren was on his arm, other men would glance enviously in his direction, and he'd marvel at his own good luck. She'd been the perfect embassy wife: charming, witty, always ready with the repartee. And she'd been beautiful, in a way any

man could appreciate. She'd known it, too. Maybe that
had been the problem.

The woman sleeping on this bed was nothing like
Lauren. Sarah had called herself plain. She'd felt a sense
of wonder that a man like Geoffrey had married her. It
must have been painful to learn that her marriage had
been nothing but a sham. Nick knew all about pain;
he'd lived through it himself four years ago. In a way,
he'd never recovered. After his divorce he'd promised
himself he'd never be hurt again. So here he was, stubbornly single. At least the bitterness had faded. At least
he was still human enough to look at Sarah and think
of the possibilities.

The possibilities? Who was he kidding? There were none.
Not until they learned the truth about Geoffrey.

Sarah wasn't ready to abandon what for her had been a
happy marriage. It was obvious she still loved her husband.
She wanted to believe in him. The perverse part about it
all was that this very loyalty to Geoffrey was what made
Sarah so appealing. Loyalty.

Nick turned and gazed out the window. In the street
below, the same black car was parked. The Company was
still watching them. He waved, wondering what in God's
name had happened to the quality of spies these days. Then
he closed the curtain and went to lie down on the other bed.

The daylight was disconcerting. He couldn't sleep.
Tired as he was, he could only lie there with his eyes
closed and think.

What exactly am I doing here? he wondered. Boarding the
plane last night had been an impulse of pure anger. He'd
thought Sarah had lied to him; she had hammered the last
nail in the coffin of his career, and he had meant to find

her and get to the truth. Instead, here he was, not ten feet away from her, daydreaming about the possibilities.

He glanced over at her bed. She was sleeping so soundly, so peacefully, like a tired child. Yet she wasn't a child, and he was too aware of that fact. He remembered how it had felt this morning to touch her hair, to feel her face against his shoulder. Something began to stir in his belly, something very, very dangerous. It had been a long time since he'd had a woman, and Sarah looked so soft, so near....

He closed his eyes, suddenly angry at his own lack of control. Why was he putting himself through this unnecessary agony? The smart thing to do would be to go home and let the CIA handle the whole affair. But if they let anything happen to her, he'd never forgive himself.

Gradually, fitfully, Nick drifted toward sleep. A vision intruded: a woman with amber eyes. He wanted to reach out and touch her, but his hands became tangled in the long strands of her hair. Sarah, Sarah. How could anyone not think you beautiful? His hands moved leadenly, caught in a web too thick to penetrate. Beyond his grasp, Sarah faded away. He was alone. As always, he was alone.

IN ONE OF Roy Potter's back rooms, a radio report came over the receiver. "O'Hara left Lieberman's office forty minutes ago," the agent called in. "Now he's back at the Kenmore. Haven't seen the woman for an hour. Curtains are drawn. Looks like they're hitting the sack."

"And I'll bet ya two bangers it's not to sleep," Potter muttered to his assistant. Agent Tarasoff barely smiled. Tarasoff had no sense of humor, no sense of fun. His style of dressing was absolutely correct: a conservative gray suit, a tie in dull blues and silvers, a plain white shirt, and all of it spotless. Even the way Tarasoff ate his roast-beef sandwich was boring. He took neat little nibbles, wiping his fingers between bites. Now Potter, on the other hand, ate like a normal person. No pussyfooting around. He just ate and got it over with. Potter gulped down his last bite of corned-beef sandwich and reached for the transmitter.

"Okay, guys, just stick it out. See who wanders by."

"Yes, sir. Have you got anything on the Kenmore folks?"

"Clean Brits. Plain old B and B types, widow and two sons."

"Check. We've seen 'em."

"How're you guys situated?"

"Can't complain. Got a pub right across the street."

"Has he spotted you yet?"

"Afraid so, sir. He flipped us a bird some time back."

Tarasoff made a sound that might have been a chuckle. But when Potter glanced over at him, all he saw was the same impassive face.

"Geez, he's on to you already? What'd you guys do? Go up and introduce yourselves?"

"No, sir. He saw us way back, after we left the station."

"Okay. It's one-thirty. You can clock yourselves out in two hours. Keep alive."

Potter hung up, crumpled the waxed paper from his lunch and tossed it at the trash can. It missed by a mile, but he didn't feel like getting up.

Tarasoff rose and retrieved the crumpled paper. "What do you make of all this, Mr. Potter?" he asked, neatly dropping the trash into the can.

Potter shrugged. "Wild-goose chase? I hope not."

"Should we be looking at this Nick O'Hara in a different light?"

"What do you mean?"

"Is it possible there's something more complex involved? Could he be under deep cover for someone?"

Potter burst out laughing. "O'Hara? Let me tell you something about him. He's not the deep-cover type. Too damned honest. Thinks he's on a quest for the Holy Grail or something. You know, the kind of guy who spends all day worrying about dead whales." Potter eyed Tarasoff's half-eaten roast-beef sandwich. His stomach was still growling. "You gonna finish that thing?"

"No, sir. You can have it."

Potter took a bite and almost choked. Horseradish. Why did folks have to go and ruin perfectly good roast beef? But there was no point wasting it. "O'Hara's smart enough, I guess," he said between bites. "I mean, in an intellectual sort of way—all theory, no practice. Speaks about four languages. Not a bad consular officer. But he just doesn't operate in the real world."

"It's strange, though," said Tarasoff. "Why should he get mixed up in this affair? He's jeopardized his career. It doesn't make sense to me."

"Tarasoff, have you ever been in love?"

"I'm married."

"No, I mean *in love?*"

"Well, yes, I suppose so."

"You suppose so. Hell, that's not love. By love, I mean something red-hot, something that'll make you go crazy, risk your life. Maybe even get married."

"He's in love? With Sarah Fontaine?"

"Why not?"

Tarasoff shook his head gravely. "I think he's under deep cover."

Potter laughed. "Never underestimate the power of hormones."

"That's what my wife always says." Tarasoff suddenly frowned at Potter's arm. "Sir, you'd better wipe up that mustard. It'll ruin your jacket."

Potter glanced down at the yellow blob on his sleeve. Another day, another stain. He looked around for a napkin, then gave up and reached for a scrap of memo paper. It was a note he'd scrawled to himself earlier in the week: *Mail alimony checks!* Dammit, late again. If he got over to the post office right now, the checks might arrive by Tuesday....

He tossed the memo at the trash can. It missed. With a groan he forced himself out of his chair. He was reaching down for the scrap of paper when the door opened. "Yeah?" he asked. Then he fell silent.

Puzzled, Tarasoff turned and looked at the man standing in the doorway. It was Jonathan Van Dam.

Potter cleared his throat. "Mr. Van Dam. I didn't know you were in London. Is there new business?"

"No. Actually it's old business." Van Dam settled into Potter's chair and carelessly brushed aside the mound of crumpled waxed paper and Styrofoam cups before sliding his briefcase on the desk. "An odd bit of information has come to my attention, and I really can't account for it. Perhaps you can shed some light."

"Uh—information?"

"Yes. I've had a tap on Sarah Fontaine's phone. To my surprise I learned she had a call from her husband a few days ago. Rather amazing feat, don't you think? Or has long-distance service improved that much?"

Potter and Tarasoff looked at each other. "Mr. Van Dam," said Potter, "I can explain...."

"Yes," said Van Dam. He wasn't smiling. "I think you should."

ON THE HIGH cliffs above Margate, Nick and Sarah stood with their faces against the wind. Gulls dove from the teal-blue sky, and their cries pierced the air like a hundred voices raised in mourning. The sun was shining brightly, and the sea sparkled like broken glass. Even Sarah was stirring to life under the healing touch.

Since starting out from London that morning, she'd shed her sweater and scarf. Now, dressed in a white cotton shirt and the old gray skirt, she paused in the sunshine and drank in its warmth. She was alive. For the past two weeks, she'd somehow forgotten that fact. She'd wanted to bury herself along with Geoffrey—or who she'd thought was Geoffrey. Only now, as she felt the salt wind in her face, did life seem to creep back into her body. She'd survived Geoffrey's death; now she would survive his resurrection. To think how deeply she'd loved him! Now she could barely recall the feeling. All she had left were images, freeze-frame memories of a man she'd hardly known.

"Sarah?" Nick touched her arm and nodded toward the path. His hair was wild and windblown, his face ruddy in the sunshine. In his faded shirt and trousers, he looked more like a fisherman than a bureaucrat. "How much farther?" he asked.

"Not far. It's at the top of the hill."

As they walked up the path to Whitstable Lane, she found herself watching him. He strode easily, without effort, as though he'd spent all his life scaling cliffs. Once again, she wondered about Nick O'Hara. Whatever his reasons for being here, she knew this much: she trusted him. There was no point questioning his motives. He was a friend; that was all that mattered.

Nick turned and squinted down the path. The town of Margate was nestled below at the foot of the cliff. There was no sign of pursuit. They were alone.

"I wonder why they're not following us," said Nick.

"Maybe they're tired."

"Well, let's keep moving. At least we've got some breathing room now."

They turned and continued walking.

"You don't like the CIA, do you?" she asked.

"No."

"Why not?"

"They're a different breed. I don't trust them. And I especially don't trust Roy Potter."

"What did Mr. Potter do to you?"

"To me? Nothing. Except maybe get me shipped back to Washington."

"Is Washington that bad?"

"It's not the place foreign service careers are made."

"Where are they made?"

"Hot spots. Africa. South America."

"Yet you were in London."

"London wasn't my first choice. They offered me Cameroon, but I had to turn it down."

"Why?"

"Lauren. My ex-wife."

"Oh." So that was her name, Lauren. Sarah wondered what had gone wrong between them. Had it been like so many other failed marriages, in which there was a gradual drifting apart? Boredom? She couldn't imagine ever being bored of Nick. He was a man of many layers, each one more complex than the last, each waiting to be discovered. Could a woman ever really know him?

They walked in silence, past the row of mailboxes and around the curve leading to Whitstable Lane. The cottage came into view, a small white house behind a low picket fence. The old grounds keeper was nowhere in sight.

"This is the house," she said.

"Then let's find out who's home," said Nick. He walked up to the front door and rang the bell. There was no answer. The door was locked. "Sounds like it's empty," he said. "All the better."

"Nick?" she called, following him around to the back door. She found him jiggling the knob. It was unlocked.

Slowly the door swung open. The shaft of daylight swept across a polished stone floor. At their feet lay a single shattered china plate. Nothing else appeared out of place. The kitchen drawers were closed. Copper pots hung in rows on an overhead rack. On the window sill sat two wilted plants. Except for the soft drip of a leaky faucet, the house was eerily silent.

Sarah jumped when Nick touched her arm. "Wait here," he whispered. His footsteps crunched loudly on the broken china as he walked through the kitchen and disappeared into the next room. As she waited for him, her eyes slowly explored the strange surroundings. She was standing in the very heart and soul of the house. Here was where Eve had cooked, where she and Geoffrey had laughed and eaten together. Even now, the room seemed to resonate with their presence. Sarah didn't belong here. She was the intruder.

"Sarah?" Nick was calling from the doorway. "Come take a look."

She followed him into a sitting room. Leather-bound books lined the wall shelves; china figurines sat in a row on the mantelpiece. In the fireplace were the ashes from Eve's last fire. Only a desk had been disturbed. Its drawers had been pulled out and dumped. A pile of correspondence—mostly bills and advertisements—had been ripped open and tossed on the floor.

"Robbery wasn't the motive," he said, nodding at an obviously antique pewter goblet on the mantelpiece. "I think someone was after information. An address book, maybe. Or a phone number."

She gazed around the room. It would have been a cozy place, with the flames crackling and the lights burning low. She could picture Eve sitting quietly in the leather chair, smoke trailing from her cigarette. Would there be music? Yes, of course, Mozart and Chopin. There were the records, stacked by an old phonograph. The ashtray was still full of butts. Fear must have made her light one cigarette after another. Here, alone in the shadows, Eve must have jumped every time the windows rattled or the floor creaked.

A few feet away, Sarah saw an open door. She felt herself drawn toward it by an inexplicable and painful fascination. She knew what lay beyond, yet she couldn't stop herself from going in.

It was the bedroom. With gathering tears she stood at the foot of the double bed and looked at the flowered coverlet. This was another woman's bed. In her mind she saw Geoffrey lying here, with his arms around Eve. The vision filled her with such pain she could barely refrain from screaming. How many nights had he slept here? How many times had they made love? As he lay in this bed, hadn't he ever missed Sarah, just a little?

These were questions only he could answer. She had to find him. She had to know, or she'd never be free.

In tears she bolted from the room. A moment later she was standing alone near the edge of the cliff, staring out to sea. She scarcely heard Nick's footsteps as he walked up behind her.

But she did feel his hands settle gently on her shoulders. He said nothing; he merely stood there, a warm, solid presence. It was precisely what she needed from him: the silence. And the touch. As the waves churned below, she closed her eyes and felt his breath in her hair.

She'd been married to Geoffrey and she'd never really known him. Here was Nick, a man she'd met just two weeks ago. Already their lives had mingled inextricably. And now she desperately wanted him to pull her closer, to gather her into his arms.

How did things get so crazy? she wondered. Was it just the loneliness? The grief? She wanted to turn to him, to be held by him, but she knew it was more than simple desire. It was also need. She was afraid and vulnerable, and Nick was the only safe anchor in her world. It was the wrong reason to fall in love.

Pulling away, she turned and faced him. He stood very still and erect. His eyes were the color of smoke. The wind whipped his shirt. In the sky above, gulls soared and circled like a silver cloud.

"I have to find Geoffrey," she said, her words almost lost in the gulls' cries. "And you can't come with me."

"You can't go off on your own. Look what happened to Eve—"

"They don't want *me*! They want Geoffrey. And I'm their only link. They won't hurt me."

"How are you going to find him?"

"He'll find *me*."

Nick shook his head, and his hair danced wildly in the wind. "This is crazy! You don't know what you're up against."

"Do you? If you know, Nick, you have to tell me."

He didn't answer. He only stared at her with eyes that had darkened to tarnished silver. *What does he know?* she wondered. *Is he somehow part of all this?*

She turned and kept walking. Nick followed her, his hands jammed deeply into his pockets. They stopped at the row of mailboxes, where Whitstable Lane curved into the cliff path. An old man in a postal uniform tipped his hat and rode away on his bike, down the path to Margate. He had just delivered the mail. Sarah reached into the slot marked 25. Inside were another catalog and three bills, all addressed to Eve.

"She won't be needing them," Nick pointed out.

"No. I guess not." Sarah stuffed the bills into her purse. "I was hoping there'd be something…."

"What did you expect? That he'd write you a letter? You don't even know where to start, do you?"

"No," she admitted. Then she added stubbornly, "But I'll find him."

"How? Don't forget, you've got the CIA down there, waiting for you."

"I'll lose them. Somehow."

"And then what? What happens if Eve's killer decides to come after you? You think you can handle him on your own?"

She broke away and headed down the path. He seized her arm and pulled her around.

"Sarah! Don't be stupid!"

"I'm going to find Geoffrey!"

"Then let me come with you."

"*Why?*" she cried, her word lost in the wind.

His answer caught her completely off guard. In one swift motion, he pulled her into his arms. Before she could react, before she could even comprehend what was happening, his mouth came down on hers. The force of his embrace crushed the very breath from her lungs. The cry of the gulls faded, and the wind seemed to carry her up and away, until she lost all sense of where she was. As if by their own accord, her arms found their way around him, to clutch at the hard curve of his back. Willingly her lips parted; at once he was exploring her mouth, devouring her with an animal's hunger. Nothing mattered anymore, nothing but Nick, the taste of his mouth, the smell of the sea on his skin.

The gull cries turned into screams as reality rushed in. Sarah wrenched herself free. His expression mirrored her own look of surprise, as though he, too, had been swept up by something he couldn't explain.

"I guess that's why," he said softly.

She shook her head in confusion. He had kissed her. It had happened so fast, so unexpectedly, that she could barely take in what it all meant. She did know this much: she had wanted him. She still wanted him. With every second that passed, her hunger grew.

"Why did you do that?"

"It just happened. Sarah, I didn't mean to—" Suddenly agitated, he turned away. "No, dammit!" he blurted out, wheeling around to look at her again. "I take it back! I sure as hell *did* mean to do that!"

She retreated, more confused than ever. What was wrong with her? Only days ago, she'd thought herself desperately in love with Geoffrey. Now, at this moment, Nick O'Hara was the only man she wanted. She could still taste him on her lips, could still feel his hands pulling her against him, and all she could think of was how good it would feel to kiss him again. No, she couldn't have him near her. Not now, not after this.

"Please, Nick," she said. "Go back to Washington. I have to find Geoffrey, and you can't be with me."

"Wait. Sarah!"

But she was already walking away.

They were quiet as they approached the village. She didn't know what to say to him anymore. It had been easier when they were simply friends, when they were only two people searching for answers. Now just looking at him ignited fires deep inside her, fires she'd never known existed.

Last night she'd been so tired and afraid, she'd been almost glad to share his room. Today everything had changed. She had to leave him. As soon as they reached London, she would pack her bags and walk out of the Kenmore. Finding Geoffrey was something she could only do alone.

By the time they entered Margate, she'd hardened her resolve. Nothing he could say would change her mind. But by God, he'd try; she could see it in his face, in the stubborn set of his jaw. He wasn't through with her yet. It would be a long drive back to London.

Like two strangers walking side by side, they headed for Nick's rented M.G., which was parked on a street lined by tiny shops. Just behind the M.G. was the same black Ford that had tailed them all the way from London. The CIA. So they'd given up all pretenses of subtlety. They were operating in the open now. That would make it easier for Sarah to lose them.

One of the agents was silhouetted against the tinted window. As they walked past, she glanced through the windshield; there was absolutely no movement inside the car. Nick noticed it, too. He paused and tapped on the window. The agent didn't move, didn't speak. Was he sleeping? It was hard to tell through the dark glass.

"Nick?" she whispered. "Is something wrong with him?"

"Keep moving," he said softly, nudging her toward the M.G. "I want you to get inside the car." Calmly he unlocked her door. "Get inside and stay there."

"Nick—"

He was cautiously approaching the Ford. Burning curiosity drew her to follow him; she stood right behind him on the sidewalk as slowly, carefully, he took hold of the passenger door. The agent still hadn't moved. Nick hesitated only a second, then jerked the door open.

The agent's shoulder slumped sideways. A face slid past the window, a face with wide, staring eyes. An arm flopped out of the car and dangled into the street. Nick reeled away in horror as bright red droplets spattered the sidewalk.

Chapter Eight

SARAH SCREAMED. IN THE NEXT INSTANT, gunfire spat out the windows of the Ford, sending both Nick and Sarah diving for cover. Nick's body landed squarely on hers as they hit the concrete. She couldn't move. She couldn't even speak; all the breath had been slammed out of her by the impact.

Nick rolled aside and shoved her forward. "The car—get in!" he barked.

His harsh command jarred her into action. Like a terrified animal, she scrambled into the M.G. Gunfire shattered store windows, and all around them, people were screaming. Nick dove in behind Sarah, crawling over her and landing in a heap under the steering wheel. His keys were already out as he slid onto the seat.

The engine roared to life. Sarah struggled to close her door, but Nick yelled, "Get down! Get the hell down!" She sank to the floor.

Blindly he sent the car in reverse. It thudded into the Ford. Nick shifted to first, jammed the wheel to the right, and floored the gas pedal. They jerked forward. Sarah was thrown back helplessly against the seat. The car swerved wildly into the street. They were hurtling aimlessly, toward an inevitable collision. She braced herself.

But the crash never came. There was only the rumble of the engine and Nick's coarse oath as he shifted into third gear.

"Close your door!" he ordered.

She looked over at him. He had both hands on the steering wheel and his eyes on the road. They were safe. Nick was in control. Outside, the narrow streets of Margate hurtled by.

She tugged the door shut. "Why are they trying to kill us?"

"Good question!" A lorry appeared from nowhere. Nick swerved aside. From behind came the screech of tires and the other driver's angry shout.

"That agent—"

"His throat was slit."

"Oh, God...."

A sign marked Westgate loomed ahead. Nick shifted into fourth. They had left Margate behind them. Empty fields now whipped past the windows.

"But who, Nick? Who's trying to kill us?"

Nick shot a glance in the rearview mirror. "Let's hope we're not about to find out."

She snapped her head around in horror. A blue Peugeot was closing in fast. She caught only a glimpse of the driver, a flash of reflective sunglasses.

"Hold on," said Nick. "We're going for a ride...." He floored the pedal, and the M.G. cut recklessly through traffic. The Peugeot shot off after them. It was a larger, clumsier car; it pulled into the wrong lane and almost clipped a van. The error cost it a split second of speed; the Peugeot fell behind. But traffic was getting thin. On the open stretch, there'd be no contest. The Peugeot was too fast.

"I can't lose him, Sarah!"

She heard the desperation in his voice. They were doomed, and there was nothing he could do about it. *It's all my fault*, she thought, *all my fault that Nick's going to die.*

"Put on your seat belt," he instructed. "We've run out of options."

Out of options. A nice way of saying they'd reached the end. She watched as the Peugeot hurtled relentlessly toward them. Through the windshield she saw the driver, a glare of sunlight on his silvered glasses. There was something monstrous, something inhuman, about a man whose eyes you couldn't see.

She buckled the seat belt and glanced at Nick. His profile was hard and cool, his gaze fixed ahead on the road. He was too busy to look terrified. Only his hands betrayed him. His knuckles were white.

The road forked. To the left a sign pointed to Canterbury. Nick veered left, throwing her hard against the seat belt. The Peugeot almost missed the turnoff. It skidded onto the shoulder, then zoomed after them onto the Canterbury highway.

Nick's voice, low and steady, penetrated the cloud of fear that had formed in her brain. "The bullets'll be flying any second. Get your head down. I'll keep us on the road as long as I can. If we crack up, get out and run like hell. The gas tank could blow."

"I won't leave you!"

"Yes, you will."

"No, Nick!"

"*Dammit!*" he shouted. "*Just do what I say!*"

The Peugeot was right behind them, so close Sarah could see the driver's teeth, bared in a smile. "Why aren't they shooting?" she cried. "They're close enough to hit us!"

The Peugeot nudged their back bumper. Sarah clung to the door as Nick jammed the wheel right, then left. The Peugeot skidded and fell behind a few yards.

"That's why." Nick answered. "They want to run us off the road."

Again there was a thump, this time against the left bumper. Nick swerved again. The Peugeot roared up beside them. The cars were neck and neck. Paralyzed by terror, Sarah found herself staring through the window at the face of a killer. His blond hair—so pale it was almost white—fell jaggedly above the mirrored sunglasses. His cheeks were sunken, his skin was dull as wax. He was grinning at her.

Only vaguely did her mind register the obstacle ahead. She was hypnotized by the man's face, by the death's-head grin. Then she heard Nick's sharp intake of breath. Her eyes snapped ahead to the curve, to the car stalled in the road.

Nick spun the wheel right, flinging them into a lane of oncoming traffic. Tires shrieked. They pitched wildly out of control as cars swerved to avoid them. Green fields spun past Sarah's eyes, and then she focused on Nick's hands as he fought the steering wheel. She scarcely registered the metallic thud, the shattering of glass, somewhere behind them.

Then the world came abruptly to a halt. They found themselves staring wide-eyed at a field of astonished cows. Sarah's heart began to beat again. Only then did she remember to take another breath. In that same instant, Nick hit the gas pedal and turned the M.G. back onto the highway.

"That'll slow 'em down," he said. His understatement struck her as somehow hilarious.

She looked back. The Peugeot was lying on its side in the field. Standing in the mud beside it was the blond driver, the man with the death's-head grin. Even from that distance, she could see the fury in his face. Then he and the Peugeot shrank into the distance and vanished.

"You okay?" asked Nick.

"Yes. Yes…" She tried to swallow but her mouth felt drier than sand.

Nick grunted. "One thing's obvious. You sure as hell can't go off alone."

Alone? The very thought terrified her. No, she didn't want to be alone. Never again! But how much could she count on Nick? He was no soldier; he was a diplomat, a man behind a desk. Right now he was operating on pure instinct, not training. Yet he was all that stood between her and a killer.

The road forked again. Canterbury and London lay to the west. Nick turned east, onto the road marked Dover.

"What are you doing?" asked Sarah, turning in dismay as they bypassed the London exit.

"We're not going to London," he said.

"But we need help—"

"We *had* help. Didn't do us a lot of good, did it? So much for protective surveillance."

"London will be safer!"

He shook his head. "No, it won't. They'll be waiting for us there. This whole fiasco proves we can't count on our own people. Maybe they're just incompetent. Maybe it's something worse…."

Something worse? Did he mean betrayal? She thought the nightmare was over, that they'd simply knock on the embassy door in London and be swept into the protective arms of the CIA. She'd never considered the possibility that the very people she trusted would want her dead. It didn't make sense!

"The CIA wouldn't kill its own man!" she pointed out.

"Maybe not the Company itself. But someone inside. Someone with other connections."

"What if you're wrong?"

"Dammit, think about it! The agent didn't just sit back while someone cut his throat! He was taken by surprise. By someone he knew, someone he trusted. There's got to be an insider involved. Someone who wants us out of the way."

"But I don't know anything!"

"Maybe you do. Maybe you just don't realize it."

She shook her head frantically. "No, this is crazy. *It's crazy!* Nick, I'm just an average woman. I go to work, I go shopping, I cook dinner—I'm not a spy! I'm not like—like Eve...."

"Then it's time we started thinking like her. Both of us. I'm new to this game, too. And it looks like I'm in just as deep."

"We could fly home—to Washington—"

"You really think it's safer there?"

No, she thought with mounting despair. He was right. Home would be no safer. They had nowhere to run.

"Then where do we go?" she asked desperately.

He glanced at his watch. "It's twelve o'clock," he said. "We'll ditch the car and get the Hovercraft in Dover. It'll be a quick ride to Calais. We'll take the train to Brussels. And then you and I are going to vanish. For a while, at least."

She stared numbly at the road. A *while?* she wondered. *How long is a while? Forever? Will I be like Eve, always running, always looking over my shoulder?*

Just an hour ago, on the cliffs of Margate, it had been so clear what she needed to do—she had to find Geoffrey and get to the truth of her marriage. Now it was down to something more elemental, a goal so stark that nothing else mattered.

She had to stay alive.

She'd think about Geoffrey later. She'd take the time to wonder where he was and how she'd find him. She *had* to find him; he was the only one who had the answers. But now she couldn't look that far ahead.

She saw how tightly Nick gripped the steering wheel. He was afraid, too. That was what terrified her most—the fact that even Nick O'Hara was afraid.

"I guess I have to trust you," she said.

"It looks that way."

"Who else can we trust, Nick?"

He looked at her. The answer he gave had an awful ring of finality. "No one."

Roy Potter grabbed the receiver on the first ring. What he heard next made him hit the recording button. Through the crackle of a trans-Channel connection came the voice of Nick O'Hara. "I've got one thing to say."

"O'Hara?" shouted Potter. "Where the hell—"

"We're dropping out, Potter. Stay off our tails."

"You can't go off in the cold! O'Hara, listen! You need us!"

"Like hell."

"You think you're gonna stay alive out there without our help?"

"Yeah. I do. And you listen good, Potter. Take a close hard look at your people. Because something's rotten in the State of Denmark. And if I find out you're responsible, I'm going to see they nail your ass to the wall."

"Wait, O'Hara—"

The line went dead. Muttering a curse, Potter hung up. Then he looked reluctantly across the desk at Jonathan Van Dam. "They're alive," he said.

"Where are they?"

"He wouldn't say. We're tracing the call right now."

"Are they coming in?"

"No. They're going under."

Van Dam leaned across the desk. "I want them, Mr. Potter. I want them soon. Before someone else gets to them."

"Sir, he's afraid. He doesn't trust us—"

"I'm not surprised, considering this latest foul-up. Find them!"

Potter grabbed the phone, silently hurling every oath he knew at Nick O'Hara. This was all his fault. "Tarasoff?" he barked. "Did you get that number?... What the hell does that mean, *somewhere* in Brussels? I already know he's in Brussels! I want the damned address!" He slammed the receiver down.

"Simple surveillance," said Van Dam. "That was your plan, wasn't it? So what happened?"

"I had two good agents on the Fontaine woman. I don't know what went wrong. One of my men's still missing, and the other's in the morgue—"

"I can't be bothered with dead agents. I want Sarah Fontaine. What about those train stations and airports?"

"The Brussels office is already on it. I'm flying out tonight. There's been activity in their bank accounts—big withdrawals. Looks as if they plan to stay under a long time."

"Watch those accounts. Circulate their photographs. To local police, Interpol, everyone who'll cooperate. Don't arrest her, just locate her. And we need a psychological profile on O'Hara. I want to know that man's motives."

"O'Hara?" Potter snorted. "I can tell you all you need to know."

"What do you think the man'll do next?"

"He's new to the game. Wouldn't know the ropes of picking up a new identity. But he speaks fluent French. He could move around Belgium without raising an eyebrow. And he's smart. We might have trouble."

"What about the woman? Could she blend in as well?"

"Doesn't know any foreign languages, to my knowledge. Totally inexperienced. She'd be helpless on her own."

Tarasoff entered the office. "Got the address. It's a pay phone, center of town. No chance of tracking him down now."

"Who does O'Hara know in Belgium?" asked Van Dam. "Any friends he'd trust?"

Potter frowned. "I'd have to check his file…."

"What about Mr. Lieberman in the consular division?" suggested Tarasoff. "He'd know about O'Hara's friends."

Van Dam gave Tarasoff a look of appraisal. "Good start. I'm glad someone's thinking. What else?"

"Well, sir, I wonder if we should look at other angles, other themes running this man's life…." Tarasoff suddenly noticed the dark look Potter was flashing at him. He added quickly, "But of course, Mr. Potter knows O'Hara inside and out."

"What themes are you referring to, Mr. Tarasoff?" prodded Van Dam.

"I keep wondering if he's—well, working for someone."

"No way," said Potter. "O'Hara's an independent."

"But your man makes a good point," said Van Dam. "Did we miss something when we vetted O'Hara?"

"He spent four years in London," said Tarasoff. "He could have made numerous contacts."

"Look, I know the guy," insisted Potter. "He's his own man." Van Dam didn't seem to hear him. Potter felt as if he was shouting from the wrong side of a soundproof window. Why did he always feel like the outsider, the slob with mustard on his ten-year-old suit? He'd worked like hell to be a good agent, but it wasn't enough, not in the eyes of men like Van Dam. What Potter lacked was *style*.

Tarasoff had it. And Van Dam—why, his suit was definitely Savile Row, his watch a Rolex. He'd been smart to marry money. That, of course, was what Potter should have done. He should have married rich women. Then they'd be paying *him* alimony.

"I'll expect results soon, Mr. Potter," Van Dam said as he pulled on his overcoat. "Let me know the minute something turns up. How you handle O'Hara after that point is your affair."

Potter frowned. "Uh—what does that mean?"

"I'll leave it up to you. Just make it discreet." Van Dam left the room.

Potter stared in puzzlement at the closed door. What exactly had he meant by "I'll leave it up to you?" Oh, he knew what he'd *like* to do to Nick O'Hara. O'Hara was just another high-minded career diplomat. Potter knew the breed all too well. They looked down their noses at spooks. None of them appreciated the dirty work Potter had to do. Hell, *someone* had to do it! When things went well, he got no credit. But when things went wrong, guess who got the blame?

Those invectives he and O'Hara had hurled at each other a year ago still rankled. Mainly because he knew, deep down, that O'Hara had been right. Sokolov's death had been his fault.

This time he couldn't afford any mistakes. He'd already lost two agents. Even worse, he'd lost track of the Fontaine woman. By God, there'd be no more screwups. Even if he had to search every hotel in Brussels, he'd find them.

FOR REASONS OF his own, Jonathan Van Dam was just as determined to find them. Somehow O'Hara had managed to foul up what should have been a simple operation. He was the unexpected factor, the one little detail that no one had predicted, just the sort of thing that gives an operative nightmares. What really troubled Van Dam was something Tarasoff had suggested, that O'Hara could be more than just a man in love. Was he working for someone else?

Van Dam stared down at his plate of mixed grill and considered this last disturbing possibility. He was sitting alone in his favorite London restaurant. The food wasn't bad here. The lamb chops were tender and pink, the sausages homemade. The chips were dry, true, but he never ate them anyway. He liked the candlelight and the soft hum of conversation. He liked seeing other people around him, if only anonymously. It helped him focus on the problem at hand.

He finished his chop and, sitting back, slowly sipped a glass of fine port. Yes, that young Tarasoff had brought up a good point. It was dangerous to assume anything was as it seemed. Van Dam, better than most people, knew that. For two years he'd endured what outsiders had called a happy marriage. For two years he'd shared a bed with a woman he could barely stand to touch. He had dutifully nursed her out of her gin binges, put up with her rages and, afterward, her remorse. Through it all he'd laughed in silence at the inane comments her friends had made. "You know, Jonathan, you've made Claudia so happy!" or "You're so good for her!" or "You're both so lucky!" Claudia's death had stunned everyone—most of all, perhaps, Claudia herself. The bitch had thought she'd live forever.

Yes, the port *was* excellent. He ordered another. A woman two tables away was staring at him but he ignored her, knowing, by some strange and certain instinct, that she had a fondness for spirits. Like Claudia.

The matter of Sarah Fontaine and Nick O'Hara returned to mind. He knew that finding a man like O'Hara, a man who spoke fluent French, would be impossible in a city as big as Brussels. Sarah Fontaine was a different matter. All she had to do was open her mouth at the wrong time, and the game would be up. Yes, better to concentrate on finding her, not O'Hara. She was the easier quarry. And after all, she was the one they really wanted.

HUGGING HER LEGS to her chest, Sarah sat on the hard mattress and checked her watch again. Nick had been gone two hours, and all that time she'd been sitting like a zombie, listening for his footsteps. And thinking. Thinking about fear, wondering if she'd ever feel safe again.

On the train from Calais, she had struggled against panic, against the premonition that something terrible was about to happen. All of her senses had become acutely raw. She'd registered every sound, every sight, right down to the loose threads on the ticket taker's jacket. Details took on new importance. Their lives might hang on something as trivial as the look in a stranger's eye.

The trip had gone smoothly—they'd made it to Brussels without a hitch. Hours had passed, dulling the sharp edges of fear until terror gave way to mere gnawing anxiety. For the moment she was safe.

But where was Nick? Surely he would come back for her? She didn't want to think of the other possibilities. That he'd been caught. Or that he'd come to his senses and bailed out of a hopeless situation. She wouldn't blame him if he had bailed out. What man in his right mind would stick around waiting for death?

She rose and went to the window. Dusk was blotting out the city. Through a gray drizzle, the rooftops of Brussels hovered unanchored, like ghosts.

She flicked on the one bare lightbulb. The room was small and shabby, a mere box on the second floor of a run-down hotel. Everything smelled of dust and mildew. The double mattress was lumpy. The wood floor was covered only by a single small throw rug, which was worn and stained. A few hours ago, she hadn't cared what the room looked like. Now the four walls were driving her mad. She felt trapped. She craved fresh air, and even more than that, food. Their last meal had been breakfast, and her body was screaming to eat. But she had to wait until Nick returned.

If he returned.

Downstairs a door slammed. She spun around and listened as footsteps thumped up the stairs, then creaked heavily along the hall. A key jiggled in the lock. The knob turned. Slowly the door squealed open. She froze. A stranger loomed on the threshold.

Nothing about him seemed familiar. He wore a black fisherman's cap, pulled low over his eyes. A cigarette butt, trailing smoke, dangled carelessly from his mouth. He brought with him the reek of fish and wine, a smell he wore as distinctly as the tattered jacket on his shoulders. But when he looked up, Sarah suddenly found herself laughing with relief. "Nick! It's you!"

He frowned. "Who else would it be?"

"It's your clothes—"

He regarded his jacket with distaste. "Isn't this gross? Smells like the original owner died in it." He stubbed out the cigarette and tossed her a brown-paper package.

"Your new identity, madame. I guarantee no one'll recognize you."

"Oh, brother. I'm afraid to look." She opened the package and removed a short black wig, a packet of hairpins and a singularly hideous wool dress. "I think it looked better on the sheep," she sighed.

"Look, no fair grousing about the dress. Just be glad I didn't put you in a miniskirt with fishnet stockings. Believe me, I thought about it."

She looked dubiously at the wig. "Black?"

"It was on sale."

"I've never worn one of these before. Which way does it go? Like this?"

His hoot of laughter made her flush. "No, you've got it backward. Here, let me do it."

She wrenched it off her head. "This isn't going to work."

"Sure it'll work. Hey, I'm sorry I laughed. You just have to get the thing on right." He grabbed the pins from the bed. "Come on, turn around. Let's get your hair out of the way first."

Obediently she turned and let him pin up her hair. He was terribly awkward; she could have done the task more efficiently by herself. But at the first touch of his hands, a warmth, a contentment, seemed to melt through her body; she never wanted the feeling to end. It was so soothing, so incredibly sensuous, having a man stroke her hair, especially a man with hands as warm and gentle as Nick's.

As the tension eased from Sarah's shoulders, Nick felt the tension in his own body mounting to unbearable heights. Even while he struggled with the hairpins, he found himself staring at the smooth skin on the back of her neck. His gaze slipped down, tracing the delicate bones of her spine to the collar of her blouse. The strand of hair felt like liquid fire in his hand. The heat surged like a current up his fingers, straight to his gut. The old fantasy rose to mind: Sarah standing before him in his bedroom, her breasts bared, her hair loose about her shoulders.

He forced himself to concentrate on what he was doing. What *was* he doing? Oh yes. The wig. With clumsy fingers he began slipping in hairpins.

"I never knew you smoked," she murmured drowsily.

"I don't anymore. Gave it up years ago. Tonight's just for show."

"Geoffrey used to smoke. I couldn't get him to quit. That's the only thing we ever fought about."

He swallowed thickly as a strand tumbled loose and fell softly on his arm.

"Ouch. That pin hurts, Nick."

"Sorry." He placed the wig on her head and turned her toward him. The expression on her face—a mingling of doubt and resignation—made him smile.

"I look stupid, don't I?" she sighed.

"No. You look different, which was the whole idea."

She nodded. "I look stupid."

"Come on, try the dress."

"What is this?" she asked, holding up the garment. "One size fits all?"

"I know it's big, but I couldn't pass it up. It was—"

"Don't tell me. On sale, right?" She laughed. "Well, if we're a pair, we ought to fit together." She glanced at his tattered clothes. "What are you supposed to be, anyway? A bum?"

"From the odor of this jacket, I'd say I'm a drunk fisherman. Let's call you my wife. Only a wife would put up with a slob like me."

"All right, I'm your wife. Your very hungry wife. Can we eat now?"

He went to the window and looked down at the street. "I think it's dark enough. Why don't you change?"

She began to undress. Nick gazed steadily out at the night and struggled feverishly to ignore the tempting sounds behind him: the rustle of the blouse as it slid from her shoulders, the whisper of the skirt as it fell past her hips.

And it suddenly occurred to him what a ridiculous situation he was in.

For four years Nick O'Hara had managed to stay sanely independent. For those same four years, he'd kept his emotional doors tightly closed against women. And then, quite unexpectedly, Sarah Fontaine, of all people, had slipped in a back entrance. Sarah, who was obviously still in love with Geoffrey. Sarah, who in the course of two and a half weeks had managed to get him fired from his job, shot at and nearly run off the road. It was a spectacular beginning.

He couldn't wait to see what came next.

Chapter Nine

IN A TAVERN THICK WITH LAUGHTER and smoke, they sat at a wobbly table and split a bottle of burgundy. The wine was rough and undisciplined; farmer's wine, thought Sarah, as she downed her third glass. The room had grown too warm and too bright. At the next table, old men swapped tales over bread and ale and their laughter rang in her ears. A cat strolled through the chairs and quietly lapped at a saucer of milk by the bar. Hungrily Sarah took in every sight, every sound. It was so good to be out of hiding. So good to be out in the world again, if only for a night! Even the flecks of red wax on the tablecloth struck her as strangely beautiful.

Through the haze of cigarette smoke, she saw Nick smiling at her. His shoulders drooped in the tired slouch of a man who has labored long and hard all his life. Day-old stubble darkened his jaw. She could hardly believe he was the same man she'd met in a sleek government office only two weeks ago. But then, she was not the same woman. Fear and circumstances had changed them both.

"You did justice to your meal," he said, nodding at the empty plate. "Feeling better?"

"Much better. I was starved."

"Coffee?"

"In a bit. Let me finish my wine."

Shaking his head, he reached across the table and pushed her glass aside. "Maybe you'd better stop. We can't afford to get careless."

She regarded the displaced wineglass with irritation. As usual, Nick O'Hara was trying to run her life. It was time to fight back. Deliberately she slid the glass in front of her. "I've never been drunk in my life," she said.

"It's a very bad time to start."

Gazing at him steadily, she took a sip. "Is that a hobby of yours? Ordering people around?"

"What do you mean?"

"Since the day we met, you've been in total control, haven't you?"

"Over you? Or the situation?"

"Both."

"Hardly. Skipping off to London was your bright idea. Remember?"

"You never did say why you followed me. You were angry, weren't you?"

"I was mad as hell."

"Is that why you came? To wring my neck?"

"To be perfectly honest, I considered it." He raised the glass of wine to his lips and stared at her over the rim. "But I changed my mind."

"Why?"

"It was the way you looked at the police station. So exposed. Defenseless."

"I may be stronger than you think."

"Is that so?"

"I'm not a kid, Nick. I'm thirty-two years old. I've always taken care of myself."

"I'm not calling you incompetent. You're a very bright woman. A well-respected researcher."

"How do you know?"

"I've seen your security file."

"Oh, yes. That mysterious file. So what did you learn?"

He sat back. "Let's see. Sarah Gillian Fontaine, graduated University of Chicago. Co-researcher on half a dozen papers in the field of microbiology. Successful grant applicant for the last two years—not bad in this era of tight federal budgets. Oh, you're obviously bright." He paused. Quietly he added, "I also think you need my help."

They fell silent as the waiter came by to collect the bill. When the man was once more out of earshot, Nick said with dead seriousness, "I know you can take care of yourself, Sarah. Under ordinary circumstances. But these aren't ordinary circumstances."

She couldn't argue that point. "Okay," she sighed. "I'll admit it, Nick. I'm scared. And I'm tired. Tired of having to be careful all the time. Tired of checking the street before I walk. Wondering who's a friend and who isn't." She returned his steady gaze. "But don't underestimate me, Nick. I'll do anything to stay alive."

"Good. Because before this is over, you may have to turn into a dozen different women. Remember, you're not Sarah Fontaine anymore. You can't be, not in public. So leave her behind."

"How?"

"Make someone up. Down to the very last detail. *Become* that person. Now describe yourself. Who are you?"

She thought it over for a moment. "I'm—I'm a fisherman's wife…struggling to make ends meet…."

"Keep going."

"My life isn't easy. I'm tired a lot. And I have children—six of them—screaming all the time."

"Good. Go on."

"My husband, he…" She suddenly focused on Nick. "I mean you…you're not home very much."

"Often enough to give you six children," he pointed out with a smile.

"It's a crowded flat. All of us screaming at each other."

"Are we happy?"

"I don't know. Are we?"

He cocked his head thoughtfully. "Since I'm one half of this fabricated couple, I'll put in my two cents' worth. Yes, we're happy. I love my children, all five girls and a boy. I also love my wife. But I'm drunk a lot and I'm not very gentle."

"Do you beat me?"

"When you deserve it." Then he added softly, "But afterward I'm very, very sorry."

All at once they were staring at each other, the way two strangers do when they realize, for the first time, that they know each other well. His eyes softened. She suddenly found herself wondering how it would feel to lie beneath him in their hard bed. To feel the crushing weight of his body on hers. Though Geoffrey had been a gentle lover, there had been something cool and passionless about him. She sensed that Nick would be very different. He would take her like a starved man.

With an unsteady hand, she reached for her wineglass. "How long have we been married?" she asked.

"Fourteen years. I was twenty-four. You were…only eighteen."

"Then I'm sure my mama didn't approve."

"Neither did mine. But it didn't matter." He brushed his hand across hers. The touch of his fingers left her tingling. "We were crazy about each other."

Something about the tone of his voice made her stop speaking. This game of make-believe, so lighthearted a moment ago, had somehow changed. She heard the blood roaring in her ears, and everything melted away—the roomful of strangers, the laughter, the smoke. There was only Nick's face and his eyes, bright as silver, staring at her.

"Yes," he said again, so softly she barely heard him. "We were crazy about each other."

The sound of her glass hitting the table jerked her back to reality. She watched, bewildered, as a river of burgundy trickled across the tablecloth. The noise of the tavern suddenly swelled and burst over her.

Nick was already out of his chair, a napkin in hand. She sat mutely as he blotted up the wine. *I'm drunk,* she thought. *I must be drunk to be acting like this….*

"Sarah? What's wrong?"

Her chair flew backward as she bolted from the table and out of the tavern. The night air was like a cold slap in the face. Halfway down the alley she heard Nick's footsteps; he was running after her. She didn't stop until he grabbed her from behind and whirled her around. They were standing in the middle of a square. The buildings shone like gold in the lamplight. Around the shuttered flower carts, bruised petals lay scattered and fragrant on the cobblestones.

"Sarah. Listen to me."

"It's make-believe, Nick!" she said, trying desperately to pull free. "That's all it is! Just a silly game we're playing!"

"No. It's not a game anymore. Not for me."

He pulled her against him, pulled her so abruptly that she didn't have time to fight or even to feel surprised. She was only aware of the dizzy sensation of falling through darkness and of the jolt as she landed against his chest. She had no time to recover, no time to even draw the next breath.

Nick tasted of wine, of that rough farmer's burgundy, and she reeled like a drunken woman. She tried to make sense of what she felt, but there was no logic in this moment. Her lips parted. Her hands found their way to the back of his neck, and she felt the dampness of his hair.

"Sarah. Oh, Sarah," he groaned, pulling away to look at her. "It's not a game. It's real. More real than anything I've ever known."

"I'm afraid, Nick. Afraid of making another mistake. The way I did with Geoffrey—"

"I'm not Geoffrey. Hell, I'm just an ordinary guy, pushing middle age, not very rich. Probably not even very bright. I haven't got a hidden agenda. I just—Sarah, I'm *lonely*. I have been, for so long. I want you. Enough to get myself into one hell of a lot of hot water…."

With a sigh he drew her against him. She buried her face in the reeking wool jacket, but she no longer cared how it smelled; she only cared that Nick was wearing it, that it was his shoulder she was resting against, his arms that were holding her so tightly.

The drizzle turned to rain, and the drops splattered on the cobblestones. Laughing, Nick and Sarah dashed across the windows, past lovers huddled beneath an umbrella, past a bakery that smelled of coffee and bread.

By the time they'd climbed the stairway to their room, they were soaked. She stood beside the bed, rainwater dripping from her clothes, as Nick bolted the door. He turned and watched silently as she pulled the wig off and shook her hair free. Damp copper waves fell to her shoulders. The light above cast strange shadows on his face. Water trickled from his wet hair and down his cheek.

He came toward her, his eyes burning. At the touch of his hands on her face, she shivered. Gently he covered her mouth with his. She tasted the wine again and then the rain, trickling down his cheek to her lips. His hands slid down her neck, to the top button of her dress. One by one the buttons came undone, and then the dress sagged open. As their mouths drank each other in, his fingers slid beneath the fabric of her dress. He took her breast in his hand.

They were both shivering now, but beneath their rain-soaked clothes, fires were raging out of control.

He shrugged off his jacket, letting it fall heavily to the floor. His wet shirt was like ice against her naked breasts. The light bulb above seemed to sway and recede. They sank to the mattress and the bedsprings creaked as his weight came down beside her. With eager hands he peeled off his shirt and threw it onto the floor. She remembered what she'd thought earlier that night, that Nick would not take her gently; he'd take her like a starved man.

But did she want him to? She was just as starved as he was; surely he sensed it! He also sensed her confusion. Frowning, he drew back and gazed at her. "You're shaking, Sarah," he whispered. "Why?"

"I'm afraid, Nick."

"Of what? Me?"

"I don't know. Of myself, I think.... I'm afraid of feeling guilty."

"About making love?"

She closed her eyes tightly. "Oh, God, what am I doing? He's alive, Nick! My husband's alive...."

Slowly his hand slid away from her breast and moved to her face, willing her to look at him. He was studying her, trying to see through her eyes, into her mind. His gaze stripped away all her defenses; never had she felt so naked. "What husband, Sarah? Simon Dance? Geoffrey? Some ghost who never existed?"

"Not a ghost. A man."

"And you'd call what you had a marriage?"

She shook her head. "No. I'm not stupid."

"Then let him go, Sarah!" He pressed his lips to her forehead and his breath warmed her hair. "Let the memories go. They weren't real. Get on with your life."

"But there's a part of me that still wonders...." She sighed. "I've learned something about myself, Nick, something I don't like. I loved an illusion. That's what he was, nothing but a dream. But I wanted him to be real. I made him real because I needed him." She shook her head sadly. "Need. That's what destroys us, you know. It makes us blind to everything else. And now I need you."

"Is that so bad?"

"I'm not sure of my motives anymore. Am I falling in love with you? Or am I just talking myself into it because I need you so much?"

Slowly, reluctantly, Nick began to button up her dress. "You won't know the answer to that one," he said, "until you're safe. Not till you're free to walk away from me. That's when you'll know."

She touched his lips. "It's not that I don't want you, Nick. It's just that…" Her voice faded.

He could see the inner struggle in her eyes, those utterly trusting, open windows that concealed no secrets. He wanted her. So badly, in fact, that just looking at her now was enough to awaken that familiar ache. He wanted her, but the time and circumstances were all wrong. She was still in a state of shock. And even if there'd never been a husband, Nick didn't think Sarah was a woman who gave herself easily to any man.

"You're disappointed," she said softly.

He forced a smile to his lips. "I'll admit it."

"It's just that—"

"Don't, Sarah." He hushed her. "There's no need to explain. Just lie here with me. Let me hold you."

She buried her face against the naked warmth of his shoulder. "Nick, my guardian angel."

His laughter was quick and gentle. "And here I was all set to tarnish the old halo!"

In silence they lay together, and the flames that had raged so brightly between them were slowly beaten back to a warm glow. If only they could find a cottage on a moor where they'd never be found! But those were wild, unreasonable dreams. Even if they came true, she wouldn't be content. Not while the past remained unresolved. Not while she still wondered about Geoffrey.

"What are we going to do, Nick?" she whispered.

"I'm working on it."

"We can't keep running."

"No. We could stretch the money out a few months,

maybe. But even if it lasted forever, this cloud would always be hanging over our heads. You'd always wonder. You'd never really be free...." He looked at her with new intensity. "You have to close that part of your life," he said. "To do that, you have to find him."

He might as well have said they had to fly to the moon. It was just as impossible. How could they search all of Europe for one man? Even worse, how could they find him and not be caught themselves? They were innocents, forced into a game they didn't understand, a game with unseen players and unknown stakes, except one—their lives.

"We haven't got much to go on," said Nick. "I had to take a gamble today. I called Roy Potter."

She jerked out of his arms and stared at him. "You *called* him?"

"From a pay phone across town. Look, he already knows we're in Brussels. He's probably got an eye on our bank accounts. I guarantee that withdrawal we made this afternoon is now blinking on a CIA computer somewhere."

"Why did you call? I thought you didn't trust him!"

"I don't. But what if I'm wrong? What if he's really okay? Then at least I've got him thinking. Now he'll take a closer look at his people, if he hasn't already."

"He'll be searching for us...."

"Brussels is a big city. And we can always move on." His gaze turned insistent. "Sarah, I could have all the contacts in the world, but the rest is up to you. You were married to Geoffrey. Think, Sarah. Where would he go?"

"I've thought about it so long. I just don't know."

"Could he have left you a message? Somewhere you haven't looked?"

"I've only got my purse."

"Then let's start with that."

She grabbed the purse from the nightstand and emptied the contents onto the bed. There was only the usual clutter of a woman's handbag, plus the unopened bills they'd taken from Eve's mailbox.

Nick picked up the wallet and gave her a questioning glance.

"Go ahead," she said. "I don't have any secrets. Not from you."

One by one he slipped out the credit cards, then the photographs. For a few seconds, he paused at Geoffrey's picture before laying it on the bed. Over the years, snapshots of nieces and nephews had found their way into her wallet, and now they all spilled out.

"You've practically got a whole photo album in here," he observed.

"I don't have the heart to throw them away. Don't you carry any pictures?"

"Only my driver's license."

As he went through the scraps of paper she'd tucked away in various pockets—the phone numbers, the business cards, the little reminders—she found herself wondering why he carried no photographs. Had his divorce been that unfriendly? And why had there been no other women in his life since then? It reminded her how much she had to learn about him.

She put on her glasses and began to open Eve's mail.

There were three bills. After scanning the electricity statement, she flipped to the credit-card bill. Eve had used it only twice last month. Both items were purchases made at Harrod's, and both were listed as women's apparel.

She slit open the third bill. It was for the telephone. Quickly she glanced over the list of charges and was about to set it aside with the other two bills when one word leaped out at her from the bottom of the page: *Berlin*. It was a long-distance call, made on an evening two weeks earlier.

She clutched Nick's arm. "Look at this! The last entry."

His eyes widened, and he snatched the bill from her fingers. "This call was made the day of the fire!"

"She told me she tried to call him, remember? She must have known where he'd be in Berlin—"

"But to be so careless—to leave a trail like this—"

"Maybe it wasn't to him directly. Maybe this is a go-between. A contact. She didn't know what had happened to him or where he was. Nick, she must have been at wit's end...so she called Berlin. I wonder what this number is."

"We can't try it. Not yet."

"Why not?"

"A long-distance call at this point might scare off any contact. Let's wait till we hit Berlin." He began to throw things back into her purse. "Tomorrow we'll catch the commuter line out of the city. From Düsseldorf we can get the express. I'll buy all the tickets. I think it's better if we board separately and meet inside the train."

"What happens when we get to Berlin?"

"We'll call the number and see who answers. I've got an old friend in the Berlin consulate, Wes Corrigan. He might be able to do our legwork."

"Can we trust him?"

"I think so. We were posted together in Honduras. He was okay...."

"You said we couldn't trust anyone."

He nodded soberly. "We've got no choice, Sarah. It's a risk we have to take. I'm gambling on friendship...." He suddenly saw the worry in her eyes. Without a word he took her in his arms and pulled her down with him onto the pillows. It was a feeble attempt to banish the fear they both felt.

"What an awful feeling, to be caught without a future," she whispered. "If I look too far ahead, all I see is Eve."

"You're not Eve."

"That's what scares me. Eve knew what she was doing. She knew how to survive. Now she's dead. What chance do I have?"

"If it's any small comfort, you have me."

She touched his face and smiled. "Yes. I have you. Why am I so lucky?"

"Windmills, I guess."

"I don't understand."

"Lieberman said they used to call me Don Quixote, for all my tilting at windmills. Funny. I never knew I cut such a ridiculous figure."

"Am I another one of your windmills?"

"No. Not you." His lips brushed her hair. "You're more than that, now."

"You don't have to stay with me, Nick. I'm the one they want. You could go home—"

"Shh, Sarah."

"If you left me, I'd understand. Really I would."

"And what would you do on your own? You can't speak a word of German. Your French is—well, it's...quaint. No, you need me."

There it was again. *Need.* Yes, he was right. She needed him.

"Besides," he said, "I can't leave you now."

"Why not?"

He laughed softly. "Because I'm now an unemployed bum. And when this is all over, I plan to live off your income."

She rose up on her elbow and gazed at him. He was squinting up drowsily, and the bare lightbulb cast strange shadows over his face. "Nick. My sweet Don Quixote." Gently she lowered her mouth to his and placed a kiss on his lips. "Here's to Berlin," she whispered.

"Yes," he murmured, pulling her against him. "To Berlin."

DAWN, BRIGHT AND BEAUTIFUL. The train tracks, which a moment before had been a wet, dismal gray, suddenly gleamed like gold in the morning light. Wisps of steam curled from the rails. On the platform where Sarah now stood, commuters were already shedding raincoats and scarves. It would be warm today, and as bright as an April day should be. Schoolgirls dressed in uniforms lingered in the sunshine with their eyes closed and their faces turned like flowers to the sky. It had been a long, wet winter for Belgium, and the country was yearning for spring.

Nick and Sarah stood a dozen yards apart on the platform, exchanging only the briefest of glances. Nick was unrecognizable. With his cap pulled low and a cigarette hanging precariously from his mouth, he slouched against a platform post and scowled at the world.

From the distance came the clackity-clack of an approaching train. It was a signal that drew people from their benches. Like a wave, they flowed to the platform's edge as the train to Antwerp rolled gently to a stop. A stream of departing passengers emerged: businessmen in wool suits, students in regimental blue jeans and backpacks, smartly dressed women who would soon return home with their shopping bags full.

From her position near the end of the queue, Sarah saw Nick crush his cigarette under his heel and board the train. Seconds later, his face appeared at a window. They did not look at each other.

The line grew shorter. Only a few yards more, and she would be safely on board. Then, from her peripheral vision, came a strange flash of light. A sudden premonition of fear made her turn slowly toward its source. It was sunshine, reflected off a pair of silvered glasses.

She froze. By the ticket window stood a man with pale hair, a man whose gaze was fixed on the train door. Though he was partly hidden behind the platform post, Sarah saw enough of his face to recognize him. Her blood ran cold. It was the same man who'd stared at her through the window of the blue Peugeot. The man with the death's-head grin.

And she was headed straight for his line of vision.

Chapter Ten

HER FIRST IMPULSE WAS TO TURN and run, to lose herself in the vast crowd of commuters. But any sudden movement now would surely draw his attention. She couldn't turn back. The man would see her break away and he would wonder. She had to keep moving forward, hoping against hope that he wouldn't recognize her.

Frantically she searched the train for the window where she'd seen Nick's face. If only she could signal for help! But the window was too far behind; she couldn't see him.

At the head of the line, an elderly passenger had dropped his ticket on the ground. Slowly he bent down to retrieve it. *Dear God, please hurry!* she prayed. The longer she stood here, the longer she could be studied. Swallowing her panic, she struggled to assume the role she'd chosen, that of a sickly Belgian wife. Keeping her eyes lowered, she clutched her purse tightly in her arms. Beneath her breast her heart was thudding. The black wig felt like a blessed shield against the man's eyes. Perhaps the wig would be enough. The man was looking for a woman with reddish-brown hair. Perhaps he wouldn't notice her.

"Madame?"

She flinched at the hand on her arm. An old man was tugging at her sleeve. Stupidly she stared at him as he spoke to her in loud, rapid French. She tried to jerk her arm away, but he trailed after her, waving a woman's scarf. Again he repeated his question and pointed to the ground. With sudden comprehension she shook her head and gestured that no, she had not dropped the scarf. The old man shrugged and walked away.

Almost in tears, she turned to climb aboard. But someone stood in her way.

She raised her head and saw her own terrified face reflected in a pair of mirrored sunglasses.

The blond man smiled. "Madame?" he said softly. "Come..."

"No. No!" she whispered, backing away.

He moved toward her and something in his hand glinted, an object whose image burned its way like a hot iron into her brain. She thought of the arc the four-inch blade would follow; she anticipated the pain of its thrust. She felt herself falling dizzily backward and then realized it wasn't her own movement, but the train's. It was leaving her behind.

She caught a glimpse of the train door receding slowly down the final fifty yards of the platform. Her last chance to escape.

Sarah sensed the man moving closer. His momentum carried him forward, toward a prey he thought would turn and run.

And she did run. But in the opposite direction. Instead of turning to flee, she dashed past him, after the departing train.

The unexpected move bought her a precious split second. He was caught totally off balance.

The train was picking up speed. Only a dozen yards of platform were left before it would move beyond her reach. Her feet seemed weighted with lead; she heard his footsteps behind her, and they were gaining. With her heart close to exploding, she sprinted the last few yards. The grab bar hovered only inches away. Then her fingers touched cold steel. She fought to hold on, to pull herself aboard.

She scrambled onto the steps and collapsed, gasping for air. Buildings and gardens flashed by, fast-moving images of light and color. The ache in her throat dissolved into an incomprehensible sob of relief. *I made it,* she thought. *I made it....*

A shadow swung across the sunlight. The step creaked with a terrible new weight, and a chill settled like frost on her shoulders, a foreshadowing of her own death. She had no strength left to fight and nowhere left to retreat. She could do nothing but huddle there as the man towered above her.

The pace of the train quickened. It pounded in her head and drowned out everything else, even the thudding of her heart. *You can't be real,* she thought. *You're not a man, you're a nightmare!*

Paralyzed, she watched as he bent toward her, blotting out the last bits of sunshine. She waited to be swallowed up in his shadow.

Then, from somewhere behind her, came a low sound of rage. She sensed the movement more than saw it, a savage thrust of a foot as it connected with flesh. The shadow looming before her toppled backward with a groan.

The blond man seemed to hang forever, suspended in an endless fall. Sunlight flickered on the sallow face; the glasses slid away. Almost as if by magic, he dropped from the steps, and his parting curse was lost in the train's clatter. She caught one last glimpse of him, scrambling to his knees in the gravel below, and then he disappeared from view. Somehow she was still living, breathing; the nightmare had been shaken free.

"Sarah! My God...."

Rough hands wrenched her upward, away from the edge, away from death. With a shudder she fell into Nick's arms. There he held her so tightly she could feel the drumbeat of his heart.

"It's all right," he murmured over and over. "It's all right."

"Who is he?" she cried. "Why won't he leave us alone!"

"Sarah, listen to me. *Listen!* We've got to get off this train. We've got to change course before he intercepts us—"

And then what? she wanted to scream. Where did they go next?

He glanced at the scenery hurtling past. They were moving too fast to jump off. "The next stop," he said. "We'll have to travel some other way. Walk. Hitchhike. Once we cross the Dutch border, we can catch another train east."

She clung to him, not really hearing his words. The danger had taken on wild, irrational proportions. The man in the sunglasses had turned into something more than human. He was supernatural, beyond any horror that existed in the real world. She closed her eyes, and in her mind she saw him waiting for her at the next train station, and the next. Even Nick could not hold him off forever.

She stared ahead at the train tracks and prayed that the next stop would come soon. They had to get off before they were trapped. Blending into the countryside was their only chance.

But as far as she could see, the tracks stretched on without end. And it seemed to her that the train had turned into a steel coffin, bearing them straight into the arms of a killer.

KRONEN EXAMINED HIS bruised face in the mirror, and a wave of unspeakable anger rose inside him like hot magma. For the second time, the woman had escaped. He had had her in his grasp, there on the platform, but she had startled him by dashing off in an unexpected direction. Then, to be kicked like an animal off the train just as he'd caught up with her—that was the part that enraged him most.

Kronen slammed his fist into the mirror. Twice, this man, Nick O'Hara, had gotten in his way. Who was he, anyway? CIA? A friend of Simon Dance? Whoever he was, he'd be a dead man when Kronen found him and Sarah again.

Finding them, however, was going to be a difficult matter. They had disappeared. By the time Kronen's associates had intercepted the train at Antwerp, the woman and her companion had vanished. They could be anywhere. He had no idea where they were headed or why.

He'd have to call the old man again for help. The prospect made Kronen at first apprehensive and then angry—at the woman, for escaping, at her companion, for interfering. She'd pay dearly for all the trouble she'd caused him.

Kronen put on his sunglasses. The bruise was plainly visible over his right cheekbone. It was a humiliating reminder that he'd been bested by such an unassuming creature as Sarah Fontaine.

But this was only a temporary setback. The old man would be looking for her, and his eyes were everywhere, even in the most unexpected places. Yes, they would find her again.

She couldn't hide forever.

IT WAS THE pigeons flapping overhead that awakened Sarah. She opened her eyes. By the gentle light of dusk, she saw smooth stone walls, the fluttering of wings and the mill's wooden shaft revolving slowly. A pigeon settled on a window ledge high above and began to coo. The gears of the windmill creaked and groaned, like the timbers of an old ship. As she lay there in the straw, she was filled with a strange sense of wonder, and a fear that she had few such moments left to live. Oh, but she was so hungry for life! She'd never *known* such hunger. Only now, as the pigeons flapped and the sunlight faded, did she realize how precious each moment had become. And she owed them all to Nick.

She turned and smiled at him. He was sleeping beside her in the straw, his hands clasped behind his neck, his chest rising and falling. Poor, exhausted Nick. They had hitched a ride across the Dutch border; then they had walked, miles and miles it seemed. Now they were less than a mile from the next train station. But Sarah had balked at the thought of boarding another train. We'll wait until dark, he'd said. They'd found a place to rest, a windmill in the fields, and in their stone tower they'd both dropped immediately to sleep.

Berlin, she thought. *Will we ever make it?*

She curled up against Nick and listened to his steady breathing. With a shudder he awakened, and his arm came around and encircled her.

"It'll be dark soon," she whispered.

"Mmm-hmm."

"I wish we never had to leave this place."

He sighed deeply. "So do I."

For a moment they lay together, listening to the creak of the gears, to the sails flapping in the wind. Suddenly he laughed.

"How ironic," he said. "Brave Don Quixote, hiding out in a windmill. I can hear 'em now, laughing in London."

"Laughing? Why?"

"Because dumb O'Hara's back in trouble."

She smiled. "In trouble, maybe. But not dumb. Never dumb."

"Thanks for the vote."

She studied him curiously. "You sound so bitter, Nick. Is the foreign service that bad?"

"No. It's a great job. If you can smother your conscience. When you join up, they make you sign this paper. It says, essentially, 'When in public, I swear to always toe the party line.' I signed it."

"Big mistake, huh?"

"When I think of all the asinine policies I had to uphold. And then there were the cocktail parties. Night after night of standing around, trying not to get drunk on the sherry. The games we used to play with the Russians! Baiting Ivan, we called it. We were like little kids, trying to learn each other's secrets."

"Ah. Diplomacy is hell."

He smiled. "But not as bad as war."

"I used to think you were just another bureaucrat."

"Yep, that's me, shuffling papers all day."

"Oh, Nick, you're the most unbureaucratic man I know! And believe me, I've known quite a few!"

"Men?"

"No, silly. Bureaucrats. Those guys in Washington who dole out my grant money. You're not like them. You're... *involved.*"

"Damn right I'm involved," he said with a laugh.

"Not just with me. With the world. Most people can't be bothered with anything outside their immediate existence. But you go out and fight for strangers."

"No, I don't. I used to. When I was in college, all those issues mattered to me. Believe it or not, Tim Greenstein and I once spent a very cold night in jail. We got arrested for illegal assembly on the chancellor's doorstep. But you know, these days, people don't seem to care about the world anymore. Maybe we all got older." He touched her face. "Or maybe we all found more important things to care about."

The pigeons suddenly flapped their wings, and straw fluttered down like bits of gold raining in from the window. They both sat up, and he began picking the pieces of straw from her hair.

"And what were you like in college?" he asked. "Very well-behaved, I'd imagine."

"Diligent."

"Of course."

"Up until now I was very good at ignoring distractions."

"Such as men?"

She tapped his nose lightly and grinned. "Such as men."

For a long time they looked at each other. Her ears were filled with the sound of her own heartbeat and the creak of the mill as it turned in the wind.

"Now I wonder what I missed," she whispered.

"You did what was important to you. That's what matters. You liked your work, didn't you?"

She nodded. Rising, she went to the doorway and looked at the newly plowed fields. "Yes. There's something nice about having the big picture right there, in my microscope. Being able to move it closer or farther away with just the flick of a lens. It's all so safe, so under my control. But you know, it never struck me till now. There are no windows in my laboratory. No windows to look out of…" She shook her head and sighed. "Now it seems like nothing's under my control anymore. But I've never felt more alive. Or more afraid of dying."

"Don't talk about it, Sarah. Don't even think about it." He came up behind her and turned her around so that she was facing him. "We'll just take one day, one moment, at a time. That's all we can do."

"I know."

"You're strong, Sarah. In some ways you're stronger than I am. Only now do I realize that…."

He kissed her then, kissed her hard and long, like a man hungry for the taste of her. In the stone tower above, the birds cooed, and the last light of day faded. Blessed night, the safety of darkness, fell over the fields.

With a groan Nick drew back, breathing heavily. "If we keep this up, we'll sure as hell miss the train. Not that I'd mind, but…" He pressed his lips once more against hers. "Now's the time to move. Are you ready?"

She took a deep breath and nodded. "I'm ready."

THE OLD MAN had a dream.

Nienke was standing before him with her long hair tied in a delft-blue kerchief. Her wide, plain face was streaked with garden dirt, and she was smiling. "Frans," she said, "you must build a stone path through the rosebushes so our friends can walk among the flowers. Now they have to walk around the bushes, never through the center, where all the pretty lavenders and yellows are. They miss them completely. I have to lead them through, and then their shoes get muddy. A stone path, Frans, like the one we had in our cottage in Dordrecht."

"Of course," he said. "I'll ask the gardener to build it."

Nienke smiled. She came toward him. But when he reached out to touch her, her blue kerchief suddenly vanished. What had once been Nienke's hair was now a bright halo of fire. He tried to tear it off before it engulfed her face, but great clumps of hair came off in his hands. The more he tried to tear the flames away, the more hair and flesh he pulled off. Bit by bit, trying to save her, he tore his wife apart. He looked down and saw that his arms were on fire, but he felt no pain, nothing at all, except a silent scream exploding in his throat, as he watched Nienke leave him forever.

IT TOOK WES CORRIGAN a good five minutes to answer the pounding on his back door. When he finally opened it, he could only stand there in his pajamas and bathrobe, blinking in surprise at his nocturnal visitors. Two people stood outside. At first glance he thought them strangers. The man was tall, white-haired, unshaven. The woman was dressed in a nondescript sweater and a gray cap. Their breath steamed in the cool night air.

"What's happened to the old sense of hospitality?" asked Nick.

Wes gaped. "What the—Nick? Is that *you?*"

"Can we come in?"

"Uh, yeah! Sure!" Still dazed, Corrigan gestured them into his kitchen and closed the door. He was a short, compact man in his midthirties. Beneath the harsh kitchen light, his skin was sallow and his eyes were puffy with sleep. He looked at his two visitors and shook his head in bewilderment. Then his gaze settled on Nick's white hair. "My God. Has it been that long?"

Nick shook his head and laughed. "Talcum powder. But any wrinkles you see are mine. Is anyone else in the house?"

"Just my cat. Nick, what the hell is going on?"

Nick strode past him, out of the kitchen and into the living room.

"Was I supposed to know about all this?" called Wes. There was no answer from Nick. He turned to Sarah just as she pulled off her cap. "Uh, hello. I'm Wes Corrigan. And who're you?"

"Sarah."

"Yeah, nice to meet you. Is this Nick's idea of a cheap date?"

"The street looks clean," said Nick, stalking into the kitchen.

"Sure, it's clean. They sweep it every Thursday."

"What I meant was, you're not under surveillance."

Corrigan looked sheepish. "Well, actually I live kind of a dull life. Hey, come *on*, buddy. What gives?"

Nick sighed. "We're in a little trouble, Wes."

Corrigan nodded. "I was starting to come to that conclusion. Who's after you?"

"The Company. Plus or minus a few others."

Wes stared at him incredulously. Quickly he went to the kitchen door, glanced outside and slid the bolt shut. He turned back to Nick. "You've got the *CIA* after you? What'd you do? Sell a few national secrets?"

"It's a long story. We're going to need your help."

Wes nodded tiredly. "I was afraid of that. Look, sit down, sit down. God, the kitchen's a mess. I don't usually entertain at two in the morning. I'll make us up a fresh pot of coffee. You hungry?"

Nick and Sarah looked at each other and smiled. "Famished," said Sarah.

Corrigan went to the refrigerator, "Bacon and eggs, coming up."

It took them an hour to tell him everything. By that time the coffeepot was empty, Nick and Sarah had polished off half a dozen eggs between them, and Corrigan was wide-awake and worried.

"Why do you think this guy Potter's involved?" asked Wes.

"He's obviously the case officer. It was his word that got Sarah released. He must've ordered those agents to tail us to Margate. But in Margate things all went wrong. While the Company isn't exactly a tight outfit, they don't usually screw up this royally without a little help. Someone had that agent killed. Someone who then proceeded to fire on us."

"The man with the sunglasses. Whoever he is." Wes shook his head. "I don't like what you're up against."

"Neither do I."

Corrigan looked thoughtful. "So you want me to check out the file on Magus. Could be tough, Nick. If they've got it super-classified, I'm not going to be able to touch it."

"Get us what you can. We can't do it alone. Until Sarah finds Geoffrey and gets some answers, we're out in the cold."

"Yeah. That's a mighty uncomfortable place to be."

He walked them to the back door. Outside, the stars were burning in a crisp clear sky.

"Where are you two sleeping?" asked Wes.

"We have a room near the Ku-damm."

"You could sack out on my floor."

"Too risky. We were lucky to get through the East German checkpoint. By now they know we're in the city. If they're smart they'll be watching your house soon."

"So how do I get hold of you?"

"I'll phone you. The name'll be Barnes. Get back to me from an outside line. It's better if you don't know where we are."

"Don't you trust me?"

Nick hesitated on the doorstep. "You know it's not that, Wes," he said, nudging Sarah into the darkness.

"Then what is it?"

"This is nasty business. It's better if you don't get too deeply involved."

Nick and Sarah turned and headed into the night. But as they left, they heard Wes say behind them, softly, "Buddy, you just got me involved."

As DAWN BRIGHTENED outside their window, Sarah lay snuggled in Nick's arms. Despite their exhaustion, neither of them could sleep; too much depended on what happened today. At least they were no longer alone. Wes Corrigan was on their side.

Nick stirred, his breath suddenly warming her hair. "When this is over," he whispered, "I want us to be just like we are now. Just like this."

"When this is over…" She sighed and stared up at the bare white ceiling. "I wonder if it'll ever be over. If I'll ever go home again."

"We'll go home. Together."

She looked at him with longing. "Will we?"

"I promise. And Nick O'Hara always keeps his promises."

She turned her face into the hollow of his shoulder. "Oh, Nick. I want you so much. I don't know anymore if I'm blind or scared or in love. I'm so mixed up."

"No, you aren't."

"Aren't you confused? Just a little?"

"About you? No. It sounds crazy, Sarah, but I really think I know you. You're the first woman I can say that about."

"What about your wife? Didn't you know her?"

"Lauren?" His voice, so warm and gentle a moment before, all at once sounded hollow. "Yeah. I guess I did know her. When it was over."

"What went wrong, Nick?"

He lay back against the pillows. "You know the old saying? That there are two sides to every story? Our marriage was a perfect example. If you asked Lauren what went wrong, she'd say it was my fault. She'd say I didn't understand her needs."

"And if I asked you?"

He shrugged. "As time passes you get a sense of perspective. I guess I'd have to say it was no one's fault, really. But I can't forget what she did." He turned to Sarah with such a look of sadness that she could almost reach out and touch his pain. "We were married—oh, three years. She liked Cairo. She liked the embassy whirl. She was an outstanding foreign service wife. I think that's one reason she married me. She thought I could show her the world. Unfortunately my career required going to places she didn't quite consider civilized."

"Like Cameroon?"

"That's right. I wanted that post. It would only have been for a year or two. But she refused flat out to go. Then I got offered London, which made her happy. It might have all worked out eventually. Except…" His voice trailed off. Sarah felt his arm stiffen beneath her shoulder.

"You don't have to tell me, Nick. Not if you don't want to."

"People always say time heals all wounds. But sometimes it doesn't. You see, she got pregnant. I found out in London. She didn't tell me—the embassy doctor had to come up and slap me on the back with the news. Told me I was going to be a father. I was—hell, Sarah, for about six short hours I was so high they had to peel me off the ceiling. Then I got home. I found out she didn't want it."

There was nothing Sarah could say to ease his pain. She could only hope that when he'd finished talking, he'd find some comfort in her arms.

"Sometimes I wonder," he said. "I wonder what it would have looked like. Whether it would have been a boy or a girl. What color its hair would've been. I catch myself counting the years, thinking of all the birthdays it never had. I don't have much family. I wanted that baby. I practically begged her for it. But Lauren called it an inconvenience." He looked at Sarah with bewilderment in his eyes. "An *inconvenience*. What was I supposed to say to that?"

"There's no answer you can give."

"No. There isn't. That's when I realized I didn't know her. We had all kinds of fights then. She flew home and…took care of the problem. She never came back. I got the divorce papers a month later. Special delivery. It's been four years now."

"Do you ever miss her?"

"No. I was almost relieved when the papers came. I've been on my own ever since. It's easier that way. No pain. Nothing." He touched her face and a smile formed on his lips. "Then you walked into my office. You with your funny glasses. The first day I saw you, I wasn't paying attention to your looks. But you took off those glasses and then all I saw were your eyes. That's when I wanted you."

"I'm going to throw those old glasses away."

"Never. I love them."

She laughed, grateful for the kind and funny things lovers say. For the first time in her life, she almost felt beautiful.

A breeze blew in the open window, carrying with it the faint smell of exhaust from the street below. Berlin was waking up. Sounds of traffic drifted in: the honk of a horn, a bus roaring by. The night was over. It was time to make that phone call.

"Sarah? Have you thought about what happens when we find him?"

"I can't think that far ahead."

"You still love him."

She shook her head. "I don't know who I loved anymore. Not Simon Dance. Maybe the man I loved never existed. He was never real."

"But I am," whispered Nick. "I'm real. And unlike Geoffrey Fontaine, I've got nothing to hide."

Chapter Eleven

IS THIS WHERE I'LL FIND HIM?

The thought played over and over in Sarah's mind as they rode the bus north, past broad, clean streets, past avenues where shopkeepers were out in the early morning sunshine, sweeping the sidewalks.

A half hour earlier, they had called the number on Eve's phone bill and learned it was a flower shop. The woman on the other end had been courteous and helpful. Yes, the shop was easy to find. It was several miles north of the Ku-damm. The bus stop was only a block away.

It was not a good part of town. Sarah watched as the broad streets gave way to alleys littered with glass and a neighborhood of squat, shabby houses. Here, children played in the streets, and old men sat dully on their porch steps. Was Geoffrey hiding in the back room of one of these houses? Was he waiting for her in the basement of a flower shop?

At a street corner, they stepped off the bus. A block away they found the address. The shop was small, with dirty windows. On the sidewalk just outside sat plastic buckets overflowing with roses. A tiny brass bell tinkled as they opened the door.

The smell of flowers overwhelmed them. Inside, a plump woman of about fifty smiled at them across a counter piled high with satin ribbons and roses and baby's breath. She was making bouquets. For a few seconds, her gaze lingered on Sarah, then it settled on Nick. "*Guten tag,*" she said.

Nick nodded. "*Guten tag.*" Casually he wandered about the shop, noting the refrigerators with their sweating glass doors and the shelves of vases and china figurines and plastic flowers. Near the door was a funeral wreath, packed in cellophane and ready for delivery. The shop woman clipped the thorns from the roses and began to wind wire ribbon around the stems. It was a bride's bouquet. She hummed as she worked, not at all perturbed by the silence of her two visitors. At last she put the bouquet down and her eyes met Sarah's.

"*Ja?*" she asked softly.

Sarah pulled out Geoffrey's picture and placed it on the counter. The woman stared at it but said nothing.

Nodding at the photograph, Nick asked her a question in German. She shook her head. "Geoffrey Fontaine," he said. The woman didn't react. "Simon Dance," he said. Again the woman only stared at him blankly.

"But you must know him!" Sarah blurted. "He's my husband—I have to find him."

"Sarah, let me—"

"He's waiting for me. If you know where he is, call him. Tell him I'm here!"

"Sarah, she doesn't understand you."

"She has to understand! Nick, ask her about Eve. Maybe she knows Eve."

At Nick's questions the woman shrugged again. She knew nothing at all about Geoffrey. Or if she did know, she wasn't talking.

To have all their hopes end like this! After traveling halfway across Europe, they had reached nothing but a dead end. Sick with disappointment, Sarah slipped the picture back into her purse. The German woman calmly turned her attention to wrapping the bouquets in green tissue paper.

Sarah turned miserably to Nick. "What do we do now?"

He was staring off in frustration at the funeral wreath. "I don't know," he muttered. "I just don't know."

The shop woman began tearing off sheets of tissue paper. The soft ripping noise made Sarah shudder.

"Why here?" she murmured. "Why would she call this place? There had to be a reason."

Sarah wandered to the refrigerator and stared through the glass at the buckets of carnations and roses. The smell of flowers was beginning to sicken her. It reminded her too vividly of a painful day on a cemetery hilltop just two weeks ago. "Please, Nick," she said quietly. "Let's leave."

Nick dipped his head at the shop woman. "*Danke schön.*"

The woman smiled and beckoned to Sarah. Puzzled, Sarah went to the counter. The woman held out a single rose with a tissue-wrapped stem and murmured, "*Auf wiederschen.*" Then, gazing steadily, the woman gave the rose to Sarah. Their eyes met. It was only the briefest of looks, but in that instant Sarah understood its significance; something had just been passed to her. Something for her eyes only.

Nodding, she accepted the rose. *"Auf wiedersehen!"* she said. Then she turned and followed Nick out of the shop.

Outside, Sarah clutched the rose tightly in her fist. Her mind was racing; the stem felt like a hot poker. It took all her willpower not to tear away the tissue paper and read the message she knew was written inside. But something about the woman's eyes had conveyed another message, a warning. A look that said, *You are in danger, from someone nearby.*

But the only person nearby was Nick.

Nick, the man she trusted, the man she loved.

Since Geoffrey's disappearance, Nick had been her friend, her protector. Whenever she'd needed him, he'd been there. Had it been mere coincidence? Or had it all been planned? If so, it had worked brilliantly. They had picked the right man for the job. They had known she'd be frightened and lonely, that she'd be desperate for a friend, for someone to trust. Then, like magic, Nick had appeared in London. Since then he'd been with her almost twenty-four hours a day. Why?

She didn't want to believe it, but the answer was staring her right in the face. Surveillance.

No, she couldn't be sure. And she loved him.

But the woman's look of warning had burned into her memory; she couldn't forget it.

The bus ride seemed to take forever. All the way back, Nick's hand rested on her knee. His touch burned like a brand into her skin. She wanted to meet his eyes, but she was afraid of what she might see. Afraid that he would read her fear.

As soon as they reached the *pension*, she fled into the bathroom at the end of the hall and bolted the door. With shaking hands she peeled the tissue paper from the rose's stem. Beneath the naked light bulb by the sink, she read the message. It was in English and had been scrawled hurriedly in pencil.

Potsdamer Platz, one o'clock tomorrow.

Trust no one.

She stared at the last three words. *Trust no one.* Its meaning was unmistakable. She had been careless. She could afford to make no more mistakes. Geoffrey's life depended on her.

Savagely she ripped the note into a dozen pieces and flushed it down the toilet. Then she headed back to the room, to Nick.

She couldn't leave him yet. First she had to be certain. She loved Nick O'Hara, and in her heart she knew he would never hurt her. But she had to know: for whom was he working?

Tomorrow, in Potsdamer Platz, she'd find her answers.

"WE WERE BEGINNING to think you wouldn't make it," said Nick.

Wes Corrigan looked uneasy as he took a chair across from Nick and Sarah. "So was I," he muttered, glancing over his shoulder.

"Trouble?" said Nick.

"I'm not sure. That's what bothers me. It's like one of those old horror flicks. You're never sure when the monster's going to leap at you." He slouched down, in a vain attempt to hide in the chair's depths.

In search of a discreet meeting place, they had come to this dark café. Their table was dimly lighted by a single candle; around them were people who spoke in whispers, people who purposefully minded their own business. No one looked twice at the two men and a woman sitting at the corner table.

Almost by instinct, Sarah's eyes searched the room for a back entrance. If things went wrong, she'd need an easy escape. The door was clearly marked, but it would require a dash across the room. She picked out her route through the tables and chairs. Three seconds, that's all it should take. If it came to that, she'd be on her own. She could no longer count on Nick.

It struck her then how much her existence had changed. A few weeks ago, she'd been an ordinary woman, living an ordinary life. Now she was scouting out escape routes.

"I tell you, Nick," said Wes, after he'd ordered a beer. "This whole thing has got me spooked."

"What's happened?"

"Well, to begin with, you were right. I'm being watched. Not long after you left last night, a van showed up across the street from my house. It's been there ever since. I had to sneak out the back door, through the alley. I'm not used to this kind of life. Makes me nervous."

"Have you got anything for us?"

Wes looked around again, then lowered his voice. "First of all, I went back to review my file on Geoffrey Fontaine's death. When I called you a few weeks ago, I had all the data in front of me. The pathology report, the police report. I had a whole file of notes, the photocopy of his passport..."

"And?"

"They're missing." He glanced at Sarah. "Everything. It's *all* gone. Not just my file. It's disappeared from the computer."

"What *have* you got, then?"

"On Geoffrey Fontaine? Nothing. It's as if I never filed that report."

"They can't erase a man's existence," Sarah pointed out.

Wes shrugged. "Someone's trying to. I can't be sure who did it. We've got a big staff in our mission. It could have been any of a dozen."

They stopped talking as the waitress served their suppers: warm, crusty bread; escargots sizzling in garlic and butter; wedges of Gouda cheese.

"What about Magus?" asked Nick.

Wes dabbed a drop of butter from his chin. "I was getting to that. Okay, after I found out Geoffrey Fontaine had been dropped from the records, I hunted around for info on Magus. Except for the obvious biblical references, there's nothing under that name."

"Doesn't surprise me," said Nick.

"I'm not cleared for the top secret stuff. And I think this Magus fellow falls into that category."

"So we're left with nothing," said Sarah.

"Not exactly."

Nick frowned. "What did you find?"

Wes reached into his jacket and pulled out an envelope, which he tossed on the table. "I found Simon Dance."

Nick grabbed the envelope. Inside were two pages. "My God. Look at this!" He passed the pages to Sarah.

It was a photocopy of a six-year-old visa application. Included was a poor-quality reproduction of a passport photo. The eyes were strangely familiar. But had Sarah seen this man on the street, she would have passed him by without a second glance.

Sarah's heart was beating fast. "This is Geoffrey," she said softly.

Wes nodded. "At least that's how he looked six years ago. When his name was Dance."

"How did you get this stuff?" asked Nick.

"Whoever cleaned out Geoffrey Fontaine's file didn't bother to dispose of Dance's. Maybe the file's too old. Maybe they figured the face and name have changed, so why bother?"

Sarah flipped to the next page. Simon Dance, she saw, had had a German passport, with an address in Berlin. His occupation had been architect. He was married.

"Why did he apply for this visa?" she asked.

"It was a tourist visa," Wes pointed out.

"No, I mean *why?*"

"Maybe he wanted to see the sights."

"Or scout out the possibilities," added Nick.

"Have you checked this old Berlin address?" asked Sarah.

Wes nodded. "It's gone. Got demolished last year to make way for a high rise."

"Then we're left with no leads," said Nick.

"I've got one last source," offered Wes. "An old friend, who used to work for the Company. He retired last year. Got disgusted with the practice of spying. He just might know about Simon Dance. And Magus."

"I hope so," said Nick.

Wes rose. "Look, I can't hang around too long. That van's waiting outside my house. Call me tomorrow around noon. I should have something by then."

"Same procedure?"

"Yeah. Give me fifteen minutes after you call. I can't always get to a pay phone right away." He looked at Sarah. "Let's hope this thing's resolved soon. You must be tired of running."

She nodded. And as she gazed across the table at the two men, she thought that it wasn't the lack of sleep or the irregular meals or even the minute-to-minute fear that was wearing her down. It was the anxiety of not knowing whom to trust.

"YOU'VE BEEN AWFULLY quiet," Nick said. "Is something wrong?"

They were walking the streets back to their *pension*. Night had turned the city garish; darkness was what Sarah longed for, a place away from the traffic and the neon billboards. She gazed up at the sky, but there were no stars; there was only the gray haze of reflected city lights.

"I don't know, Nick," she sighed. She stopped and turned to him. Beneath a flashing billboard, they stared at each other as the neon lights glowed red and white and red on their faces. His eyes were impenetrably dark, the eyes of a stranger. "Can I really trust you, Nick?"

"Oh, Sarah. What a ridiculous question."

"If only we'd met some other way! If only we were like everyone else—"

He touched her face, a quiet gesture of reassurance. "What happened, happened. We take it from here. You just have to trust me."

"I trusted Geoffrey," she whispered.

"I'm Nick, remember?"

"Who *is* Nick O'Hara? I wonder, sometimes. I wonder if you're real, if you're flesh and blood. I worry that someday you'll just dissolve before my eyes."

"No, Sarah." He drew her into his arms. "After a while you'll stop wondering. You'll know I'm real. It might take a year, two years, maybe even a dozen years. But you'll learn to trust me."

Trust? she thought bitterly. Trust was something you learned as a baby, something that was supposed to keep you wrapped up and warm, like a blanket. It was one of life's cruel illusions. She'd outgrown the concept. She'd discovered how alone everyone really was.

But she hadn't outgrown desire. Or need.

A short time later, as they stood holding each other in their room, she found herself hungrily storing up what might be her last memories of Nick: his smile, his laughter, the smell of his skin. From somewhere in the building came the scratchy music of a phonograph, a German ballad, sung by a woman with a sad, throaty voice. It was a song meant for a cabaret, a song for a room of darkness and smoke. The music drifted lazily through the night, into their open window.

Nick turned off the light. The music swelled with sadness; it was a song of parting, a woman's farewell. As long as she lived, Sarah would carry that song in her heart. Then, through the shadows, Nick came to her. The music rose, note upon note of sorrow, as she buried herself in his arms. She sensed him struggling to understand. How she wanted to tell him everything! She loved him. Only now, with her trust in him stretched to a mere thread, did she recognize it. She loved him.

The music faded and died. The only sound left was their breathing.

"Make love to me," she whispered. "Please. Now. Make love to me."

His fingers slid down her face and lingered on her cheek. "Sarah, I don't understand…. There's something wrong…."

"Don't ask me anything. Just make love to me. Make me forget. I want to forget."

"Oh, God," he groaned, trapping her face in his hands. "I'll make you forget...."

All at once she was drowning in the taste of his mouth. The hunger that had always burned just beneath Nick's cool surface suddenly burst free. His fingers slid down her neck to her blouse. Slowly the fabric parted, and she felt his hand and then his mouth close eagerly over her breast. She was barely conscious of the skirt falling from her hips; all her awareness centered on what his mouth was doing to her.

She sank down into the bed. He toppled like a tree over her, crushing the breath from her lungs.

"I've wanted you," he murmured, raking his fingers through her hair, "from the very first day. It's all I've thought about, seeing you like this. Having you, tasting you." With sudden recklessness he began to tug at his shirt, and in his clumsiness a button tore loose and fell on her naked belly. He pushed the button aside and, bending down, he reverently kissed the flesh where it had lain. Then he rose up and shed the last of his clothes.

Through the window the faint city lights shone in on his bare shoulders. She could see only a faint outline of his face; he was just a shadow hovering above her, a shadow that took on fire and substance as their bodies met. Their mouths found each other. It was a frantic kiss, too passionate to be gentle; he was invading her mouth, devouring her. With both body and soul, she welcomed him in.

His entry was slow, hesitant, as though he was afraid he might hurt her. But in his fever he soon lost all restraint. He was no longer Nick O'Hara; he was something wild, something untamed. Yet even as the end came, even as he threw himself against her, there was a tenderness between them, a caring that went beyond need.

Only when he had fallen exhausted beside her and their hearts had slowed did Nick wonder again about her silence. He knew she had wanted him; she had responded in a way that had exceeded any fantasy. Just lying beside her now, feeling her head against his chest, stirred his hunger again. But something was wrong. He touched her cheek and felt the dampness. Something had changed.

Later he would ask her. After they'd spent all their passion on each other, he would make her tell him why she was crying. Not now. She wasn't ready. And he wanted her again; he couldn't wait any longer.

As he slid into her a second time, he forgot all those questions. He forgot everything. There was only Sarah, so soft and warm. Tomorrow he would remember what it was he had to ask.

Tomorrow.

"GOOD MORNING, MR. CORRIGAN. May we have a word with you?"

From the tone of his voice, Wes knew at once this was not a social visit. He glanced up from the stack of papers on his desk and saw two men standing inside the doorway. One was rumpled and on the heavy side; the other was tall and a little too sleek, even for a Company man. They were not smiling.

Wes cleared his throat. "Hello, gentlemen. How can I help you?"

The tall man sat down and looked Wes straight in the eye. "Nick O'Hara. Where is he?"

Wes felt his voice freeze up. It took him a few seconds to regain his poise, but by then it was too late. He'd given himself away. Shoving aside the stack of papers, he said, "Uh— Nick O'Hara... Isn't he still in Washington?"

The chubby man snorted. "Don't play games with us, Corrigan!"

"Who's playing games? Who are you guys, anyway?"

The tall man said, "The name's Van Dam. And this is Mr. Potter."

The Company, thought Wes. *Oh, boy, am I in trouble. Now what do I do?* He rose from his chair, trying hard to look indignant. "Look, it's Saturday. I've got other things to do. Maybe you could book an appointment for a weekday like everyone else?"

"Sit down, Corrigan."

Wes reached for the phone to call a security officer, but Potter intercepted his hand before he could hit the button. Fear shot through Wes for the first time. Verbal aggression was one thing; actually manhandling him was another. These guys were playing rough. Wes didn't like violence. Especially when it involved his own body.

"We want O'Hara," said Potter.

"I can't help you."

"Where is he?"

"I told you. Washington. As a matter of fact, I called him just two weeks ago, on a consular matter." Wes looked down at his trapped hand. "Now if you'll kindly let me go?" Potter released him.

Van Dam sighed. "Let's not prolong this nonsense any longer. We know the man's in Berlin. We also know that yesterday, you started making odd little computer searches on his behalf. Obviously he's contacted you."

"This is all pure specul—"

"Someone with your access code has been busily ferreting out data." He opened a small notebook. "Let me see. Yesterday, seven a.m., you did a search on the name Geoffrey Fontaine...."

"Yes, well, I filed a report on Fontaine's death a few weeks back. I wanted to review the facts."

"At seven-thirty you keyed in the name Simon Dance. Curious name. Any reason for that search?"

Wes was silent.

"Finally, twelve noon—your lunch hour, I presume—you requested data on someone or something called Magus. Have you, perhaps, an interest in the Old Testament?"

Wes didn't answer.

"Come, Mr. Corrigan. We both know why you're making these searches. You're doing it for O'Hara, aren't you?"

"Why do you want to know?"

Potter snapped impatiently, "We want him!"

"Why?"

"We're concerned about his safety," said Van Dam. "As well as the safety of the woman traveling with him."

"Oh, sure."

"Look, Corrigan," said Potter. "His life depends on our finding him in time."

"Tell me another fairy tale."

Van Dam leaned forward, his eyes locked on Wes. "They're in on deadly business. They need protection."

"Why should I believe you?"

"If you don't help us, you'll have their blood on your hands."

Wes shook his head. "Like I said, I can't help you."

"Can't or won't?"

"Can't. I don't know where he is. And that's the honest-to-God truth."

Van Dam and Potter exchanged glances. "Okay," said Van Dam. "Get your men set up. We'll simply have to wait it out."

Potter nodded and whisked out of the office.

Wes started to rise again. "Look, I don't know what the hell you think you're doing, but—"

Van Dam motioned him back to his chair. "I'm afraid you won't be leaving the building for a while. If you need to use the head, just let us know, and we'll send an escort with you."

"Dammit, what's going on here?"

Van Dam smiled. "A waiting game, Mr. Corrigan. We're going to sit back and see how long it takes for your phone to ring."

Chapter Twelve

IT WAS 12:50 THAT AFTERNOON WHEN the taxi let Sarah off on the edge of Potsdamer Platz. She was alone. Losing Nick had been easier than she'd thought. Thirty seconds after he'd left the room to call Wes Corrigan, she had grabbed her purse and headed out the door.

She forced herself not to think of Nick as she walked deliberately across the square. From the map she had seen that Potsdamer Platz was a point of intersection between the British, American and Soviet sectors. Cutting like a knife across the square was the Berlin Wall, which now loomed before her. No matter where one stood in the square, it was the wall that held one's gaze. People paused in the weak spring sunshine and stared at it, as if trying to see through the concrete to a different Germany beyond. Here, even in the presence of barbed wire, were ice-cream stands and laughing children and wanderers out to enjoy the light blue day.

She paused near a busload of students and pretended to listen as the teacher lectured in very precise German. But all the time, Sarah was searching for a face. Where was the woman? The beating of her heart became faster. The teacher's voice faded. Even the laughter of the children receded from her ears.

Then, despite the pounding of her heart, she heard a woman's voice; it spoke softly in passing.

"Follow me. Keep your distance."

Turning, she spotted the woman from the flower shop walking away with a net shopping bag dangling from her arm. She could be mistaken for any housewife out on her daily errands. At a leisurely pace, the woman headed northwest, toward Bellevuestrasse. Sarah followed at a discreet distance.

After three blocks, the woman disappeared into a candle shop. For a moment Sarah hesitated outside on the sidewalk. Curtains hung across the shop windows; she could see nothing beyond. At last she stepped inside.

The woman was nowhere to be seen. The smell of burning candles, bayberry and pine and lavender, filled the dimly lighted room. On display tables sat strange little creatures shaped from wax. A flame burned brightly on the figure of a twisted old gnome, slowly melting away his face. On the counter sat a candle in the shape of a woman. Melted wax had streamed down her breasts, like strands of hair.

Sarah started with surprise when an old man popped up on the other side of the counter. He nodded at her. "*Geradeaus,*" he murmured. She gave him a quizzical look. He pointed to the back of the shop. "*Geradeaus,*" he repeated, and she understood. He wanted her to move on.

With her heart in her throat, she walked past him, through a small storage room and out the back door.

Sunlight blinded her. The door slammed shut, locking immediately. She was now standing in an alley. Somewhere to her right lay Potsdamer Platz. She could hear the distant sounds of traffic. Where was the woman?

The roar of a car engine made her whirl around. From nowhere a black Citroën had appeared and was barreling down the alley, straight at her. She had no way to escape. The shop door was locked. The alley was an endless tunnel of buildings set tightly side by side. In terror she fell back, her hands pressed flat against the wall, her eyes fixed on the gleaming black hood of the Citroën, looming closer and closer.

The car skidded to a halt. The door flew open. "Get in!" hissed the woman from the back seat. "Hurry!"

Sarah peeled herself from the wall and scrambled inside.

"*Schnell!*" the woman snapped at the driver.

Sarah was thrown backward as the car jerked ahead. One block up, it turned left, then right, then left again. Sarah lost her bearings. The woman kept staring over her shoulder. At last, satisfied that no one was following them, she turned to Sarah.

"Now we can talk," she said. At Sarah's questioning glance toward the driver, the woman nodded. "He's all right. Say what you want."

"Who are you?" asked Sarah.

"I'm a friend of Geoffrey's."

"Then you know where he is?"

The woman didn't answer. Instead she said something in German to the driver. He responded by turning off the main street and heading onto a quiet park road. A short distance beyond, they stopped among the trees.

The woman tugged on Sarah's arm. "Come. We'll walk here."

Together they crossed the grass. A fine haze seemed to hang over the city, dulling the sky to a silvery blue.

"How did you know my husband?" asked Sarah.

"Years ago we worked together. His name was Simon, then." She nodded, remembering. "He was most promising, Simon was. One of my best."

"Then you're also…in the business?"

"I was. Until five years ago."

It was hard to imagine this woman as anything but a plump housewife. Her hair was already streaked with gray; her face was round and moist. Perhaps that was her strength, the fact that she looked so ordinary.

"No, I do not look the part," said the woman, reading Sarah's mind. "The best ones never do."

They walked a few paces in silence. Even here, in the midst of trees and grass, the smell of the city hung in the air. "Like Simon, I was one of the best," the woman confided. "And now even I am afraid."

They stopped and looked at each other. The woman's eyes were like two brown raisins pressed into a face of bread dough.

"Where is he?" asked Sarah.

"I don't know."

"Then why did you ask me here?"

"To warn you. As a favor to an old friend."

"You mean Geoffrey?"

"Yes. In this business we have few friends, but the ones we do have mean everything to us."

They began to walk again. Sarah looked back and saw the black Citroën, waiting for them by the road.

"I last saw him a little over two weeks ago," the woman continued. "What a shock, to meet after all this time! I knew Simon had left the business. Yet here he was in Berlin, carrying his tools once again. He was worried. He thought he had been betrayed by the people he was working for. He was going to drop out of sight."

"Betrayed? By whom?"

"The CIA."

Sarah halted, an expression of amazement on her face. "He was working for the CIA?"

"They forced him into it. He had skills—he knew things that made him vital to their operation. But too many things were going wrong. Simon wanted out. He came to me for a few essentials. I provided him with a new passport, identity cards. Things he'd need to leave Berlin, once he'd disposed of his old identity. For a few hours, we visited." She shook her head sadly. "The turns our lives have taken! I saw your photograph in his wallet. That's how I recognized you yesterday. He told me you were a very…delicate person. That he was sorry you'd been hurt. When he left he promised I'd see him again someday. But that night I learned about the fire. I heard a body had been found."

"Do you think he's dead?"

"No."

"Why not?"

"If he's dead, then why are they still following *you*?"

"You mentioned a CIA operation. Does it have anything to do with a man called Magus?"

The woman's eyes showed only a faint trace of surprise. "He should not have told you about Magus."

"He didn't. Eve did."

"Ah. Then you know about Eva." The woman gave her a searching look. "I hope you aren't jealous. We can't be jealous in this work." She smiled. "Little Eva! She must be close to forty now. And still beautiful, I imagine."

"You mean—you haven't heard?"

"Heard what?"

"Eve is dead."

The woman froze, all color drained from her face. "How did it happen?" she whispered.

"A back alley in London…just a few days ago."

"She was tortured?"

Sarah nodded, feeling sick at the memory.

Swiftly the woman scanned the park. Except for the driver in the Citroën, there was no one else in sight. "Then we've no time to waste," she said, turning to Sarah. "They'll be coming for me. Listen to what I'm going to say. After we part you will not see me again. Two weeks ago, when your husband came to me, it was on business. Deadly business."

"Magus?"

"Yes. What's left of him. Five years ago the three of us were given an assignment. It was—how should I put it—to terminate with extreme prejudice. Our target was Magus. Simon planted the explosives in his car. The old man always drove himself to work. But on that one morning, he stayed home. His wife took the car instead."

The woman's voice held Sarah in a trance. She was afraid to hear the rest; she could already guess what had happened.

"The woman died instantly, of course. After the explosion the old man ran out of the house and tried to pull her from the car. The flames were terrible. But somehow he survived. And now he wants us."

"Vengeance," murmured Sarah. "That's what he's after, then."

"Yes. Against us all. Me. Eva. And most of all, Simon. He has already found Eva."

"What do I have to do with all of this?"

"You're his wife. You're their link to Simon."

"What should I do? Should I go home—"

"You can't go home. Not now; perhaps never." She looked toward the Citroën.

"But I can't run forever! I'm not like you—I don't know how to live this way. I need help. If you can just tell me how to find him…."

The woman studied Sarah for a moment, sizing up her chances of survival. "If Simon is still alive, then he is in Amsterdam."

"In Amsterdam? Why?"

"Because that is where Magus is."

THE PHONE SEEMED to ring forever. Nick's fingers tapped nervously against the booth. Where the hell was the operator? he wondered.

"American Consulate."

Instantly Nick snapped to attention. "Mr. Wes Corrigan," he said.

"One moment, please." There was a pause. Then another voice came on. "You're calling for Mr. Corrigan? I believe he's somewhere in the building having lunch. I'll page him. Please hold."

Before he could protest, she cut him off. For five minutes he waited on the line. Then, just as he was about to hang up, she returned.

"I'm sorry. He's not answering. But he's due back any minute for a meeting. Can I take a message?"

"Yes. Tell him Steve Barnes called. It's about my passport trouble."

"Your number?"

"He knows it." Nick hung up.

By their arrangement, Wes would leave the embassy grounds and use an outside line to call Nick's pay phone. Nick would give Wes fifteen minutes to get back to him. If there was no call, he'd try again later. But something told him he was taking a risk, waiting around for the phone to ring. This last exchange with the operator worried him. Especially that pause at the beginning. He glanced at his watch. It was 1:14 p.m. He'd wait until one-thirty.

Someone tapped on the booth. A young woman was standing outside, waving a coin. She wanted to use the phone. With a silent oath, he left the booth and waited as she made her call. The conversation seemed to last for hours. At 1:25 she was still talking. He held up his watch and pointed at the time, but the woman merely turned her back on him.

Cursing, he started up the street. But he had already waited too long.

Out of a crowd of pedestrians standing on the corner emerged a man in a charcoal-gray suit. He was walking toward Nick. Something about the way the man reached into his jacket told Nick he was in trouble. In one smooth motion, the man crouched and brought up his hands. Nick found himself staring into the barrel of a gun.

"Freeze, O'Hara!" shouted Roy Potter from somewhere behind him.

Nick spun to his right, poised to bolt into the busy street. Instantly two more guns appeared. A cold steel barrel was pressed against his jugular. He heard the resounding click of a pistol hammer being cocked. For a few seconds, no one moved, no one breathed. A few feet away in the street, a limousine screeched to a halt and the door flew open.

Slowly Nick turned to look at Potter, who was now cautiously edging forward, his gun aimed squarely at Nick's head. "Put the damn thing away, Potter," said Nick. "You're making me nervous."

"Get in the car," Potter commanded.

"Where are we going?"

"To a little debriefing with Jonathan Van Dam."

"Then what happens?"

Potter's grin was distinctly unpleasant. "That all depends on you."

"WHERE IS SARAH FONTAINE?"

Nick slouched down in the leather chair and gave Van Dam his best go-to-hell look. He was surprised to find himself in such comfortable surroundings. He'd expected glaring lights and a hard bench, certainly not the expensive armchair in which he was now sitting. He had no doubt things would soon get less pleasant.

"Mr. O'Hara, I'm getting impatient," said Van Dam. "I asked you a question. Where is she?"

Nick merely shrugged.

"If you care at all about her, you'll tell us where she is, and you'll tell us fast."

"I do care," said Nick. "That's why I'm not telling you anything."

"She won't last a week out there. She's inexperienced. Frightened. We've got to bring her in—now!"

"Why? You need her for target practice?"

"You're a royal pain in the ass, O'Hara," muttered Potter, who stood sulking a few feet away. "Always have been, always will be."

"I'm crazy about you, too," Nick grunted.

Van Dam pointedly ignored the interchange. "Mr. O'Hara, the woman needs our help. She's better off under our wing. Tell us where she is. You may be saving her life."

"She was under your wing at Margate. What kind of protection did you give her then? What the hell is going on?"

"I can't tell you."

"You want Geoffrey Fontaine, don't you?"

"No."

"You arranged her release in London. Then you followed her. You thought she'd lead you right to Fontaine, didn't you?"

"We already know she can't."

"What's that supposed to mean?"

"We're not after Fontaine."

"So tell me another story."

Potter couldn't stay silent any longer. "Dammit!" he blurted out, his palms slapping the desk. "Don't you get it, O'Hara? Fontaine was one of *ours*!"

The revelation stunned Nick into a momentary silence. He stared at Potter. "You mean—he's with the *Company*?"

"That's right."

"Then where is he?"

Potter sighed, looking suddenly tired. "He's dead."

Nick sat back, floored by the new information. All the running, all the searching, had been for nothing. They'd crossed half of Europe in pursuit of a dead man. "I—I seem to have a major gap of knowledge here. Enlighten me. Who's after Sarah?"

Van Dam broke in, "I'm not sure we can—"

"We've got no choice," said Potter. "We've gotta tell him."

After a pause Van Dam nodded. "Very well, then. Go ahead, Mr. Potter."

Potter paced as he talked, moving like an old bulldog between the chairs. "Five years ago, one of Mossad's top agents was a man named Simon Dance. He was part of a team of three. The other two were women: Eva Saint-Clair and Helga Steinberg. They were assigned a routine termination job, but the operation got fouled up. Their target survived. Instead the man's wife was killed."

"Dance was a hired assassin?"

Potter halted and scowled at Nick. "Sometimes, O'Hara, you've gotta fight fire with fire. The target in this case was the head of a worldwide terror cartel. These guys don't operate on ideology; they do it for hard cash. A hundred big ones gets you a bombing. Three hundred will sink you a small ship. If you're a do-it-yourselfer, they'll get you the equipment. A crate of Uzis. A surface-to-air missile. Anything your little heart desires, for a price. There's no way to deal with a club like that, except on terms they understand. The job had to be done, and Dance's team was the best."

"But the target got away."

"Unfortunately, yes. Within a year a contract was out on all three Mossad agents, with the biggest price on Dance's head. By that time they had wisely dropped out of sight. Helga Steinberg, we think, is still in Germany. Dance and Eva Saint-Clair vanished. For five years no one knew where they were. Then, three weeks ago one of our London agents was sitting in his favorite pub when he just happened to overhear a voice he recognized. He'd worked with Dance some years ago so he knew that voice. That's how we found out about Dance's new identity: Geoffrey Fontaine."

"How did he come to work for the Company?"

"I persuaded him."

"With what?"

"I tried the usual. Money. A new life. He didn't want any of it. But he did want one thing: to be able to live without any more fear. I pointed out to him that the only way was to go back and finish the job on Magus, the man he should have terminated. For years I'd been trying to track Magus myself, without luck. I traced him only as far as Amsterdam and I needed Dance's help. He agreed."

Magus, thought Nick. The old man, the magician. At last he was beginning to understand. "Couldn't do the job yourself," he said. "So you hired a hit man for the good old U.S.A."

"Oh, yeah. Yeah, tell me your old-fashioned diplomacy's any damned good in this situation. A bullet, at least, gets results."

"The easy answer to everything. Just blow off their heads. So what went wrong? Why didn't your hit man deliver?"

Potter shook his head. "I don't know. In Amsterdam Dance got…nervous. He took off like a scared rabbit. For some weird reason, he flew to Berlin and checked into that old hotel. That night there was a fire. But you know about that. And that's the last we heard of Simon Dance."

"It was his body in the hotel?"

"We've got no dental records to prove it, but I'm in-clined to think it was. No one else from Berlin has been re-

ported missing. Dance hasn't surfaced anywhere. How it
happened is anyone's guess. Murder? Suicide? Both are possibilities. He was depressed. Tired."

Nick frowned. "But if he died in that hotel—then who
called Sarah?"

"I did."

"*You?*"

"It was a composite message, spliced together from
recordings of his voice. You see, we'd tapped his London
hotel room."

Nick's fingers tightened around the armrest as he fought
to keep his voice steady. "You wanted her here in Europe?
You're telling me you set her up as a target?"

"Not a target, O'Hara. Bait. I heard Magus still had the
contract out on Dance. Obviously he didn't believe Dance
was dead. If we could make him think Sarah knew something, he might make a move on her. So we drew her to Europe. We were hoping Magus would show his hand. The
whole time, we had our eyes on her. That is, until you
pulled her underground."

"You *bastards*," cried Nick. "She was nothing more to you
than a—a goat tied to a stake!"

"There are deeper issues here—"

Nick shot to his feet. "*To hell* with your issues!"

Van Dam shifted uncomfortably in his chair. "Mr. O'Hara,
please sit down. Try and see the broader situation...."

Nick turned on Van Dam. "Was this your bright idea?"

"No, it was mine," Potter admitted. "Mr. Van Dam had
nothing to do with it. He found out about it later, when he
showed up in London."

Nick looked at Potter. "You? I should've known. It smells
like your kind of job. So what've you got planned next?

Shall we tie her up in the town square with a big sign say-ing Fair Game?"

Potter shook his head and said quietly, "No. The opera-tion's over. Van Dam wants to bring her in."

"Then what happens?"

"It will soon be plain to everyone involved that Fontaine's really dead. They'll leave her alone. We'll have to find Magus some other day."

"What about Wes Corrigan? I want him let off the hook."

"Already done. There'll be no harm to his career. Not a mark'll show up on his personnel file."

Slowly Nick sat down. He gave Potter a long, hard look. His decision and its consequences rested on only one thing: Could he trust these men? Even if he couldn't, what choice did he have? Sarah was alone out there, hiding from a killer. She'd never survive on her own. "If this is some kind of scam—"

"There's no need to threaten me, O'Hara. I know what you're capable of."

"No," said Nick. "I don't think you do. And let's hope you never find out."

"WHERE WILL I FIND HIM in Amsterdam?" Sarah asked the woman.

They were walking through the trees to the Citroën. The ground was damp, and Sarah's heels sank deeply into the young grass.

"Are you certain you wish to find him?" asked the woman.

"I have to. He's the only one I can turn to for help. And he's waiting for me."

"You may not survive this search. You know that, don't you?"

Sarah shivered. "I'm barely surviving now. Every moment I'm afraid. I keep wondering when and how it'll end. If it will be painful." She shuddered. "They used a knife on Eve."

The woman's eyes darkened. "A knife? Kronen's trademark."

"Kronen?"

"Son of the Devil, we used to call him. He is Magus's favorite."

"He wears sunglasses? And he has blond, almost white hair?"

The woman nodded. "You've seen him, then. He'll be looking for you. In Amsterdam. In Berlin. Wherever you go, he'll be waiting."

"What would you do if you were me?"

The woman looked at Sarah thoughtfully. "In your place? With your youth? Yes, I would do what you're doing. I would try to find Simon."

"Then help me. Tell me how I can find him."

"What I tell you could kill him."

"I'll be careful."

The woman searched Sarah's face, once more weighing her chances. "In Amsterdam," she said, "there is a club, the Casa Morro. On the street Oude Zijds Voorburgwal. It is owned by a woman named Corrie. She was once a friend to Mossad. To all of us. If Simon is in Amsterdam, she will know how to find him."

"And if she doesn't?"

"Then no one will know."

The Citroën's door was already open. They climbed in and the driver headed toward the Ku-damm.

"When you see the Casa Morro, don't be shocked," the woman said.

"Why would I be shocked?"

The woman laughed softly. "You'll find out." She leaned forward and spoke to the driver in German. "We can drop you off near your *pension*," she told Sarah. "Is that what you wish?"

Sarah nodded. To reach Amsterdam she would need money, and Nick was carrying most of their cash. Tonight, when he was asleep, she could lift it from his wallet and leave Berlin. By morning she'd be miles away. "I'm staying just south of—"

"We know where it is," said the woman. She muttered a few more words to the driver. Then she turned to Sarah. "There is one last thing. Be careful whom you trust. That man you were with yesterday—what is his name?"

"Nick O'Hara."

The woman frowned, as if trying to place the name. "Whoever he is," she said, "he could be dangerous. How long have you known him?"

"A few weeks."

The woman nodded. "Don't trust him. Go alone. It's safest."

"Whom can I trust?"

"Only Simon. Tell no one what I've told you. Magus has eyes and ears everywhere."

They were nearing the *pension*. The street outside looked so exposed, so dangerous. Sarah felt safer in the car; she didn't want to get out. But the Citroën had already slowed down. She was reaching for the door handle when the driver suddenly cursed and floored the gas pedal. Sarah's shoulder slammed against the door as they swerved away from the curb and shot back into the traffic.

"*Nach rechts!*" the woman shouted, her face instantly taut with fear.

"What is it?" cried Sarah.

"CIA! They're all over this street!"

"*CIA?*"

"Look for yourself!"

They were coming up fast on the *pension*. Like all the other buildings on this street, it was a featureless box of gray concrete, distinguished only by a splash of shocking red graffiti scrawled on its front wall. On the sidewalk next to the graffiti stood two men. Sarah recognized them both. Planted solidly on his two short legs was Roy Potter, who squinted up the street in their direction. And standing close by, his face frozen in disbelief, was Nick.

He seemed unable to move, unable to react. As the Citroën roared past, he could only stand and stare. Just for an instant, his eyes met Sarah's through the car window. He grabbed Potter's arm. Both men dashed into the street after the Citroën in a futile attempt to grab the car door. That's when she understood. At last it was clear.

Nick had been working with Potter all along. Together they'd engineered a plan so intricate, so well acted, that she'd been totally taken in. Nick was with the Company. She'd just seen the proof, there on the sidewalk. He must have returned to the room and found her missing. Then he'd sounded the alarm.

Sarah collapsed against the seat in shock. She heard Nick's voice one last time as he shouted her name. Then the sound faded away, drowned out by the engine's roar. All of Sarah's strength was gone. She huddled against the car door like a hunted animal. She *was* a hunted animal. The

CIA was after her. Magus was after her. No matter which way she fled, someone's net would be closing in.

"We'll have to leave you at the airport," said the woman. "If you board a plane immediately, you may have time to get out of Berlin before they can stop you."

"But where are you going?" cried Sarah.

"Away. We take a different route."

"What if I need you? How can I find you—"

"You can't."

"But I don't even know your name!"

"If you find your husband, tell him Helga sent you."

The sign for Tegel Airport came up too quickly. There was so little time to gather her courage, so little time to think. Before she was ready, the Citroën stopped at the curb. She had to climb out. She didn't have a chance to say goodbye to Helga. As soon as Sarah's feet hit the pavement, the door slammed and the car sped off.

Sarah was alone.

On the way to the ticket counter, she glanced through the cash in her wallet. There was barely enough for a meal, much less a plane ticket. She had no choice. She'd have to use her credit card.

Twenty minutes later a flight took off for Amsterdam. Sarah was on it.

Chapter Thirteen

AFTER IT LEFT TEGEL AIRPORT, THE BLACK Citroën headed south toward the Ku-damm. Helga had to make one last stop before she left Berlin. She knew she was taking a big chance. The CIA had seen her license plate; they could trace her address. Death was closing in fast. Already Eva was gone. She would have to call Corrie, tell her to warn Simon. And she would ask her about this man, Nick O'Hara. Helga wondered who he was. She didn't like new faces. The most dangerous enemy in the world is the one you do not recognize.

She would have to abandon the car and board the train to Frankfurt. From there she could move south to Switzerland and Italy, or west to Spain. It didn't matter where she went; what mattered was that she left Berlin. Before Eva's fate caught up with her, too.

But even spies can be sentimental. Helga couldn't leave the city without her few precious possessions. To anyone else they were worthless things, but to Helga they were bits and pieces of a life she'd left behind: photographs of her sister and her parents, all of whom had died in the war; a half dozen love letters from a boy she would never forget; her mother's silver locket. These things reminded her of her humanity, and she would never leave without them, even under threat of death.

Her driver understood why they were stopping at the house. He knew it was useless to argue. He took her home one last time and sat in the car while she ran inside to collect her belongings.

From all the secret places in her bedroom came those few treasured items. They were packed, along with her pistol, in the false bottom of a satchel. Then clothes were thrown on top, the old skirts and housedresses she favored for their lack of distinction. She glanced out the window and saw the Citroën parked in the street below. What a pity to abandon such a fine car, she thought, but she had no choice.

She closed the window and headed downstairs. Outside, the sunlight made her blink. For a few seconds, she stood on the porch and let her eyes adjust before she locked the door. Those few seconds saved her life.

From the street came the screech of tires. Almost simultaneously, gunfire ripped the afternoon silence. Bullets spattered the Citroën. Helga threw herself to the porch, behind a row of clay tulip pots. Gunfire burst out again, and shards of glass rained down from the windows above her head.

Desperately she rolled beneath the railing and threw herself into the flower bed behind the porch, dragging the satchel with her. She had only a few seconds to act, a few seconds before the assassin would move in to finish the job. Already she heard his car door slam. He was coming.

She reached in the satchel. The false bottom slid open. Her hand closed around cold steel.

The footsteps moved closer. He was climbing the steps now; for him it would be a straight shot into the flower bed.

But she beat him to it. She raised the pistol, aimed and fired. The man's head was flung backward as a bright blotch of scarlet sprang out above his right eye. He fell, smashing through the far railing, and toppled like a disjointed doll among the garden tools.

Helga didn't bother to check his condition. She knew he was dead. The man's companion didn't wait around to confirm her marksmanship, either. He was already back in the driver's seat. Before she could aim and fire again, the car had roared off and disappeared.

One look at the Citroën told her her driver could not have survived. She had time for only a twinge of regret, but no tears. She had trusted the man. While they hadn't been lovers, they had been colleagues and they had worked well together these past five years. Now he was dead.

She grabbed the satchel and walked briskly down the street. A block away she broke into a run. To remain in Berlin any longer would be foolish. She had made one costly mistake, and she had survived; next time she might not be so lucky.

BLOOD WAS EVERYWHERE.

Nick shoved through the crowd of onlookers, across a street littered with broken glass, toward the black Citroën. Voices were shouting around him in German; on the sidewalk ahead, ambulance attendants crouched next to a body.

Nick fought to get through, only to find himself blocked by a policeman. But he was close enough to see the dead man lying on the sidewalk, face exposed, eyes wide and staring. "Potter!" he shouted. But there were too many other voices, too many sirens. His cry was lost in the noise. He was utterly paralyzed, unable to move or think, just another stunned body in a crowd of onlookers, all staring at the blood. The man beside him suddenly sank to his knees and began to retch.

"O'Hara!" It was Potter, calling to him from across the street. "She's not here! There're only two men, the driver and another guy, over by the porch. Both dead."

Nick shouted back, "Then where is she?"

Potter shrugged and turned as Tarasoff approached.

Enraged by his own helplessness, Nick pushed through the crowd and walked aimlessly down the street. He didn't know or care where he was headed; the sight of blood was more than he could bear. It could just as easily have been Sarah's body lying in the street, Sarah's blood splattered all over that Citroën.

A few yards away, he sank to the curb and dropped his head in his hands. There was nothing he could do. All his hopes rested on the skills of a man he'd never trusted and an organization he'd always despised. Roy Potter and the good old CIA. Potter had never been bothered by moral questions of right or wrong; he just did what he had to, and the rules be damned. For the first time in his life, Nick could appreciate such amoral practicality. With Sarah's life at stake, he didn't care how Potter did his job, either, as long as he got her back alive.

"O'Hara?" Potter was waving at him. "Let's move it! We've got a lead!"

"What?" Nick scrambled to his feet and followed Potter and Tarasoff to the car.

"KLM Airlines," said Potter. "She used her credit card."

"You mean she's leaving Berlin? Roy, you've gotta stop that plane!"

Potter shook his head. "We're too late for that."

"What do you mean?"

"The plane landed ten minutes ago. In Amsterdam."

THE DUTCH, it is said, never close their curtains. To do so would imply that one has something to hide. At night, when the houses are lighted, anyone who walks down an Amsterdam street can look through the windows, straight into the soul of a Dutch home, and see supper tables where well-scrubbed children sit watching as their mothers spoon out applesauce and potatoes. The hours will pass, and the children will disappear to their beds. Mother and father will go to their accustomed chairs. There they will watch TV or read, all in plain view of the world.

This open-curtain policy extends even to the Wallen district of Amsterdam, where members of the world's oldest profession display their charms. In the brothel windows, ladies knit or read novels, or they look out the windows and smile at the men gawking from the street. To them it is only a business, and they have nothing to hide.

It was in this neighborhood that Sarah found the Casa Morro. The afternoon had already slipped toward dusk by the time she crossed the small canal bridge to Oude Zijds Voorburgwal. In the sunlight the city had glowed with the gentle patina of age. But with the darkness came neon lights and throbbing music and all the strange and restless people who do not sleep at night. Sarah was just one more in a street of wanderers.

In the shadows by the low stone bridge, she stood and watched the passersby. The dark waters of the canal gently slapped the boats behind her. A young man shambled by with the bent shuffle of a street addict. In the window across from her, four women in various stages of undress were displayed, the human offerings of Casa Morro. They looked like altogether ordinary women. The tallest one glanced around as someone called her name. Then, putting down her book, she rose and disappeared through the blue curtains. The other three women did not even look up. *Don't be shocked,* Helga had said. This is what she had meant. After living on the edge of death, something as commonplace as a brothel could hardly shock Sarah.

For half an hour, she observed the steady flow of men in and out the door. The three women in the window eventually departed through the curtain; two others emerged in their place. Casa Morro appeared to be a thriving business.

At last Sarah went inside.

Even the scent of perfume could not hide the building's smell of age. The odor hung like a heavy curtain over what had once been an elegant seventeenth century home. Narrow wooden stairs led to a dim hallway above. Persian carpets, worn from years of traffic, muffled Sarah's footsteps as she walked from the foyer into a sitting room.

A woman looked up from a desk. She was in her forties, black-haired, elegantly tall and rawboned. Her gaze swept across Sarah in a swift look of assessment. *"Kan ik u helpen?"*

"I am looking for Corrie."

After a pause the woman nodded. "You are American, aren't you?" she asked in perfect English.

Sarah didn't answer. Slowly she circled the room, taking in the low couch, the fireplace with its brightly polished grate, the bookcase with its shelves of obscenely humorous knickknacks. At last she turned back to the woman. "Helga sent me," she said.

The woman's face remained absolutely expressionless.

"I want to find Simon. Where is he?"

The woman was silent for a moment. "Perhaps Simon does not wish to be found," she said softly.

"Please. It's important."

The woman shrugged. "With Simon everything is important."

"Is he in the city?"

"Perhaps."

"He'll want to see me."

"Why?"

"I'm his wife. Sarah."

For the first time, the woman looked perturbed. She went to her desk and sat down. Tapping a pencil nervously, she studied Sarah. "Leave me your wedding ring," she said. "Then come back tonight. Midnight."

"Will he be here?"

"Simon is a cautious man. He'll want proof before he comes anywhere near you."

Sarah removed her ring and gave it to the woman. Her hand felt naked without it. "I'll be back at midnight," she said.

"Madame!" the woman called as Sarah turned to leave. "There are no guarantees."

Sarah nodded. "I know." The woman's warning had not been necessary; Sarah had learned that nothing was guaranteed. Not even her next heartbeat.

CORRIE WAITED ONLY a moment after Sarah left. Then she walked outside and down the block, to a pay telephone where she dialed an Amsterdam number. It was answered immediately.

"The woman Helga called about was just here," said Corrie. "Long hair, brown eyes, early thirties. I have her wedding ring. It is gold, inscribed Geoffrey, 2-14. She will be back at midnight."

"She's alone?"

"I saw no one else."

"And that man Helga mentioned—O'Hara—what did your friends find out?"

"He's not CIA. His involvement appears to be purely...personal."

There was a pause. Corrie listened carefully to the instructions that followed. Then she hung up and returned to the Casa Morro, where she placed the wedding ring on a pedestal in the front window where it would be easily visible from the street.

Corrie smiled when she thought of what would happen when the woman returned. Sarah looked like all the other straitlaced types who so despised working women like Corrie. All of her life, Corrie had sensed the disdain of those "virtuous women." She'd wanted to fight back, but how can one spar with cold silence? Tonight the tables would be turned. It was a brazen way to do things, putting this woman Sarah on display, but Corrie didn't question her instructions.

In fact, she rather relished them.

IN A QUIET coffeehouse a mile away, Sarah sat on a hard wooden bench and stared at the candle on the table. Her life—what there was of it—had somehow come to this strange and lonely point in time. Outside, the world went about its business. Cars honked on the street, young men and women laughed and shouted as they walked in the night. But Sarah's universe was made up of this table and this room. Had she ever existed before this moment? She could hardly remember. *Was I ever a child?* she wondered. *Did I ever laugh and dance and sing? Was there ever a time when I wasn't afraid?*

She didn't ask these questions out of self-pity. She felt only bewilderment. In two weeks she'd lost touch with everything she'd once called familiar. Closing her eyes, she hungrily pictured her old bedroom, the mahogany nightstand, the brass alarm clock, the chipped china lamp. She went over every detail, the way one goes over a favorite photograph. Her old life, before fear had swept it away forever.

Strange, she thought, how one learns to keep going. Now her money was running low. She was alone. She didn't know where she was headed or how she would get there. But she had learned one thing about herself: She was a survivor.

Today had proved it. The pain of Nick's betrayal still cut like a knife; she would never recover from a wound that deep. Yet somehow she'd found the strength to move on. Surviving had turned into something automatic, something one did by way of instinct. All those false, pretty dreams of love had been left behind. Now she had only one clear goal in mind: to live long enough to end this nightmare.

In a few hours, she'd be with Geoffrey again. He would see to her safety. Moving in this world of shadows was second nature to him. And even if there was no love between them, she did believe he cared, just a little. It was the one hope she had left.

She dropped her head as a profound weariness settled on her shoulders. She'd walked for miles through the streets of Amsterdam. Both body and soul had been battered, and she longed to sleep, to forget. But as she closed her eyes, the memories returned: the taste of Nick's mouth, the way he laughed so gently when they made love. Angrily she forced the images from her mind. What had once been love was now turning to cold fury. At Nick for betraying her. At herself for being unable to give up the memories. Or the longing.

He had used her, and she'd never forget that. Never.

"THERE'S NO WORD on Sarah," said Potter as he walked into Nick's Amsterdam hotel room. He was carrying two cups of coffee. He closed the door with his foot and handed a cup to Nick.

Nick watched Potter flop into a chair and wearily rub his eyes. They were both dead beat. And hungry. Somehow they'd forgotten about supper; probably a first for Potter, judging by his girth. Since leaving Berlin they'd consumed nothing more substantial than black coffee. A quick shot of caffeine was what they both needed, thought Nick as he downed his cup and tossed it into the wastebasket. It was going to be a sleepless night.

"Slow down, O'Hara," said Potter. "You're gonna eat up your stomach, gulping it fast like that!"

Nick grunted. "You don't know my stomach."

"Yeah, well, the last thing I need is to get blamed for your bleeding ulcer, too." Potter glanced at his watch. "Damn. That deli down the street just closed. I could've used a sandwich." He fished a package of broken crackers from his pocket. "Saltines. Want some?" Nick shook his head. Potter tossed the broken crackers into his mouth and crumpled the cellophane. "Bad for my blood pressure. Too much sodium but, what the hell, when you're hungry, you're hungry." He brushed the crumbs off his suit and watched Nick pace the floor. "Look, things are moving fine without you having a nervous breakdown. Why don't you just turn in?"

"I can't." Nick stopped at the window. The city of Amsterdam stretched out in an endless sea of light. "She's out there somewhere. If I only knew where…"

Potter lighted a cigarette and strode across the room for an ashtray. After sixteen hours on the job, he was looking a little frayed. His suit was rumpled and his face was pastier than usual. But if he was discouraged by the recent turn of events, he didn't show it. Potter, the bulldog. No style, no charm, just a thick body with a thick head, all dressed up in a polyester suit. "For God's sake, O'Hara." He sighed. "Turn in! Finding her is our job."

Nick said nothing.

"Still don't trust us," said Potter.

"No. Why should I?"

Potter sat down and blew out a mouthful of smoke. "Something's always eating you, isn't it? What is it about you career guys in the foreign service? You go around the world nursing your ulcers, whining about the idiots in Washington. Then you turn around in public and put on that patriotic face. Hell, no wonder our foreign policy's so screwed up. It's administered by schizophrenics."

"Unlike central intelligence, which is run by sociopaths."

Potter laughed. "Yeah? At least we get things done. Matter of fact, you might be interested to hear I just got off the line to Berlin. We've turned up some info on those two dead men."

"Who were they?"

"The driver of the Citroën was German, once connected to Mossad. The neighbors had a notion he and Helga Steinberg were brother and sister, but it's obvious now they were just associates."

"Helga," Nick murmured thoughtfully. "She's the link we need. If we could find her…"

"Not a chance. Helga Steinberg's too good. She knows every trick in the book."

"What about that hit man?"

Potter sat back down and blew out a cloud of smoke. "The hit man was Dutch."

"Any connection to Helga?"

"None. Obviously he was just carrying out a contract. But she got him first." He grinned. "What a shot! I'd like to meet the broad someday. Hopefully not in a dark alley."

"The man had no record at all?"

"Nothing. His papers indicated he was a sales rep for some legitimate company, here in Amsterdam. Did a lot of traveling. But there's one interesting thing. It may be just the slipup we've been waiting for. Two days ago there was a transfer of funds to the man's account. A big transfer. We traced the source to another firm, the F. Berkman company, also here in Amsterdam. They import and export coffee. F. Berkman has been in business ten years. It has offices in a dozen countries. Yet it barely shows a profit. Funny, don't you think?"

"Who's this F. Berkman?"

"No one knows. The company's run by a board of directors. None of them have ever met the man."

Nick stared at Potter. The same thought had occurred to them both. "Magus," said Nick softly.

"That's what I wondered."

"Sarah's right smack in his territory! If I were her, I'd be running like hell in the other direction!"

"Seems to me she's done a lot of unexpected things. She's sure not behaving like your everyday scared broad."

"No," said Nick, sinking tiredly onto the bed. "She's not your everyday scared broad. She's smarter."

"You're in love with her."

"I suppose I am."

Potter regarded him in wonderment. "She's some change from Lauren."

"You remember Lauren?"

"Yeah. Who could forget her? You were the envy of every guy in the embassy. Tough luck, about your divorce."

"That was one hell of a mistake."

"The divorce?"

"No. The marriage."

Potter laughed. "I'll let you in on a secret, O'Hara. After two divorces I've finally figured it out. Men don't need love. They need their meals cooked and their shirts ironed and maybe a little action three times a week. But they don't need love."

Nick shook his head. "That's what I thought, too. Until a few weeks ago…"

The phone by the bed suddenly rang.

"Probably for me," said Potter, stubbing out his cigarette. He started across the room, but Nick had already grabbed the receiver.

For a moment there was only silence. Then a man's voice asked, "Mr. Nick O'Hara?"

"Yes."

"You'll find her at the Casa Morro. Midnight. Come alone."

"Who is this?" demanded Nick.

"Get her out of Amsterdam, O'Hara. I'm counting on you."

"Wait!"

The line went dead. Cursing, Nick slammed the receiver down and ran for the door.

"What—where you going?" called Potter.

"Some place called Casa Morro! She'll be there!"

"Hold on!" Potter grabbed the phone. "Let me call Van Dam. We need backup—"

"I'm on my own on this one!"

"O'Hara!"

But Nick was already gone.

FIVE MINUTES AFTER Nick left his hotel, the old man received a call. It was his informant.

"She's at the Casa Morro."

"How do you know this?" asked the old man.

"O'Hara was called. We don't know by whom. He's already left. The Company will be following shortly—you haven't got much time."

"I'll send Kronen for her now."

"What about O'Hara? He'll be in the way."

The old man made a sound of dismissal. "O'Hara? A minor detail," he said. "Kronen can deal with him."

JONATHAN VAN DAM hung up and walked briskly from the phone booth. It had started out as a mild spring evening, but now a chill had crept in with the mist and he found himself buttoning his overcoat. The thought of returning immediately to the warmth of his hotel room was tempting. First, though, he had to stop at a drugstore. A simple excuse was all he needed, a bottle of antacid for an upset stomach, or perhaps some milk of magnesia for sluggish digestion. Should anyone ask, he would have a reason for his short absence from the hotel.

He stopped at an all-night pharmacy. The clerk barely looked up from his magazine as Van Dam walked in and surveyed the shelves of medicine. There was something comforting about seeing all those good American brands. It made him feel close to home. The doorbell tinkled and another customer wandered in, a man in a black overcoat. The man was hacking loudly as he paused by the cold remedies and rubbed his hands together. Van Dam selected a bottle of Maalox, for which he paid eight guilders, and walked out into the mist.

It took him ten minutes to reach the hotel. He opened the Maalox, poured a therapeutic dose down the drain and changed into his pajamas. Then he waited in bed by the phone.

In a short while, things would be happening at Casa Morro. He didn't like to think about it. In all his years with the Company, he'd never once felt bullets whistle past his cheek, never once engaged in violence. He'd certainly never killed a man—in person, that is. When violence was necessary, he'd done it secondhand. Even his wife Claudia's death had been arranged at a comfortable distance. Van Dam disliked the sight of blood. He had been a continent away when Claudia was shot by the prowler. By the time he returned home, the blood had been cleaned up and the floor waxed. It was as if nothing at all had changed, except that he was free, and also extremely wealthy.

But a month later he'd received a note. "The Viking has talked to me," was all it said. The Viking. The man who'd pulled the trigger.

Van Dam had been paralyzed by fear. He'd thought of disappearing, to Mexico perhaps, or South America. But every morning he'd awakened in the bright sunshine of his bedroom and thought, *No, I can't leave my home, my comforts....* So he'd waited. And when the old man at last made contact, Van Dam had been ready to deal.

Information was all that was asked of him. It was minor data at first, the budget of a particular consular office, the takeoff schedule of transport planes. He suffered only a few pangs of guilt. After all, it wasn't the KGB he was dealing with. The old man was merely an entrepreneur, unconcerned with global politics. He could not be considered the enemy. Van Dam could not be considered a traitor.

Before long, though, the demands grew serious. They always arrived without warning. Two rings on the telephone, then silence, and Van Dam would find a package left in the woods or a note stuffed in a tree hollow. He'd never laid eyes on the old man. He didn't even know his real name. He was given a phone number, to be used only in emergencies. The few times he'd used it, the calls had been brief and mediated by a series of clicks and pauses—obviously a string of radio patches, designed to make tracing the calls impossible. Van Dam had found himself trapped by a captor who had no name and no face. But it was not a disagreeable arrangement. He was still safe. He had his house and his fine suits and his brandy. In truth, the old man was a most benign master.

"IT'S MIDNIGHT," SAID SARAH. "Where is he?"

Corrie swept a strand of long black hair off her face and looked up from her desk. "Simon wants proof."

"He's seen my wedding ring."

"Now he wants to see you. But from a safe distance. You'll have to look the part. Go upstairs, second room on your right. Look in the closet. I think the green satin will suit you."

"I don't understand."

The woman sat back and smiled. The lamplight fell fully on her face, and for the first time, Sarah saw the wrinkles around her eyes and mouth. Life hadn't been kind to this woman. "Just put on the dress," she said. "There's no other way."

Sarah climbed the stairs to a hall lighted dimly by a single Tiffany lamp. The room was unlocked. Inside she found a wide brass bed and a closet full of gowns. She changed into the green satin dress and glanced at herself in the mirror. The thin fabric clung to her breasts, and her nipples stood out plainly. But modesty meant nothing to her now. Staying alive was all that mattered. For that she'd wear anything.

Downstairs, Corrie eyed her critically. "You're so thin," she sniffed. "And take off your glasses. You can see without them, can't you?"

"Well enough."

Corrie gestured toward the front window. "Go, then. I'll watch your purse. Take a book if you like, but sit with your face toward the street, so he can see you. It will not take long."

The heavy velvet curtains parted. Sarah stepped through into a cloud of perfumed air. What struck her first were the faces, staring at her from the street, all of them strangers'. Was Geoffrey's among them?

"Sit," said one of the whores, nodding toward a chair. Sarah sat down and was handed a book. She opened the cover and looked intently at the first page. The book was written in Dutch. Even though she couldn't read a word, it was still a shield between her and the men outside. She clung to it until her fingers ached.

For what seemed like forever, Sarah sat as still as a statue. She heard laughter drifting in from the street. Footsteps rained on the cobblestones. From the disco a block away came the steady beat of music. Time slowed down and stopped. Her nerves were stretched to the breaking point. Where was he? Why was it taking so long?

Then, through the noise surrounding her, she heard her name. The book slid from her nerveless fingers and thudded to the floor. She felt the blood drain from her face as she looked up.

Nick was staring incredulously through the window. "*Sarah?*"

Her reaction was instantaneous. She ran. She bolted through the velvet curtains and dashed up the stairs to the room where she'd found the dress. It was mindless flight, the instinct of a desperate woman fleeing from pain. She was afraid of him. He was out to hurt her, to hurt Geoffrey.

If she could just reach the room and lock him out...

But as she scrambled through the door, Nick grabbed her arm. She jerked herself free and flung the door in his face, but he'd already forced his way in. Stumbling backward, she retreated as far as she could, until the backs of her legs collided with the bed. She was trapped.

Shaking uncontrollably, she screamed at him, "Get out!"

He moved forward, his hands held out to her. "Sarah, listen to me—"

"You bastard, I hate you!"

He kept moving closer. The distance between them inexorably melted away. She swung at him. The blow struck him so hard her fingers left red welts on his cheek. She would have hit him again, but he grabbed her wrists and hauled her toward him.

"No," he said, "listen to me. Dammit, will you listen!"

"You *used* me!"

"Sarah—"

"Was it fun? Or was it a chore, bedding the widow for the good old CIA?"

"Stop it!"

"Damn you, Nick!" she cried, flailing helplessly against his grasp. "I loved you! I loved you…." Somehow she found the strength to wrench free again, but her momentum carried her backward and she toppled across the bed. He came down on top of her, his hands closing over her wrists, his body covering hers. He was too heavy to push away. She couldn't fight him any longer. All she could do was lie beneath him, sobbing and struggling vainly, until her strength was gone and she was limp and exhausted.

At last, when he knew all the fight had left her, he released her hands. Slowly, tenderly, he pressed his lips against her mouth.

"I still hate you," she said weakly.

"And I love you," he said.

"Don't lie to me."

He kissed her again, and this time his lips lingered, unwilling to part from hers. "I'm not lying, Sarah. I never have."

"You were working for them all along—"

"No. You're wrong. I'm not with them. They cornered me. Then they told me everything. Sarah, it's over. You can stop running."

"Not until I find him."

"You can't find him."

"What do you mean?"

The look he gave her said everything. Even before he spoke, she knew what his answer would be. "I'm sorry, Sarah. He's dead."

His words hit her like a physical blow. She stared at him, stunned. "He can't be dead. He called me...."

"It wasn't him. It was a Company trick. A recording."

"Then what happened to him?"

"The fire. That was his body they found in the hotel."

She closed her eyes in pain as his words sank in. "I don't understand. I don't understand any of this," she cried.

"The Company set you up, Sarah. They wanted Magus to make a move on you. They hoped he'd get careless. Reveal his whereabouts. But then they lost us. That is, until Berlin."

"And now?"

"It's over. They've called off the operation. We can go home."

Home. It had a magical sound, like a fairy-tale place she no longer believed existed. And Nick was somehow magical, too. But the arms wrapped around her now were made of flesh, not dreams. Nick was real. He'd always been real.

He rose and pulled her from the bed, tugging her in an arc that ended in his arms. "Let's go home, Sarah," he whispered. "First thing in the morning, let's fly the hell out of here."

"I can't believe it's over," she murmured. "I can't believe you're really here...."

In answer he turned her face to meet his. It was the gentlest of kisses, not one of hunger, but of tenderness; it told her she was safe, that she'd always be safe, as long as Nick O'Hara was around.

Tucked under his arm, she walked with him down the hall, toward the stairs. It would be cold outside. But he would keep her warm, the way his jacket had kept her warm on that rainy day in London. They reached the top of the stairs. The foyer came into view, right below them. And Nick stopped dead in his tracks.

At first she didn't understand. All she saw was his shocked face. Then her eyes followed the direction of his gaze.

Below them, at the foot of the steps, a dark pool of blood was soaking into a blue Persian rug. And flung out across the wood floor, her hair mingling with her own blood, was Corrie.

Chapter Fourteen

A SHADOW FELL ACROSS THE FOYER WALL. Someone was walking in the sitting room, just out of sight. The shadow grew larger; it was approaching the stairs. Nick and Sarah couldn't flee through the street exit without passing through the foyer, crossing the killer's line of view. There was only one other way to run, and that was up the hallway.

Nick grabbed Sarah's hand and hauled her toward a far staircase. From the sitting room came a woman's cry, running footsteps, then two sharp thuds—bullets muffled by a silencer. The hall seemed to stretch on forever. If the killer started up the stairs now, he'd spot them.

Panic sent Sarah scrambling up the narrow staircase to the room above. They had reached the attic. Nick softly closed the door, but there was no lock. They left the lights off. Through a tiny window came the faint glow of a city night. Scattered in the darkness about their feet were vague shapes and shadows: boxes, old furniture, a rack of clothes.

Nick ducked behind a trunk, pulling Sarah into his arms. She pressed her face against his chest and felt the pounding of his heart.

From downstairs came the crack of splintering wood. Someone was kicking the doors open. Methodically, he made his way down the hall, toward their staircase. *Please stop,* she prayed. *Please don't search the attic....*

Nick pushed her to the floor. "Stay down," he hissed.

"Where are you going?"

"When the chance comes, *move.*"

"But Nick..." He'd already slipped away into the darkness. The footsteps were coming up the attic staircase.

Sarah hugged the floor, afraid to move, afraid to even breathe. The steps creaked closer and closer. With no time left, she searched frantically in the darkness for a weapon, for something with which to defend herself. The floor around her was bare.

The door flew open, slamming into the wall. Light flooded in from the stairway.

In that same instant, she heard the unmistakable sound of a fist colliding with flesh, then a heavy thud shook the floor. She leaped up to find Nick grappling with the killer, a man she'd never seen before. They rolled across the floor, over and over. Nick threw a second punch, but the blow glanced off the killer's cheek. Nick's advantage had been surprise—he wasn't a trained fighter. The killer, bloodied as he was, managed to break free and slam his fist upward into Nick's stomach. Nick grunted and rolled away. The killer dove across the floor toward a pistol lying a few feet away.

Still stunned by the last blow, Nick couldn't move fast enough. The killer's fingers closed around the gun. Desperately Nick lunged for the other man's wrist, but he could only reach his forearm. Slowly, inexorably, the barrel turned toward Nick's face.

Sarah didn't have time to think, only to react. Nick's death was inches away. She sprang from the trunk. Her foot shot up in a clumsy arc and connected with the killer's hand. The pistol flew up and clattered somewhere beyond a pile of boxes. The killer, thrown off balance, couldn't fend off the next blow.

Nick's fist caught him squarely on the jaw. With a look of total surprise, the killer fell backward. His head slammed against a trunk. He slumped to the floor, knocked out cold.

Nick staggered to his feet. "Get going!" he gasped.

She led the way down the attic staircase to the second-floor hallway. Nick was a few paces behind her. Shattered stained glass from the Tiffany lamp littered the carpet. As she sprinted toward the stairs, she suddenly thought of Corrie's body in the foyer. It made her sick to think of running through the blood, but she'd have to do it to reach the front door.

She headed down the stairs, forcing her feet to keep moving. It would take only a few steps to cross the floor, then she'd be out. She'd be safe.

She didn't see the man waiting in the foyer until it was too late. His movement was only a flash, like a snake striking from the shadows. Pain clawed her arm. She was wrenched sideways, into an embrace so tight she couldn't scream. A gloved hand and the heartless gleam of a gun swept past her field of vision. The weapon was not aimed at her; it was aimed at the top of the stairs, where Nick was standing.

The gun went off.

Nick jerked backward, as if punched in the chest. Blood blossomed across his shirt. Sarah screamed. Again and again she screamed Nick's name as she was dragged toward the door. The cold night air hit her face. Bright lights blurred past, and then she was thrust into the back seat of a car. The door slammed shut. She looked up; a gun was pointed at her head.

Only then did she see Kronen's face, the pale blond hair, the waxy smile. In a thousand train stations, in a thousand cities, he had waited for her. It was the face of her nightmares.

It was a face from hell.

VAN DAM WAS still sitting by the phone when Tarasoff called him with word of the bloody fiasco. O'Hara was in the emergency room. The Fontaine woman hadn't been found. Shaken by the news, Van Dam managed to sound appropriately upset.

After the call he rose and began to pace the room. He was uneasy. He worried about this newfound link to the F. Berkman company. That transfer of funds to a contract killer had been incredibly careless. Now Potter sniffed blood, and the persistent little bastard would never let up. Roy Potter was like a dog with his teeth sunk in too deep to let go. Somehow he had to be thrown off track; Van Dam's future depended on it. If the old man were captured, he was likely to be a pragmatist. He would use whatever chips he had to bargain for freedom. And what he had was information: specifically, names. Van Dam's would be among the first revealed.

Events were piling up too fast. If the worst happened, would he have time enough to escape?

Prison. Van Dam shuddered. Soon after Claudia's death, he'd thought about prison, about being shut away in a small, dark room. He'd thought of the four walls, pressing in around him. He'd thought of unwashed bodies and rough hands and things that happened between men who were trapped together. He'd been terrified by those thoughts, and now the terror returned.

He decided to pack, just in case. In minutes the suitcase was ready. He considered his sequence of action. Lock the door. Take the stairs. Hail a taxi. He'd go straight to the Russian embassy. It was a move he'd reserved for only the most desperate of situations, a move he'd hoped to avoid. He'd never cared for the Russians. He wondered how it would be, spending all the years of his life in a dreary Moscow flat. God, no. Was that what lay ahead?

But surely the Russians would treat him well! They made special arrangements for defectors, gave them large flats and abundant privileges. He wouldn't be left to starve. He would be taken care of.

When he was a boy in West Virginia, he and his mother had lived in a two-room shack owned by the mining company. His mother would dump their trash in the woods out back, and when he went to use the outhouse at night, he'd hear the rats, hundreds of them, an army watching from the darkness. He'd do anything to avoid that walk to the outhouse. He would huddle in his bed, fighting the cramps, the urgency. For Van Dam poverty had been more than uncomfortable; it had been horrifying.

He was too deep in thought to notice the footsteps in the hallway. The sudden knock on his door made him jerk around in fright.

"Yes?"

"Status report, sir. May I come in?"

Shaking with relief, Van Dam called through the door: "Look, Tarasoff just called me. Unless there's something new..."

"There is, sir."

Some instinct made Van Dam slide the chain in place. He opened the door a crack.

Just as he did, the door flew open and slammed into his face. Wood splinters rained on the carpet. Van Dam staggered backward, almost knocked senseless by the pain.

He tried to focus. A man was standing in the doorway, a man dressed entirely in black, a man who should be dead. Van Dam's gaze slowly took in something else, something the man was holding. *Why?* he wanted to scream. His whole universe shrank to the size of a small deadly circle, the mouth of a gun.

"This is for Eva," said the man.

He pulled the trigger three times. Three bullets ripped into Van Dam's chest and exploded.

The impact hurled Van Dam to the floor. His scream of pain dribbled to a gurgle, then faded to silence. He had one last, brief image of light as he lay there, a few short seconds that filled him with wonder. It was only the glow of a hotel lamp. Then, bit by bit, the light was blotted out, like dusk falling gently into night.

SARAH HUDDLED ON the wood floor and hugged her knees to her chest. Her teeth were chattering. The room was unheated, and the green satin dress provided little warmth. She had been thrust into darkness. The only light came through a small window high above; it was moonlight, glowing through the clouds. She wondered what time it was. Three o'clock? Four? She'd lost track of the hours. Terror had turned this night into an eternity.

She closed her eyes tightly, but all she could see was Nick's face, his look of surprise and pain, and then the blood, spreading magically across his shirt. A terrible ache rose in her chest, an ache that flooded her throat and spilled out into tears that ran down her cheeks. She dropped her face against her knees, and the tears soaked the satin dress, turning it cold and wet. *Please be alive!* she prayed. *Dear God, please let him be alive!*

But even if he was alive, she was beyond his help. She was beyond anyone's help. In the darkness it had come to her: She was going to die. With this certainty had come a strange peace, a final acknowledgment that her fate was inevitable and that struggling against it was hopeless. She was too cold and tired to care. After days of terror, she at last saw her own death drawing near, and she was calm.

This new peace brought everything sharply into focus. Without panic clouding her every perception, she could study the situation coolly, clinically, the way she once had studied bacteria beneath the lens of her microscope. She concluded that the situation was hopeless.

She was being held in a large storeroom on the fourth floor of an old building. The only way out was through the door, which was now bolted solidly. The window was for ventilation; it was small and too high to reach. The smell of coffee permeated the air and she remembered the roasting ovens she'd seen on the ground floor, and the loading platform, covered with burlap bags stamped F. Berkman, Koffie, Hele Bonen. At the time she'd shuddered, thinking that one of those burlap bags could easily conceal her body.

There might be some small hope from the fact this building was not a residence, but a business. Workers would have to show up sometime. If she screamed, someone would hear her.

Then she remembered that it was Sunday morning. No one would be coming to work today. No one except Kronen.

She stiffened at the creak of footsteps. Someone was climbing the stairs. A door opened and banged shut. Through the cracks she saw light shining from the room next door. Two men were speaking in Dutch. One was Kronen. The other voice was low and hoarse, almost inaudible. The footsteps crossed the room and headed toward her door. She froze as the bolt squealed open.

Light burst in brightly from the next room. She fought to see the faces of the two men standing in the doorway, but at first all she could make out were silhouettes. Kronen flicked on the wall switch. What she saw in that initial flood of fluorescent light made her cringe.

The man towering above her had no face.

The eyes were pale and lashless and as lifeless as cold stones. But as the man took in her appearance, his eyes moved; it was his first sign of life. She realized she was staring at a mask. The face was covered by a featureless shield of flesh-toned rubber. Only the eyes and mouth were visible. What hair he had left grew in wispy white patches on a naked scalp. With a macabre touch of fashion, he had swathed his neck in a bright red silk scarf.

The lashless eyes settled on her face. Before he spoke she knew who he was. This was the man called Magus. The man Geoffrey should have killed.

"Mrs. Simon Dance," he said. The voice came out in a whisper. His vocal cords, like his face, must have been scarred in the fire. "Stand up, so I may see you better."

She cowered as he grabbed her wrist. "Please," she begged. "Don't hurt me. I don't know anything—really, I don't."

"But you do know something. Why did you leave Washington?"

"It was the CIA. They tricked me…."

"Whom are you working for?"

"No one!"

"Then why did you come to Amsterdam?"

"I thought I'd find Geoffrey—I mean Simon—please, let me go!"

"Let you go? Why should I?"

Her voice stopped working. She stared at him, unable to think of a single good reason why he should let her live. He would kill her, of course. All the pleading in the world wouldn't change things.

Magus turned to Kronen, who was looking profoundly amused. "This is the woman you spoke of?" he asked Kronen incredulously. "This stupid creature? It took you two weeks to find *her?*"

Kronen's smile vanished. "She had help," he pointed out.

"She found Eva without help."

"She is smarter than she looks."

"Undoubtedly." The mask turned back to Sarah. "Where is your husband?"

"I don't know."

"You found Eva. And Helga. Surely you must know how to find your own husband."

She bent her head and stared down at the floor. "He's dead," she whispered.

"You're lying."

"He died in Berlin. The fire."

"Who says this? The CIA?"

"Yes."

"And you believe them?" At her silent nod, the man turned to Kronen in fury. "This woman is worthless! We've wasted our time! If Dance shows up for her, he's a fool."

The contempt in his voice made Sarah stiffen. To Magus her life was worth nothing more than an insect's. Killing her would be as easy for him as rubbing his heel in the dirt. There would be no regret, no pity; all he'd feel would be distaste. A knot of anger tightened in her belly. With sudden violence her chin came up. If she had to die, it wouldn't be as an insect. Swallowing hard, she lashed out at him defiantly.

"And if my husband does show up," she said, "I hope he sends you straight to hell."

The pale eyes in the mask registered a faint flicker of surprise. "Hell? We'll meet down there in any event. An eternity together, your husband and I. I've already felt the flames. I know what it's like to burn alive."

"I had nothing to do with it."

"But your husband did."

"He's dead! Killing *me* won't make him suffer!"

"I don't kill for the dead. I kill for the living. Dance is alive."

"I'm just an innocent—"

"In this business," he said slowly, "there are no innocents."

"And your wife? What was she?"

"My wife?" He stared off, as though suddenly hypnotized by something on the wall. "My wife…yes. Yes, she was an innocent. I never thought she would be the one…" He turned to her. "Do you know how she died?"

"I'm sorry. I'm sorry for what happened. But can't you see it had nothing to do with me?"

"I saw it. I watched her die."

"Please, won't you listen—"

"From my bedroom window, I saw her walk through the garden to the car. She stopped beside the roses and waved.

I have never forgotten that moment. How she waved. And smiled." He tapped his forehead. "It is like a photograph, here, in my mind. The last time I saw her alive…"

He fell silent. Then he turned to Kronen and said, "Before morning move her to a safer place. Where she cannot be heard. If Dance does not come for her in two days, kill her. Make it slow. You know how."

Kronen was smiling. Sarah shuddered as he reached down and playfully ran a strand of her hair through his fingers. "Yes," he said softly. "I know how…." Suddenly his body went rigid, and his jaw snapped up.

Somewhere in the building, an alarm had gone off. Over the door a red light blinked on the warning panel.

"Someone is inside!" said Kronen.

Magus's eyes were bright as diamonds. "It's Dance," he said. "It must be Dance…."

Kronen already had his gun drawn as they ran from the room. The door slammed shut. The bolt squealed into place. Sarah was left alone, her eyes fixed on the red warning light flashing on and off.

The effect was hypnotic. Red, the universal color of alarm, the color of blood, the color of fear, went on blinking. You are going to die, it screamed at her. In two days you are going to die.

Just moments ago she had accepted her own death calmly. Now fear was pumping adrenaline by the quart into her veins. She wanted to live! In panic she lunged at the door, but it was made of solid oak and impossibly strong. Two days, her brain kept repeating. Two days, and then she'd feel Kronen's knife. The way Eve had felt it. But Sarah couldn't let herself think that far ahead. If she did she'd go mad with terror.

The light was still flashing. It seemed to blink faster and faster, accelerating with the pounding of her heart.

She fell back against the door and stared around the room. In their haste to leave, Kronen and Magus had left the lights on. For the first time, she examined her surroundings.

The storeroom was not empty. Cardboard boxes, stamped with F. Berkman, were piled in a corner. She turned first to the boxes and found only a wrinkled invoice, made out in Dutch. Then she spotted a band of strapping tape around the largest box. She tore off the tape and pulled it taut a few times, testing its strength. Used right, it could easily strangle a man. She didn't know if she had the power—or the nerve—to do it. But in her current situation, any weapon— even four feet of old tape—was a gift from heaven.

Next she examined the window. Immediately she discarded it as an escape route. She'd never fit through.

There was only one way out of the room: the door. But how was she to get out?

The stacking chairs gave her an idea. A single chair was light enough to lift and swing. Good. One more weapon. Stacked together, the chairs were so heavy she could barely drag them across the floor. Her plan just might work.

She tugged the stack of chairs to one side of the doorway and tied the strapping tape to a leg of the bottom chair. She strung out the tape and crouched on the opposite side of the doorway. She pulled her end of the tape. It rose a few inches off the floor. If her timing was right, it would work as a trip wire. It would buy her a few seconds, enough time to get through the door.

Over and over she rehearsed her moves. Then she ran through everything with her eyes closed, until she could do it blind. It had to work; it was her only chance.

She was ready. She climbed onto one of the chairs and disconnected the fluorescent light tubes in the ceiling. The room was plunged into darkness. It would be to her advantage; she now knew her way around the room in the darkness. As she was jumping off the chair, she heard what sounded like thunder. It was gunfire echoing off the buildings. Outside there were shouts, then more gunfire. The building was in an uproar. In all the confusion, her escape would be easier.

First she had to draw someone's attention. She took a chair to the window. At the count of three, she swung. The chair shattered the glass.

She heard another shout, then footsteps pounding up the stairs. She brought the chair to the doorway and groped in the darkness for her end of the tape. Where was it?

The footsteps had reached the next room and were crossing to her door. The bolt squealed. Desperately her fingers swept across the floor and came up with the tape just as the door swung open. A man lunged into the room, moving so fast she barely had time to react. She jerked on the tape. It snagged the man by the foot. His momentum almost wrenched the tape out of her hand. Something clattered across the floor. The man pitched forward and fell flat on his belly. At once he scrambled to his knees and started to rise.

Sarah didn't let him. She swung the chair, slamming it on his head. She felt, more than heard, the heavy thud against his skull, and the horror of what she'd done made her drop the chair.

He wasn't moving. But as she rummaged through his pockets, he began to moan, a low, terrible sound of agony. So she hadn't killed him. She found no gun in his pockets.

Had he dropped it? There was no time to search the dark room on her hands and knees. Better to run while she could.

She fled the storeroom and bolted the door behind her. One down, she thought with a raw sense of satisfaction. How many more to go?

Now to find her way out of the building. Three flights of stairs and then a front entrance. Could she slip through it all without being seen? No time to think, no time to plan. Every nerve, every muscle, was focused on this last dash for freedom. She was nothing but reflexes now, an animal, moving on instinct.

She dashed through the office and started down the stairs. But a few steps into her descent, she froze. Voices rose from below. They were growing louder. Kronen was climbing the steps—her only escape route was cut off.

She scrambled into the office and closed and bolted the door. Unlike the other door, it was not solid wood. It would hold them off for only a few minutes, no longer. She had to find another way out.

The storeroom was a dead end. But in the office, above the desk, there was a window....

She climbed up on the desk and peered out. All she could see was mist, swirling in the darkness. She tugged at the sash, but it wouldn't budge. Only then did she see that the window had been nailed shut. For security, no doubt. She'd have to break the glass.

Clutching the sash for support, she kicked. The first three tries were worthless; her heel bounced harmlessly off the glass. But on the fourth kick, the window shattered. Shards flew out and rained onto the tiles below. Cold air hit her face. Peering outside, she saw she was at a gable window. A few feet down was a steeply tiled roof that dropped off into darkness. What lay below? It could be a deadly three story fall to the street, or it could slope down to an adjacent roof. In the older blocks of Amsterdam, she'd seen how the buildings were crammed side by side, the roofs running in an almost continuous line. In this mist she had no way of knowing what the darkness hid. Only a fall would tell her....

The tiles would be slippery. She'd be better off bare-foot. She bent down and pulled off her shoes. With sudden alarm she noticed the blood on her ankle. Her brain registered no pain; all it noted was the brightness of the blood as it oozed steadily down her foot. Even as she stared at it, mesmerized, she was aware of new noises: Kronen's pounding on the office door, and from the storeroom the loud moans of the man she'd knocked unconscious.

Time was running out.

She stepped through the window, onto the sill. Her dress caught on a shard of broken glass; with a desperate jerk, she ripped the fabric free. For a few seconds she clung by one hand to the sash and groped for another handhold, for some way to pull herself up over the gable. But the roof was too high, and the eaves hung too far out. She was trapped.

The sound of splintering wood forced her to act. Her choice was simple now. A quick death or a painful one. To fall into the darkness, to feel a split second of terror and then to feel nothing at all, would be infinitely better than to die at Kronen's hands. She could stand the thought of dying. Pain was another matter.

She heard the door give way, followed by Kronen's shout of rage. With that shout ringing in her ears, she dropped from the window.

She landed on a roof a few feet below and began sliding helplessly down the tiles. There was nothing to grab on to, nothing to stop her descent. The tiles were too wet; she felt them slipping away beneath her clawing fingers. Her legs dropped over the edge. For an instant she clung to the roof gutter, her feet dangling uselessly. The night sky swirled with mist above her, a sky more beautiful than any she had seen, because it was her last. Her numb fingers could hold on no longer. The gutter slipped from her grasp. Eternity rushed toward her from the darkness.

Chapter Fifteen

"It's only a flesh wound."

"Get back in that bed, O'Hara!" barked Potter.

Nick stalked across his hospital room and flung the closet door open. It was empty. "Where's my damn shirt?"

"You can't walk out of here—you've lost too much blood."

"My shirt, Potter."

"In the garbage. You bled all over it, remember?"

Cursing, Nick wriggled out of his hospital top and glanced down at the bandages on his left shoulder. The pain shot they'd given him in the emergency room was wearing off. He was starting to feel as if someone had taken a sledge-hammer to his upper torso. But he couldn't lie around here waiting for something to happen. Too many precious hours had already slipped away.

"Look," said Potter, "why don't you just lie down and let me handle things?"

Nick turned on him in fury. "You mean like you've han-dled everything else?"

"And what the hell good are *you* gonna do her out there? Tell me that."

Nick turned away, grief suddenly replacing his anger. He slammed his fist against the wall. "I had her, Roy! I had her in my arms...."

"We'll find her."

"Like you found Eve Fontaine?" Nick shot back.

Potter's face tightened. "No. No, I hope not."

"Then what are you doing about it?" cried Nick.

"We're still waiting for that guy you knocked out to start talking. All we've gotten out of him so far is gibberish. And we're tracking down that other lead, the Berkman Company."

"Search the building!"

"Can't. We need Van Dam's go-ahead and we can't reach him. We also need more evidence—"

"Screw the evidence," muttered Nick, turning toward the door.

"Where you going?"

"To do some breaking and entering."

"O'Hara, you can't go there without backup!" He fol-lowed Nick into the corridor.

"I've seen your backup. I think I'd rather have a gun."

"You know how to shoot one?"

"I learn real fast."

"Look, let me clear this through Van Dam—"

"Van Dam?" Nick snorted. "That guy wouldn't clear a trip to the john!" He punched the elevator button, then glanced at Potter's clothes. "Give me your shirt."

"What?"

"Breaking and entering's bad enough. I don't need a charge of indecent exposure."

"You're nuts! I'm not giving you my shirt. I'll get it back full of bullet holes."

Nick hit the elevator button again. "Thanks for the vote of confidence."

The elevator doors suddenly whished open. Potter looked up in annoyance as agent Tarasoff stepped out. "Sir?" said Tarasoff. "We've got a new development."

"Now what?"

"Just came over the police radio. There's been a report of gunfire. The Berkman building."

Nick and Potter stared at each other.

"Gunfire!" said Nick. "My God. Sarah…"

"Where's Van Dam?" Potter snapped.

"I don't know, sir. He still doesn't answer his hotel phone."

"That's it. Let's go, O'Hara!" As the three men rode the elevator down to street level, Potter muttered to Nick, "I don't know why I should put my career on the line for you. I don't even like you. But you're right. We've gotta move in now. By the time Van Dam gives the okay, we'll all be in a damned nursing home." He glanced sharply at Tarasoff. "And that comment's off the record. You got that?"

"Yes, sir."

Potter suddenly eyed Tarasoff's build. "What size are you?"

"Excuse me, sir?"

"Shirt size."

"Uh…sixteen."

"That'll do. Lend your shirt to Mr. O'Hara here. I'm sick of looking at his hairy chest. Don't worry, I'll see he doesn't get blood all over it."

Tarasoff immediately complied, but he looked distinctly ill at ease in his undershirt and jacket. They headed for the parking garage.

"Get on the radio and have the team meet us at the Berkman building."

"Shall I keep trying to get hold of Van Dam?"

Potter hesitated as he caught Nick's glance of warning. "No," he said at last. "For now, let's keep this our own little secret."

Tarasoff gave him a puzzled look as he opened the car door. "Yes, sir."

Nick slid into the back seat. "You know, Potter," he said, easing into Tarasoff's shirt, "maybe you're not as dumb as I thought."

Potter shook his head grimly. "On the other hand, O'Hara, maybe I am," he said. "Maybe I am."

WITH A HOLLOW thud, Sarah landed on her back.

The first thing she felt was wonderment. She was alive. By God, she was alive! For what seemed like hours, she lay there in the darkness, the breath knocked out of her, the sky spinning. Then she saw the gable window, not more than fifteen feet above her, and she realized she had fallen only a short distance. She was lying on an adjacent rooftop.

Kronen's shouts jolted her into action. He was standing above at the window, barking out commands. From somewhere in the darkness below, other voices responded. His men were searching the ground for her body. They wouldn't find it. Soon they'd turn their attention to the rooftop.

She scrambled to her feet. Already her eyes had adjusted to the darkness. She could discern the faint outline of roof against sky. Then it suddenly struck her that it wasn't just her eyes; the sky had lightened. The difference was almost imperceptible; the significance was frightening. Dawn was coming. In minutes she'd be an easy target, scurrying across the tiles. Before the sun rose, she had to make her way to safety.

Flashlight beams streaked below. Footsteps circled the building, and then the men shouted again. They had not found her body.

Sarah was already crawling up the next slope of tiles. The angle was shallow, and she easily reached the apex. She slipped over the top and eased her way down toward the next roof. The mist seemed to close around her in a thick, protective veil. Her dress was soaked from the wet tiles, and the satin clung to her like a freezing second skin. Her bare feet scraped across mortar, which rubbed them raw, but the cold had numbed them so completely she felt no pain. Terror had robbed her of every distraction; the unrelenting awareness of her own death blocked everything else from her mind.

She slid off the tiles onto a flat gravel surface and ran through the lifting darkness to a rooftop door. The knob was ice-cold. The door was locked. She beat it with her fists, beat it until her hands were bruised and she was weak and sobbing. The door did not open. Whirling around, she looked for another escape route—another door, a stairway. With every second the sky brightened. She had to get off this roof! Then a man's far-off shout told her she'd already been spotted.

The next roof loomed before her, a sheer wall of slate. Except for a gable window far above and an antenna at the top, the surface was smooth as ice. She could never climb it.

The shouts came again, closer. A loose tile clattered from the roof and smashed to the sidewalk. She spun around and saw Kronen lowering himself out the broken gable window. He was coming after her.

Like a trapped bird, she circled her rooftop cage, searching desperately for a way off. At the rear of the building, there was only a sheer drop to an alley. She dashed to the other side and stared down. Far below, through fingers of mist, she saw the street. There were no balconies, no stairways, to break her fall if she jumped. There was only the wet pavement, waiting to receive her body.

She heard something clatter across the tiles. Kronen cursed; his gun had fallen to the street. He was already over the top of the second roof. In seconds he'd be on her.

Her eyes darted back to the smooth slate roof, an impassable barrier between her and safety. Staring up, she felt a cold drizzle descend on her face and mingle with her tears. *If only I could fly!* she thought. *If only I could soar away!* Then, through her tears, she sighted a black wire running down the roof from the antenna. Was it strong enough to support her weight? If it broke she might tumble over the edge to the street.

The sound of Kronen's feet hitting the gravel rooftop tore away her last threads of hesitation. Reaching for the wire, she dragged herself up the slate roof. Her toes slid down a few inches, then held. As footsteps crunched across the gravel toward her, she clambered up the roof, out of Kronen's reach.

His curse echoed off the buildings. She didn't dare look back to see if he was following. Every ounce of her concentration was focused ahead, on the soaring surface of gray slate. Her fingers ached. Her feet were raw and swollen. The roof seemed to rise forever; at any moment she expected to hear gunfire from Kronen's men on the ground below, to feel a bullet slam into her back. All she heard was the wind and Kronen's angry shouts. Even without his gun, he could easily kill her. A toss of his knife would send her hurtling to the street. But she knew that Magus wanted her alive. For now.

She kept moving, unable to see her goal, unable to judge how much farther she had to climb. Surely it couldn't be far! she thought desperately. She couldn't hold on much longer.

Her feet gave way beneath her. With a cry she felt her legs swing free. Gravity was pulling her relentlessly downward, an unshakable force she couldn't fight. Her arms were exhausted. As she struggled for a foothold, her right calf twisted into a cramp. She felt the wire slipping through her hands. Then, nudged aside by a sudden breath of wind, the mist faded and she saw, only inches away, the top of the roof.

Somehow she found the strength to drag herself upward. At last her fingers closed around the antenna. The metal felt so solid, so strong! She pulled herself those last few inches to the top. There she collapsed against the hard angle of slate, her arms hugging the sides of the roof. She had to rest, just for a few seconds. She had to let the cramp ease from her calf.

But when she raised her head and looked down at the other side, she saw there was nowhere else to go. She had reached the end of the line. No other rooftop lay below to catch her. There was only a drop to the street.

Tears of despair streamed down her face. She lowered her head and sobbed into the slate, sobbed like a terrified child at what she could not escape. The sound of her own cries drowned out everything else.

Then gradually she was aware of another sound, faint at first, but growing louder: two notes piercing the dawn, over and over. A siren.

Kronen heard it, too. He stared up at her like a man possessed. Pacing back and forth, he searched for some other way up. There was none. Cursing, he grabbed the wire and started up the roof. He was coming after her.

In disbelief she watched him climb. He was long and wiry; he moved like a monkey up the slate roof. Frantically she worked at the wire, trying in vain to disconnect it from the antenna. She'd never get it loose in time. With nowhere else to go, she backed away from the edge. She could already hear his breathing, loud and harsh, as he neared the top. She tried to stand. Tottering on bruised feet, she waited for him. The siren grew louder. Just a few moments more! That's all she needed!

Kronen's fingers closed over the top. Frozen, she watched as his head rose above the peak. His eyes locked on hers. She saw no anger or hatred; what she saw was infinitely more terrifying: anticipation. He was looking forward to her death.

"No!" she screamed, her voice piercing the mist. "No!"

She lashed out at him. Her fingers clawed at his eyes, forcing him backward, toward the edge. He grabbed her wrist, twisting it so hard she cried out. Wrenching free, she stumbled and almost lost her balance. He scrambled onto the top. Slowly he came toward her.

For a moment they stood staring at each other, the wind making them sway uneasily on the wet slate. It had come to this—the two of them alone on a rooftop. One of them would not survive. She would not let him take her alive.

His hand slid into his jacket. A knife appeared. Even in the dull gray dawn, the blade seemed to glitter. He held it easily, almost casually, as if it were nothing more than a toy.

She took another step backward. How far did she have left? How far until retreat took her to the other edge? The blade moved closer. Taking her alive was no longer his goal. He was going to kill her. Through a curtain of mist, she saw him coil for the spring. She saw the blade, thrusting toward her. Her arms crossed in front of her, an automatic gesture of protection. Pain shot through her forearm as the blade came down on naked flesh. She crumpled to her knees. His shoes creaked as he came to stand over her. His heel planted itself heavily on a fold of her dress, trapping her against the roof. She could not escape now. She couldn't even stand. In silent dread she watched the blade rise again in a deadly arc.

All her feral instincts rose to a last, desperate act of survival. With a cry she hurled herself at his knees. He staggered backward, tottering on one leg, struggling for balance. She didn't let him regain it. She lunged at his foot.

The blow swept his ankle out from under him. He twisted, clawing to hold on. The knife clattered down the slate. As he started to drop toward the street, he caught the top of the roof, but only for a second. His eyes met Sarah's; it was a look of infinite surprise. He slid away, his eyes still staring upward, his arms reaching toward the sky. She shut her eyes. Long after he hit the street below, his scream was still echoing in her ears.

She was going to be sick. The world seemed to spin around her. Dropping her head, she pressed her cheek against the cold, wet slate and fought off the nausea. There she huddled, shivering, as the sound of sirens and voices rose up from the street. She was too cold, too exhausted, to move. Only when she heard Nick's shout did she stir.

It's not possible, she thought. *I'm imagining things. I saw him die….*

Yet there he was, standing on the street, waving wildly at her. Tears sprang to her eyes. She wanted to shout that she loved him, that she would always love him, but she was crying too hard for anything sensible to come out.

"Don't move, Sarah!" shouted Nick. "We're calling for a fire truck to get you down!"

She wiped the tears away and nodded. *It's all over*, she thought, watching three more police cars pull up with sirens blaring. *It's all over….*

But she had forgotten about Magus.

A loud slam made her turn and look down. A door had opened and closed. Magus emerged on the graveled roof just below. He carried a rifle. Only she could see him. From the street where Nick and the police stood, Magus was invisible. He was a lone man, trapped on a rooftop. A man about to make one last gesture in the name of vengeance. For a moment he stood staring at her, like a man longing for the one thing he cannot have. Then slowly he raised his rifle. She watched the barrel point up at her and waited for the fatal blast.

The rifle's crack thundered over the rooftops. *Where is the pain?* she thought, *Why don't I feel the pain…?*

Then, in wonderment, she saw Magus stagger backward, his shirt splattered brightly with blood. The rifle thudded to the gravel. He made a sound, a death cry that might have been only a name. With his eyes wide open, he collapsed on his back. He didn't move.

On another rooftop something glittered. It drew Sarah's attention away from the bloodied body, beckoning her gaze with the brightness of spun gold. The sun burst through the last veil of mist. It fell in a brilliant beam upon the head and shoulders of a man standing on a high roof two buildings away. The man lowered his rifle. The wind whipped his shirt and hair. He was looking at her. She could not see his face, but she knew, in that instant, who he was. In a trance she tried to stand up. As he faded from view, she tried to reach out to him, to call him back, to thank him before he disappeared forever.

"Geoffrey!" she screamed.

The wind swept her voice up and carried it away. "No, come back! Come back!" she screamed, over and over. But all she saw was a last glimpse of golden hair, and then there was only a wet, empty roof, sparkling beneath the morning sun.

ON THE STREET below Sarah, the rifle crack echoed like thunder over the rooftops. A half dozen cops immediately dived for cover. Nick froze in alarm. "What's going on?" he cried.

Potter turned and barked to Tarasoff, "Who the hell's shooting up there?"

"Not one of ours, sir. Maybe the cops—"

"That was a rifle, dammit!"

"It was not my men," said a Dutch police officer, peering out from the safety of a nearby doorway.

Nick looked up and saw immediately that Sarah was still alive. Frantically his eyes searched the surrounding windows. Who had fired the shot? Was Sarah the target? Down here, on the street, he was totally helpless to save her. Panicking, he shouted at Potter, "For God's sake, *do something!*"

"Tarasoff!" yelled Potter. "Get your men up there! Find out where the hell that shot came from!" He turned to the Dutch cop. "How long till the ladder gets here?"

"Five, ten minutes."

"She'll be dead by then!" said Nick, taking off toward the buildings. He didn't look twice as he passed the dead body lying on the blood-spattered sidewalk. He had to get to Sarah.

"O'Hara!" shouted Potter. "We've got to clear the building first!"

But Nick was already across the street and heading for the door. The building was unlocked. Inside, he took the stairway two steps at a time. All the way up, he was terrified he would hear a second rifle shot, terrified that he'd emerge on the roof and find Sarah dead. But all he heard were his own footsteps pounding up the stairs.

Somewhere below, a door slammed shut. Potter's voice shouted, "O'Hara?"

Nick kept going.

The wide steps led to a small staircase that spiraled to the roof. He dashed up the last steps and scrambled through the door at the top.

Outside, the sun was shining. Nick halted, stunned by the sudden burst of light and by the horror of what lay in the gravel at his feet. The dead eyes of a faceless man stared up at him. A red silk scarf fluttered in the wind, as bright and alarming as the blood seeping slowly from the man's chest. Beside him lay a rifle.

The roof door flew open. Potter rushed through and almost collided with Nick.

"My God!" said Potter, staring at the body. "It's Magus! Did he shoot himself?"

From a roof above them came a sudden wail, a ghostly sound of despair. Nick looked up in alarm.

Sarah was reaching out helplessly, as though pleading with the wind. She didn't notice Nick or Potter; she was gazing into the distance, at something only she could see. What she screamed next made Nick shudder. It didn't make sense; it was the cry of a terrified woman, driven to hysteria. He turned and looked in the direction of her gaze. He saw only rooftops, wet and sparkling in the sunlight. And echoing off the buildings, he heard Sarah's voice, over and over, screaming to a man who did not exist.

When they finally brought her down from the roof, she was quiet and composed. Nick was right beside her as they lowered her onto the stretcher. She looked so small and weak and cold. There was so much blood on her arms. He was scarcely aware of what he said or did at that moment; he only knew he wanted to be near her.

Down on the street, the ambulance was waiting. "Let me ride with her," Nick muttered, brushing off Potter's restraining hand. "She needs me."

"Just keep out of their way, O'Hara."

Nick climbed in beside Sarah's stretcher. She was awake. "Sarah?"

She turned her head and gazed at him in wonder. "I thought I'd never see you again," she whispered.

"Sarah, I love you."

Potter stuck his head in the ambulance. "For God's sake, O'Hara! Give 'em some room to work in!"

Nick glanced around and saw the two attendants scowling at him.

"No, please!" Sarah pleaded. "Let him stay. I want him to stay."

Potter gave the attendants a shrug of helplessness. Grumbling, they went on with their work. From the looks they exchanged, it was obvious what they thought of this extra passenger. But they decided it was better to leave Nick alone. From experience they knew that frantic husbands could be stubborn, unreasonable creatures. And this one, obviously, was very, very frantic.

Chapter Sixteen

WITH AN OVERWHELMING SENSE OF RELIEF, Roy Potter watched the ambulance pull away from the curb. Even after it had turned the corner, he could still hear the siren's two notes piercing the quiet Sunday morning. As the sound faded into the maze of Amsterdam streets, Potter stifled a yawn and walked toward the other ambulance, which was parked a few yards away. For the first time in twenty-four hours, he could allow himself to feel tired. No, exhausted was a better word. Exhausted and triumphant. The operation was over.

Mentally he tabulated their gains. Magus and his key associate were dead. Four other men were in custody. And last, but not least, Sarah Fontaine was alive.

She would need hospitalization, of course. She had sustained nasty lacerations on her arms and feet; they'd probably require a surgeon's skill. More important, she would need immediate psychiatric attention. She'd been hallucinating, seeing ghosts on rooftops. Under the circumstances, hysteria was perfectly understandable. It might take weeks, even months, to recover from the ordeal she'd just survived. But she would recover. He had no doubt about it. Sarah Fontaine, he'd decided, was made of sterner stuff than anyone had suspected.

Potter watched as the next stretcher was loaded into the waiting ambulance. The siren would be silent this time; both men were dead. He shuddered, remembering the sight of Kronen's body on the sidewalk. Thank God the ambulance crew had cleared it away so quickly. After a night of nothing but black coffee, Potter's stomach was just waiting for an excuse to puke. Would have been damned undignified, to say the least, especially with a dozen Dutch cops standing around as witnesses.

The second stretcher was now being placed in the vehicle. It was Magus. Potter frowned, wondering at the irony of the old man's suicide. After all these years of evading capture, Magus had chosen to take his own life. Or had he? The ballistics lab would surely confirm it. Suicide was the only explanation. There had been no other gunman. None, that is, except for the one seen by Sarah Fontaine, and she'd seen nothing but a ghost.

"Mr. Potter?"

He turned. A Dutch policeman was coming toward him through the knot of bystanders.

"What is it?"

"There is a man inside who wishes to see you. An American, I think."

"Have him talk to Mr. Tarasoff."

"He said he'd only talk to you."

Potter stifled a curse. What he really wanted to do right now was crawl into bed. But he grudgingly followed the officer through the police line, into the F. Berkman building. The smell of coffee was everywhere; it reminded him he'd hardly eaten since the previous afternoon. Breakfast would taste good right now. Bacon and eggs and then an honest-to-God hot shower. Hell, he deserved it. They all deserved it. He made a mental note to put in a commendation for Tarasoff and the others. They'd held up well.

The officer nodded toward the front office. "There he is."

Potter glanced through the doorway and frowned. The man standing at the window had his back turned. He was dressed completely in black. There was something disturbingly familiar about the golden color of his hair, which was sparkling in the window's light.

Potter went in and closed the door. "I'm Roy Potter," he said. "Did you want to see me?"

The man turned and smiled. "Hello, Mr. Potter."

Potter's jaw dropped. He couldn't speak. He could only stare like a dumb animal. *What the hell is going on?* he thought. *Am I seeing ghosts, too?*

It was Simon Dance.

AN HOUR LATER Simon Dance—the man once known as Geoffrey Fontaine—finally turned and wandered back to the window. For a moment he stood there motionless, his face silhouetted against the sunlight. "So that, Mr. Potter, is what happened," he said softly. "Rather more complicated than you suspected. I thought you might appreciate hearing the facts. In return I ask only that one favor."

"If I'd only known—why the hell didn't you tell me all this before?"

"It was instinct at first. Then the explosives appeared in my hotel room. That's when I was certain. I knew I couldn't trust you. Any of you. There'd been a leak all along. High level, I'm afraid."

Potter said nothing. Somehow he'd already guessed who it might be.

"Van Dam," said Dance.

"How can you be sure?"

Dance shrugged. "Why does a man leave his warm hotel at midnight to use a phone booth?"

"When was this?"

"Last night, right after I tipped O'Hara."

"That was your call?" Cursing softly, Potter shook his head. "Then it's partly my fault. I told Van Dam about the tip. I had to."

Dance nodded. "I didn't understand his little walk to the phone booth. At first. Then I heard that Kronen and his men appeared at Casa Morro shortly afterward. That's when I knew who Van Dam had called. Magus."

"Look, I need more evidence. You don't expect me to proceed on the basis of one phone call?"

"No, no. The matter has already been taken care of."

"What do you mean?"

"You'll understand. Shortly."

"What about his motive? A man doesn't go bad without a good reason!"

Calmly Dance lighted a cigarette and shook out the match. "Motives are funny things. We all have them. We all have our secrets, our hidden agendas. Van Dam was a wealthy man, I understand."

"His wife left him millions."

"Was she old when she died?"

"In her forties. There was some kind of crime involved. A burglary, I think. Van Dam was out of the country at the time."

"Of course he was."

Potter fell silent. There it was. Motive. Yes, if you looked deep enough, you might find it, hidden in the shadows of a man's life. "I'll begin an internal investigation," he said. "Immediately."

Dance smiled. "No hurry. I doubt he'll be vanishing any time soon."

"What about you?" asked Potter. "Now that it's over, will you surface?"

Dance slowly blew out a cloud of smoke. "I don't know what I'll do yet," he said, staring off sadly. "Eva was the only thing that ever mattered to me. And I've lost her."

"There's still Sarah."

Dance shook his head. "I've caused her enough pain." He turned and looked out the window again. "Your ballistics report will reveal that Magus was killed not by his own rifle, but by a bullet fired from a distance. Promise me Sarah will never learn this fact."

"If that's what you want."

"It's what I want."

"You won't even say goodbye to her?"

"It's kinder if I don't." Dance squinted out at the street. The last police car had just driven off. The bystanders were gone. Except for the bloodstains on the curb, it looked like any Amsterdam street on a Sunday morning. "Mr. O'Hara seems like a good man," he said softly. "I think they'll be happy together."

Potter nodded. Yes, he had to admit, Nick O'Hara wasn't so bad after all. "Tell me, Dance," he said. "Did you ever love Sarah?"

Dance shook his head. "In this business love is always a mistake. No, I didn't love her. But I did not want her harmed." He gave Potter a hard look. "Next time, avoid the use of innocents in your operations. We cause enough misery in this world without making those who are blameless suffer."

Potter was suddenly uncomfortable. The whole operation had been his idea; if Sarah had been killed, he'd be the one responsible. Thank God she'd survived.

"Someday," said Dance, "I'll tell you how the operation should have been run. You're still amateurs. But you'll learn. You'll learn." He took one last puff and stubbed out his cigarette. "Now I think it's time I be on my way. I have a great deal to do."

"Will you be going back to the States? If so, I'll see what I can do to get you a new identity—"

"That won't be necessary. I've always managed best on my own."

Potter couldn't argue that point. Dance's one brief affiliation with the Company had almost proved fatal for him.

"I think perhaps a change in climate will suit me," said Dance as he walked to the door. "I have never liked the dampness. Or the cold."

"What if I need to get hold of you?"

"I'm afraid I won't be available, Mr. Potter."

"But—but how do I find you?"

Dance paused in the doorway. For a moment he was thoughtful. Then, with a smile, he said, "You can't."

IT WAS LATE afternoon when Sarah woke up. The first thing she saw was the white curtains, blowing gently beside the open window. Slowly her unfocused gazed took in the pots of red and yellow tulips, sitting in a row on the table. And then, in a chair beside her bed, she saw Nick clutching a tulip pot in his lap. He was fast asleep. His shirt was a map of wrinkles and sweat. His hair was streaked with more gray than she'd remembered. But he was smiling.

She reached over and touched his hand. With a start he woke up and looked at her with bloodshot eyes.

"Sarah," he murmured.

"My poor, poor Nick. I think you need this bed more than I do."

"How are you feeling?"

"Strange. Safe."

"You are safe, Sarah." He put the tulip pot down and took her hands. "You really are."

She gazed at the table. "Oh, look at all the flowers!"

"I guess I overdid it. I didn't know two dozen pots would go so far."

They both laughed then, a tentative laugh that quickly faded. Neither of them was ready to let go of the fear. Not yet. Too much had happened. In silence he watched her and waited.

"I did see him, Nick," she said softly. "I know I did."

"It doesn't matter, Sarah...."

"But it *does* matter. To me. Whether he was real or imagined—I saw him...." She sank back on the pillows and stared up at the ceiling. "And I'll always wonder."

"When you're scared, your mind can do funny things."

"Perhaps."

"I don't believe in ghosts."

"Neither did I. Until today."

He took her hand and pressed it to his lips. "If he was a ghost, then I owe him one. For letting me keep you."

Nick looked so rumpled, so tired, as his dark head bent down to her palm. A sudden, overwhelming wave of tenderness swept through her. He raised his head and she saw, in his tired gray eyes, the love she'd never really seen in Geoffrey's.

"I love you, Nick," she said. "And you're right. Maybe, just for a moment, I *was* seeing things. I was so scared. And there was no one else to help me. No one but a ghost."

"He's dead, Sarah. Your seeing him then—at that moment—it was just your way of saying goodbye."

There was a knock at the door. They looked up as Roy Potter stuck his head in the room. "Both awake, I see," he said cheerily. "Can I come in?"

Sarah smiled. "Of course, Mr. Potter."

Potter stared at the tulip pots and whistled. "Wow. What'd you do, O'Hara? Go into the flower business?"

"Just being romantic."

"Romantic? A slob like you?" Potter winked at Sarah. "Better tell this guy to shave. Before he's arrested for vagrancy."

She stroked the stubble on Nick's jaw. "I think he looks just wonderful."

Potter shook his head in wonderment. "Just goes to prove love really is blind." He gave Sarah a thoughtful look. "The doc says you'll be released in the morning. You feeling up to it?"

"I think so." She nodded at her bandaged arm. "It's sore. They had to put in a dozen or so stitches." Nick's arm came around her shoulder and she glanced up at him. "But I'm sure I'll be all right."

For a few seconds, Potter regarded them in silence. "Yeah," he said at last. "I think you'll be all right."

"So your operation's wrapped up?" asked Nick.

"Just about. We've still got a few…details to clean up. A few things we hadn't expected. But you know how it is in this business. For every gain you take a few losses. Those dead agents in Margate. Eve Fontaine."

"And Geoffrey," said Sarah softly.

Potter fell silent again. "Anyway," he said after a pause, "what's next for you two?"

"Home," said Nick, taking Sarah's hand. "We've got a flight back to D.C. day after tomorrow."

"And then what?"

Nick's eyes turned to Sarah. "I'll let you know," he said softly.

The room fell silent. Potter got the message, loud and clear. It was time to leave these two alone. Rising, he patted Nick on the back. "Well, good luck to both of you. I'll put in a good word with your boss, Nick. That is, if you want your job back."

Nick didn't answer. His eyes were still locked with Sarah's.

"Okay," muttered Potter as he walked unnoticed to the door. "Then I'll just tell old Ambrose that Nick O'Hara says go to hell." In the doorway he turned and glanced back one last time to see Nick pulling Sarah into his arms. They didn't say a word, but the way they held each other said everything. Potter shook his head and grinned. Yes, Simon Dance was right. Nick and Sarah would be happy together.

Suddenly the afternoon sun burst through the clouds and flooded the room so brightly Potter had to squint. At that instant, Nick took Sarah's face in his hands and kissed her. And as he watched their lips meet, it seemed to Roy Potter that all the world's shadows had suddenly vanished, taking with them forever the ghost of Geoffrey Fontaine.